Sign up for our newsletter to hear
about new releases, read interviews with
authors, enter giveaways,
and more.

www.ylva-publishing.com

Other Books by L.T. Smith

Once

BY L.T. SMITH

REVISED EDITION

Acknowledgement

It is not just because Astrid Ohletz is a great publisher, a savvy business woman, the Boss Lady, a patient teacher and guide, or a woman who strives for perfection in everything she does that makes me so happy that I am blessed enough to publish with Ylva. It is more than that. But, without rambling too much, I am grinning stupidly because she is also a very good friend. And so is Daniela. Don't think I am going to forget you. Thank you for not strangling me when you were trying to sort out my chapter headings. Very much appreciated. My neck thanks you, too.

Although *Once* has previously been released, there are many changes to be found in this edition. These are due to the skill and dedication of one woman—Day Petersen. Weirdly, or not so weirdly after all, Day worked with me on the original edit all of those years ago. It is amazing how a writer's writing style and a reader's expectation have changed over the years, but I believe my vision for the story remains intact. This is all down to Day and her talent as an editor. A very big thank you.

Once again, thank you Amanda Chron the wonderful cover you have designed for this revised edition. Even though my furry lad was not best pleased about having his adorable face replaced by a buff-looking border and "two lady luvvers", he has finally forgiven you. I think. After he has finished licking his most intimate place, I'll ask him again. I don't think his current action is a criticism of your work, but then again, he was miffed.

Finally, I would like to thank you, the reader. I hope beyond hope you enjoy this edition of *Once*. Without your support over the years, writing for me would be a thing of the past. You have shown me faith when I thought I had lost it, support when I believed I was sagging, and optimism when things seemed darker than they should. But most of all, you have been a constant point of reference in my writing—if you like what I do, then I'm doing something right.

Let's hope I don't let us both down. Enjoy.

Dedication

To living life, forging friendships, having hope, and loving with no holds barred.

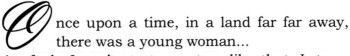nce upon a time, in a land far far away, there was a young woman...

Aw fuck. I can't start my story like that. Let me think. What about:

It was a *lovely* day...

What a load of bollocks. Here am I, wanting to spin you a tale, and I can't even decide how to begin. Should I start at the beginning, the middle? Or even begin at the end and then go backwards. I think I'm diverting into some kind of literary cul de sac. Before you know it, I will be using tired old clichés and quoting Shakespeare.

Perhaps I should set the scene. You know—paint a picture with words. Number one in the tired old cliché brigade. Setting is important, though, isn't it? It gives readers a feel for the story. Without it they will be visually bankrupt, much as I am feeling verbally bankrupt at the moment.

Okay, here we go, setting the scene, thereby readying my reader. Just a minute—you are ready, aren't you? I don't want to waste ink starting and then find you are still fiddling around in your handbag, looking for a mint.

Consider this the beginning, the setting, the start.

Now to the scene: Shall I set it with time or place, or shall I go for the gold and set it with emotion?

The latter, I believe. Visualize, if you will, a metaphorical pushing of glasses up onto the bridge of my nose, which gives me a look of intelligence.

Right. I'm ready too.

Cough.

On your marks, get set...

The Start. Formally Known as The Introduction

She said she'd love me forever. For*e*ver. Three syllables, seven letters. Go on; - count them. And those three syllables and seven letters turned out to be a one-syllable, three-letter word.

Lie.

Unless "forever" meant it was okay to treat me like pond life and then shag her work mate. If that is the case, then I'm sorry, I'm wrong; it is forever. But in *my* dictionary, "forever" means something completely different. Let's just check.

Forever / fə're.və / *adv* 1. *also* for ever, FOR ALL TIME, for all future time. 2. *also* for ever, FOR A VERY LONG TIME, for a very long or seemingly endless time (*informal*).

See? "FOR ALL TIME" and even "A VERY LONG TIME," if you want to be informal.

Don't get me wrong; I'm not a pedant. I don't typically carry a dictionary around with me and contradict people on their usage of the English language. But come on! When someone tells you they will love you forever, it usually means longer than three and a half years. Or it should.

In my own way, I loved Sue. I didn't like the way she treated me, but I loved her all the same. We had lived together for just over three years when I came home to find her rolling around on our bedroom floor with a woman I'd met briefly at their company dinner two weeks previous. The prevailing thought bouncing around in my head was *I hope I don't have to steam clean the carpet,* then I turned, walked down the stairs and out of the door.

I'd barely grabbed the handle on my car door when Sue was behind me. Gripping my arm, she spun me around and started throwing accusations. Words literally splattered on my face, words like "cold," "heartless," and the blinding one that charged me with "indifferent."

"Even when you catch me fucking someone else, you just walk away!"

What had she expected me to do?

"Why can't you show any emotion?"

Why should I? That wouldn't change the fact that she'd lied when she said she would love me forever.

In hindsight, I should have asked her the question, but all I wanted to do was get out of there, flee the scene of her crime, block it all out. I couldn't see the point in staying to listen to her blast out all my alleged shortcomings to all and sundry who happened to be passing by at something nearing a hundred shrill decibels, a level that was loud enough to make dogs howl.

And that's where my story truly begins.

The True Beginning

Sue was the longest relationship I'd ever had—forty months, to be precise. We met through a friend of a friend of a friend, which nearly made our introduction an urban myth. It was lust at first sight, and we barely knew anything about one another before we were inside each other's underwear. We scarcely even made it inside my house before we were at it. The front door clicked, and so did her bra strap.

Sex had always come easy to me, or it used to. I wasn't the type of person to form long-lasting relationships, and that suited me just fine. I actually preferred it to be just my little boy and me. When I say little boy, don't misunderstand me. I'm not a single mother, and I most assuredly never slept with a man. My little boy has the most gorgeous brown eyes and wet nose any mother could wish for. Unlike most, the child in question had four legs instead of the customary two.

Dudley, Duds for short. Black and tan, fuzzy, with a tail that wagged liked crazy taking his whole bum with it. His smile was the perfect overshot jaw of the classic Border terrier. We'd been a team long before Sue came on the scene, and I knew we still would be long after Sue had gone.

It was weird how it all kicked off, the relationship with Sue, that is. Before I knew it, we were seeing each other every night, and if I were to say I didn't enjoy having sex with her, I'd be lying. Things between us just grew. We became dependent on one another in a way that was a bit like smoking: You know it's bad for you, but you believe you need it to feel normal.

Duds found Sue suspect from the first moment he clapped his beady eyes on her. The first time I introduced them, he tried to bite her tit. To be fair, we were in the hallway, and he was just protecting his property. I should've asked her to leave there and then, because dogs are never wrong, but at that moment in time I wanted to bite her tit, too, so I kind of ignored Duds' warning. I can guarantee that gross negligence will not be repeated.

After four months of being together, Sue began to apply the pressure. Why couldn't we move in together? It would be so much easier, cheaper, fun. And on and on and on, and then on and on and on some more.

I can hear you saying, "Why didn't you just tell her to sling her hook?"

Ah, easy for you to say, but you weren't the one receiving wonderful, mind-blowing sex, were you? You weren't the one who steadily began to believe that you actually couldn't do all the things you used to do; you were suddenly dependent on another person. Even washing up. I couldn't even do that right. She systematically broke me down until I thought I would have difficulty trying not to drown in the bath.

When I agreed to her moving in, she was in, unpacked, and settled in less than twelve hours. She must have been half packed and waiting for me to give her the go-ahead. Duds was not a happy boy, as she banished him from sleeping at the foot of my bed from the very first night, claiming it wasn't healthy.

I missed him, missed the way I would wake up in the night and stretch my arm down to feel a warm wet tongue lavish my fingers with kisses. I even missed the way I would inadvertently tickle his winkle because he was sprawled on his back, snoring away.

As you might have guessed, the relationship between me and Sue wasn't easy from the start. But when she moved in, I began to see a different side to Sue than the one she had presented to me over the first six months. At first I would argue, especially when it came to Duds, but then it just became easier to go along with her. Oddly, that seemed to infuriate her even more. Arguments would start as soon as I got home from work. She didn't even wait for me to take my coat off before she was accusing me of the usual things—not appreciating her, not telling her I loved her often enough, loving that damned mutt more than I loved her. Erm, well I... Nah, you get the picture.

Eventually I didn't have the energy, or inclination, to argue. I just took it on the chin, rolled up my sleeves, and began to wash up. Badly. Sex went out the window after the second year, and I spent more time in the sunroom with Duds, reading or just "arsing about," as Sue so delicately phrased it.

I thought these things were a blip most couples went through when they first moved in together. I truly believed I loved her. Honestly.

Because, you see, she had told me she'd love me forever. And I, like a fool, believed her. It didn't even occur to me to wonder whether I wanted her to.

৪১৫৪

Self-confidence was a thing of the past. I was beginning to believe I was a worthless piece of shit. I'm not saying Sue purposely set out to make me feel that way, all I'm saying is that I felt vacant. The only thing I believed in was that she would always love me. The most sorrowful thing was that I hoped she was lying.

I felt trapped, caught like a poor fox in the woods, leg stuck in a mantrap and waiting for the end to take him. The pain wasn't physical, more an emotional rendering of the helpless, if you get my meaning. Vacancy morphed into hollowness, and hollowness seeped into an abyss, trickling away and leaving me clutching at straws, at what I once called hope, but what eventually seemed like a last ditch attempt to maintain my sanity.

Then I came home one day and saw her, saw her on the bedroom carpet with another woman. At that excruciating moment, any excuse she might have offered for her infidelity wasn't important, and I wasn't going to stick around and ask her why she was shagging someone in our home.

A few weeks after the event, she finally admitted she had wanted me to catch her in flagrante delicto, wanted me to respond in some way that would prove to her that I loved her as much she loved me.

I said the only thing that made any sense. "Bollocks."

The word conveyed an inner strength I thought had died, but by dignifying her argument with any response at all, I believed it also robbed me of what little self-respect I had left. And I wanted to keep that; she'd taken everything else.

Well, not straight away. She did give me a little time to adjust before she turned up with a removal van and wiped me out. Most of the furniture was now stacked in her apartment—unused for the most part and collecting dust. Not surprising, considering that nearly six months had passed.

When she demanded visiting rights for Duds, she went too far. Duds hated her. At the time I didn't know why, because it isn't in a dog's nature to hate, only humans have that capability. But as time went on, I began to get the whole picture.

Why would a dog that has been loved from the minute he wiggled his fat little arse into my arms until now, dodge when I lifted my hand up suddenly? And why would a dog hide when I slapped a newspaper on the side of the chair?

Mmmm. It was not rocket science.

That was the moment when things started becoming interesting. That was the moment when I thought I might choke the fucking life out of her. But I didn't. Nope. That wouldn't have been satisfying enough.

Part of me still believes that what I did next wasn't just because of what I thought she had done to Duds. I think it was because of all the times I had never fought back in the past—verbally, I mean. I am not offering this as an excuse; I'm merely trying to explain how I felt and why I did the thing I am about to confess to.

Sue opened her front door, and I smacked her right in the face. Her look of surprise was priceless, and the satisfying crunch of her nose under my fist will live with me for the rest of my life. I revelled in the sight of the once-straight feature leaning to one side and pissing blood like a soda siphon.

"Cold? Heartless? Fucking indifferent?" I grabbed the front of her shirt. The buttons tore away from the cloth. I stopped. This wasn't me, wasn't who I was. I never fought, whatever the provocation.

Grey eyes looked into mine. One emotion in them stood out above all others—fear. And I had put it there.

Duds was going crazy in the car, howling and scratching at the window in a vain attempt to get to me. He distracted me for less than the blink of an eye, and that's all Sue needed.

Bang! Knee up and meeting my crotch with the speed and precision of an all-in wrestler. And down I went. Flat on top of her. Face to face, her blood smearing on my cheek.

"You haven't heard the last of this, Beth," she spat into my face. "I'll get you, and your little dog, too."

What the fuck was that? A twisted version of *The Wizard of Oz*? Were Munchkins going to clamber out of the flowerbeds and start singing in voices that sounded as if they'd been altered by inhaling helium?

I tried to pull away from her, but she clutched me nearer so she could then push me away with extra force. I clattered onto the paving slabs and tried to stop myself from skidding. Sue shakily got to her feet, wiping the back of her hand across her nose and wincing in pain. I just sat there while the neighbourhood squatted in eerie silence, apart from the demented howling of my little wolfman.

She slowly stepped forward, and I cowered, lifting my hands to my face, believing she was going to hit me. Her shadow loomed over me and stayed, and I cowered, curled into my protective shell.

"You're not worth it."

And then the shadow left, and the sun warmed the backs of my arms and dried the tears that had trickled down my face at the introduction of her kneecap to my private parts.

I don't know how long I sat there, but by the time I struggled to my feet, both my right leg and my backside were numb. I undoubtedly looked ancient as I hobbled back to the car, where I was greeted by a very concerned bundle of fur. Duds licked all the dried tears from my cheeks. He even cleaned all the new ones that raced down my face. Bless him.

Unconditional love. If only humans could do that, I'd be set for life.

ഇറ

Things went downhill from there, really, although I'd had no sense that they could get any lower than they already were. The only time I went out was to take Dudley for his walks or to collect more work to do, as I'd stopped going to the office and did all my design work from home. My boss, Jim Adamson, had no objections, as he realized that drawings and ideas came from within, not from one's surroundings. That's what he said to me anyway. All I needed to do was to go in to the office to collect the project files allocated to me. Of course, all my accounts were small fry in comparison to what else the company offered, and mainly concentrated on local business promotion. I used to be one of the high fliers in the company, but not anymore. This was my choice, though. I didn't think I could cope with too high profile a workload.

Jim believed in me, more than I believed in myself. He actually told me to take some time to get my life in order, however long that might take.

Every day I found it more difficult to get out of bed, and not just because I'd hit Sue or found her sleeping with someone else. Maybe those points were a factor, but I think it had been building for a while. There is only so much negativity a person can take before it begins to erode the positives in life, and, to be honest, I don't think I was handling being on my own again. I know I should have been ecstatic, but that was not how I was feeling. Far from it, in fact. And if it hadn't been for the necessity of taking care of someone else, I don't think I would have even bothered to get up in the morning. What was the point? A black cloud had descended on me, and I had the distinct impression that my life had taken a swan dive off a cliff and landed on concrete.

As mums tend to do, my mum was forever phoning and trying to get me to "Get my backside" round to her place. My brother Will also wanted to come over, take me out, fix me up with a work mate, anything to take my mind off things. But I couldn't face them; I felt too fragile. After realising Sue was no longer on the scene, old friends came out of the woodwork, only to discover I was "unavailable for comment." I just wanted to be left on my own to simmer and stew and sink deeper into myself.

What I needed to do was get the facts of the case out in the open. Firstly, she said she'd love me forever. Secondly, she didn't. Should I say thirdly? Nah. I should bullet point.

- She hit Duds. Fucker.
- I hit her. Sound of cheers from the crowd!
- She kneed me in the lady garden, and it still throbs at the memory, and she wiped blood and spit all over my face.
- The grabber nicked half of my furniture. Robber.
- She made me feel worthless and stupid. Erm...
- *And* I had to steam clean my bedroom carpet.

Sorted.

Now all I needed to do was to make a similar list to counterbalance that one.

- Shower.
- Dress
- Feed Duds.
- Eat.
- Go for a walk.

And that brings me to the development stage of my tale.

The Development

Earlham Park. Beautiful—green lolling fields and a clear sky. I would say "blue sky," but this was England in October. Therefore, we have a clear sky, maybe greyish at best.

The day was cool, but not cold. It was cold enough for a jumper, and the ground was wet enough to wear boots, but all in all, it was a crisp autumn day in Norwich. The field was filled with butterfly dogs and their owners, you know, people who only walk their dogs when the sun is shining.

Duds didn't know what to do first—chase his ball, or dash around yapping happily with the biggest dog he could find. Smiling occasionally at his antics, I became lost in thought, and ignored the first rule of walking a dog: Always be alert.

But you know how it is—thoughts pop into your head and you just go with them, and before you know it, thirty minutes have flown by and you have no idea how. It's scary how we can ignore time, considering how we dwell on it so much.

Of course I had been thinking about Sue and how things had fallen apart. I was trying to put it all in perspective—from how we met to the final punch-out in front of her house. The blame was shifting from her to me and then back to her again. It was so unlike me to be violent. After I started living with Sue, I would do anything to avoid conflict, and physical contact of the "bodily harm" variety was not my style. Or hers, for that matter.

What had happened to the two of us? What had created the first chink in our relationship? I know what had triggered my outburst, but why had I felt the need to punch her, especially with no concrete evidence of her having done any harm to Duds?

The thought of Dudley being mistreated brought me back to reality with a crack.

I couldn't see him.

Couldn't see him!

Panic raced through me and choked off my breath. My heart was thumping against my ribcage.

"Duds! Come on, fella!" The shout broke the dam in my throat, and I felt the tears start to gather. "Dud... ley!"

I was running, my head whipping round trying to spot his little black body, but he wasn't there anywhere. He was gone.

Sue's words rattled around my head, the ones I laughed at: *"and your little dog, too."* I can guarantee I wasn't laughing now. She had him. As sure as I was racing down the hill screaming his name, I knew she had him. All thoughts of physical violence not being my style flew out the window. If she hurt him in any way, I would rip her apart, limb from fucking limb. But all the smacking in the world wouldn't bring him back.

Then I saw it. I couldn't believe I hadn't been on my guard, couldn't believe I hadn't followed the first rule of dog walking.

The river.

Fuck.

The river.

Duds loved the river. In the summer, I frequently took him to the shallow part so he could jump in and fetch sticks. I can't tell you how many balls he had dropped in there to sink into the murky depths of a watery grave. Now Duds had followed them. He would drown in there this time of the year. The current would be too fast for him to get back to the bank.

There was no sign of him at the river's edge. Despair shot through me, and my knees gave way and I sank to the ground. The cry that came from within me felt as if it had been ripped from my heart. I had lost everything...everything. Duds was my everything, and he was dead.

I heard a whimper. Distant, but definitely a whimper. I didn't think twice, just leapt up and vaulted into the freezing water. It seeped through my jeans and jumper and soaked my rapidly cooling skin, and I found the weight of it pulling me under. The sheer power of the water made me realise that if Duds had whimpered a second ago, there was no way he would still be whimpering now. It would be impossible for him to get back to the bank in this current.

It didn't stop me. I had to find him, alive or—

"Excuse me."

The sound of the water was nearly deafening, but I could tell that someone was calling to me from the bank. I couldn't tear my eyes away from the water. It was taking all of my effort to not be whisked along with the raging water. Duds had to be here somewhere.

"Excuse me!" The voice was a little louder, a little more insistent.

"Can't you see I'm busy?" I didn't look back, didn't even ask the voice for help.

"Is this your dog?"

The first thought that popped into my mind was that Dud's body had been washed to the shore, and the owner of the voice had found him. But then I heard the whimper again. I steadied myself and turned toward the bank.

The woman standing there was holding something black, wriggling, and *very* dry. The bundle in her arms was whimpering around a bright red ball that was clamped inside his mouth.

I bet you're thinking I sloshed to the side, clambered up the muddy bank, and had a tearful reunion with my little man. Nope. I stood there and cried. And cried. And cried. Relief? Maybe. Anger? A little bit. Shock? Almost guaranteed. But I think it was just everything pouring out at last, everything I had bottled up since splitting with Sue, or even before that.

Words seeped into my consciousness, but I couldn't respond to the woman asking me if I was okay, did I need help, to sit and stay. Sit and stay?

Water splashed and splashed, and then I felt arms enveloping me, pulling me against a solid chest. The closeness jolted me out of my misery-cum-happiness for a brief moment, and I looked into a most glorious pair of brown eyes. The sob which was in the process of being launched from my slackened mouth stopped midway.

The woman pulled me closer to her and held me for a split second before steering me towards the bank. Her arms left me briefly as she scrambled up, and then a hand extended and hovered in front of me, offering me help to reach safety.

It was a strange feeling, a tingling. Her fingertips seemed to trigger something deep inside, but I couldn't grasp the implication. My brain was frozen like the rest of my body, except for my hand. One tug and I was on the bank, falling onto my hands and knees, an excited Dudley licking my face, his ball rolling towards the water's edge. Shit. He would follow it.

But she was there again, swiftly catching the ball in one capable hand.

The funny thing was, I hadn't really had a good look at her yet. I had only seen her close up, and then it was the back of her head as she had scrambled up the embankment. One thing I knew, though, her eyes were brown, a mesmerising brown. I was kneeling on the ground, soaking wet, hair going all directions, and completely covered in mud. Not to mention being thoroughly loved by my boy, which, if you've ever seen a dog really excited at being reunited with his mum, you will know is not a flattering sight. So, when she turned to look at me, ball in hand, I felt thoroughly dishevelled, to say the least.

"You must be freezing."

"Huh?"

She stood straight, and I looked upwards so I could see her eyes again. The way she strolled over, totally controlled, her wet jeans flapping against her legs, made my stomach tighten with what I believed to be shock about what had almost happened with Dudley.

"I said, you must be freezing. You need to get out of those clothes."

"Huh?"

A smile flickered briefly over her face and then disappeared. "You're all wet...erm...the river...erm... water."

I was surprised that the heat emanating from my face didn't dry my clothes. Duds had decided to just lie across my chest and stare into my face, his breath cool against my glowing skin. I could hear his panting, my panting, and a rapid clattering inside my chest that I put down to exertion.

"Are you okay?" Her face came down towards mine, and I felt my focus moving from her eyes to her mouth, watching the words come out. "Come on. Let's warm you up."

Now there was an offer.

ℂℂ

We ended up in the café in the middle of the park, and the people who ran it gave us towels and a blanket to wrap around our legs as sodden jeans, underwear, and boots dried in the kitchen. Duds curled up in front of the fire and dozed, his ball under his chin.

"I'm Amy, by the way."

When I took her hand again to introduce myself, I got the same sensation I had before, but this time it seemed stronger. "Beth." I stared down at our intertwined fingers, maybe to try to put a name to what was happening, and before I knew it, her hand was gone.

"Here. Drink this." She passed me a steaming mug of hot chocolate, and I wrapped my hands around it, willing the heat to spread through me.

The only sounds were the clattering of the workers in the café and our slurping of hot drinks. Time seemed to drift, and the warmth I felt from the fire and the drink made me want to just curl up and sleep.

"Are you feeling warmer?" Amy's voice was filled with concern.

Not wanting to break the serenity I was feeling, I barely nodded. It had been a long time since I had felt so relaxed.

"May I ask you a question?"

My gaze shifted to her face. I saw nothing threatening there, so I nodded again.

"You don't have to answer if you don't want to."

"Go on." The words coming out of my mouth sounded crackly, as if I hadn't used my voice box for ages. After a quick cough and clearing of my throat, I said, "What do you want to know?" I placed my empty mug on the table and turned to face her.

"I was just wondering..."

She looked embarrassed, and I was thinking, *Shit*, but I just stared at her and waited.

"Erm...I was just wondering...why on earth were you in the river at this time of year?" She shifted nervously, and her bum crunched on the plastic seat. "I mean, it's freezing in there."

"Tell me about it. But I didn't have time to think, just wanted to save Dudley."

"But he was with me."

"I know that *now*, but at the time..." I started to cry again.

"Hey. Come on. Everything's okay now."

I tried stop the flow of tears, but it was beyond my control. I felt so low, so beaten. My head slumped forward into my waiting hands, and I just let it all out.

Hands slipped around my shoulders, and arms caught me, even though I wasn't falling. The warmth and smell of her flooded through me, and the tender murmurs trickling over my forehead made me want to stay there indefinitely.

"Come on, Beth. He's safe. Look at him. Come on."

I lifted my eyes to look at Duds, who was at my knee, one paw on the blanket, his eyes full of worry.

"I was having a cup of tea when he came in a while ago. I think he was trying to get some treats."

Dud's eyes shifted guiltily for a split second.

"And then he wanted to play ball."

Did I see my dog lick his lips, as if he was going to speak up to deny it?

"I went out to find who he was with, but I couldn't see anyone. He went ballistic. Kept on racing ahead and then running back to me, as if he wanted me to follow him."

I stroked his fuzzy head; tender licks covered my fingers. My dog was Lassie. Or Skippy, the bush kangaroo.

"Next thing I knew, we were at the river, and I had to hold him to stop him coming in after you. Didn't I, fella?" Amy stroked Dudley's head, him obviously lapping up the attention from the both of us.

Our fingers met, only briefly, but the sensation was there again.

"I'd better go." I stood up sharply, wanting to flee the scene, failing to recall that I was naked from the waist down. Until the blanket fell from me, of course. "Shit...erm...sorry...and... Oh crap!" I clutched at the blanket, which made her laugh. Such a musical laugh.

Her hand grabbed at the edge of the blanket to preserve my modesty, but she inadvertently grabbed my crotch.

Recoiling in an embarrassment of her own, Amy fell backwards onto the floor, exposing herself in the process.

What a pair of lemons—both of us flashing our girly bits in the middle of a café in the centre of Earlham Park. Could things be any more embarrassing?

Only time had the answer.

৪৩৫৪

How does one follow such an exhibition? You can either dress quickly to save further humiliation and run for your life, or you can laugh. Amy chose the latter. She sat on the floor, trying to pull the blanket over her, but her laughter was making her weak. I was opting for a quick getaway. My blanket was *firmly* in place by this stage, and I was on a one-way trip to the kitchen to gather my belongings.

Her mirth stopped me, and I just looked at her laughing. Her head thrown back, her brown hair flew backwards and then forwards as her body shook. A tickle of a chuckle rose up my throat and rested patiently just behind my lips.

She tried to get up and tangled her legs in the blanket, hitting the floor like a sack of potatoes. Unfortunately, I was trying to help her up, and she took me down with her. I landed awkwardly, half on and half off her jiggling frame.

It was an opportunity not to be missed by Dudley, who thought it was a game. All four paws simultaneously landed on the centre of my back, his ball thwacking me on the back of my head and pushing my face forward. The crunch of Amy's skull against mine stopped her laughing for a moment, and her widened eyes looked into mine. Jesus. We were so close, I could feel her breath. I knew my eyes flared in shock, as did hers, but when a very wet nose poked itself around and licked my face, then hers, she guffawed loudly.

And so did I. Real hearty laughs, the ones good for the soul. I tried to get up, but I couldn't. My legs kept tangling with the blankets and bringing me back down on top of Amy. Buster Keaton sprang to mind.

"Hold up...hold up. I...I...can't breathe." Amy was trying to control herself, panting and laughing, laughing then panting. "If we just stop," she froze and so did I, "then maybe we could do this properly, before we lose every shred of our dignity."

Slowly, gradually, we puzzled ourselves apart. The cool rush of air reminded me of where I was and what I was wearing.

"I'm so sorry." What else could I say? "God. I can't believe this." Not the most coherent of apologies, but I wasn't feeling very coherent or rational. How *do* you apologise for making someone jump into icy water, sit half-naked in a café, and then be the cause of her exposing herself to all and sundry? Words failed me.

"What for? I haven't had this much fun in ages." Her face was open and honest, and so beautiful, natural...and apparently waiting for a response.

"For...for *this*." My hand gestured wildly at her dishevelled frame and half-covered torso. "For getting you all wet." She sniggered. "Erm and erm... Aw shit." My face was beetroot red. I wouldn't have thought twice about having commented on how wet I'd made her if she hadn't sniggered. "I'd...I'd better go."

It was amazing how nimbly she got to her feet, surprising me with her swiftness and sureness of foot.

I shook my head and then turned to get the clothes for my bottom half.

We dressed in silence as Duds watched patiently from the wings, red ball clamped in his mouth. His little eyes looked from me to Amy and then back, his head bobbing comically.

After thanking the owners and offering to pay for the drinks and assistance, we went back to the car park. Amy walked me to my car, and then stooped to ruffle Dudley's hair.

"Thanks." Brown eyes looked into mine. "I don't know what I would've done without you. You're a lifesaver."

"My pleasure." Amy's smile radiated a genuine happiness, and my chest heaved and relaxed as she lectured Duds. "And you stick by your mum. Don't want her jumping in rivers too often, do we?"

And then I left, leaving her standing in the car park, waving and laughing. Dudley stood on the parcel shelf of the car and wagged his tail until she was out of sight. If I'd had a tail, I would have wagged mine, too.

Then it dawned on me—I didn't know her surname, didn't know anything except that her name was Amy. No address or phone number. Nothing.

My imaginary tail stopped wagging, and I drove away, taking one last look in the rear view mirror, just in case she might still be in view.

෫෨ଈ

For a moment here I deliberated where I should pick up the tale, whether or not it would be best to jump a ways ahead. I have decided that proceeding to the middle sounds good.

Maybe you're wondering, "What happens now?" or even "I don't give a shit. Where's the sex?"

But, like me, you have to be patient, although my patience was the forced result of not having the foresight to ask Amy even a little about herself. I wanted to kick myself for not thinking things through and reeling off a list of thoughtful questions, but at the time it had felt right to just sit and be.

As a result, I went to the park, and then back to the park, and then again and again and again, for about a week. Park. Park. Park. Like a dog with a speech impediment. Every afternoon, about the same time as the day we'd met Amy there, Duds and I trekked to the park on the off chance we would spot her and maybe have a chat.

No such luck.

But I persevered, and Duds thought I was the bee's knees and the cat's pyjamas for taking him out for walks in his favourite place. And I was beginning to make an effort to look halfway human—not wearing my scruffiest jeans, and even combing my hair. It didn't matter, though, because within five minutes of being out in the exposed elements, I always looked like something the cat had either dragged home or thrown up.

Of course, I was definitely following the first rule of dog walking and the one for bird watching—always be on the lookout for something, or someone.

It was exactly one week later when Duds decided it was high time he dropped his ball into the river, and then he apparently expected me to go in and get it. Thankfully, it was in a shallow section, although the string of non-biodegradable words coming from my mouth would have indicated otherwise. The stick I found was huge, almost a caber, and way too big to be using to fish for a little ball.

Wrestling with the stick was no easy feat, especially with an excited dog spurring me on with high yaps of encouragement. The ball seemed to be laughing at me when I heard a familiar voice behind me.

"You're not jumping in again, are you?"

I spun around, nearly going arse over tit into the water.

Amy grabbed my arm to stop me, and the branch escaped and drifted away in the current.

"Thank you. Again." I could feel a blush colour my face and hoped she hadn't noticed.

"You've gone all red."

Shit.

"Do you think you should sit down? Maybe you overdid it."

I nodded, taking on the role of "She Who is Close to Passing Out" with gusto.

Amy helped me lower myself to the ground and then plonked herself down next to me. Dudley looked at us both with disgust, and then continued to stare at the spot where his ball was bobbing.

It was lovely just to sit there, taking in the surroundings, listening to the birds. The view was beautiful, absolutely breathtaking. The park grounds weren't bad either. Amy was facing the river, profile in view, fingers draped over her raised knee. And I was mesmerised.

It was a good job that Dudley whimpered, because just as I turned away from Amy to look at Duds, she was turning to face me. A split second earlier, and I would've been caught gawping.

But I didn't get up; she did. Without a second's hesitation, she kicked off her trainers, pulled off her socks, and waded into the water to get Dudley's ball. She bent down out of my view, and then suddenly stood with the errant ball clutched tightly, water trickling off her hand. My little man went mad, excited mewling noises emanating from his mouth.

"Here you go, fella."

The ball whizzed past me, followed by a black and tan streak.

Her laugh was heart-warming, and my face nearly split in half with the smile that came from the place deep inside which is the source of smiles for perfect occasions. Before I knew it, she was beside me, trainers and socks in hand, her glistening feet looking decidedly blue.

"How did you know?"

She turned to me, her brown eyes so deep and enchanting that I nearly missed the half smile on her lips.

"It didn't take a genius. You with a huge stick, stabbing the water, and him," her head tilted towards the returning hero, "whinging at the side the whole time we were sitting here."

It was simple when I looked at it like that.

She wiped the water off her feet, but the moisture clung to them and kept her from putting her socks back on.

Then I thought of the clean white handkerchief in my coat pocket. "Here. Use this." I passed the linen to her and nodded at her feet. "The least I can do."

Why did I feel like a teenager—full of self-consciousness and hormones—when she smiled at me? Then I said the only thing I could think of. "He loves his ball."

Classic me. I wanted to tell her she had the most enchanting eyes I had ever seen and her smile could warm the coldest heart, but I was still in teenager mode. I was surprised I didn't shove her over, or worse, put her in a headlock.

She was tying her laces and didn't see me slap my forehead.

"Fancy a coffee?"

"Yap!"

Trust Dudley to get in there before me. Thinking about it now, he was just as entranced with Amy as I was. His eyes were full of adoration, his ball almost forgotten. Almost.

"Well, that settles it. Coffee, it is. Isn't that right, Duds?" I chucked his chin, stood up, and offered her my hand.

She paused before she took it. Or should I say hesitated? Then she grinned and slipped her fingers into mine, nearly pulling me over as she got up.

"Let's see if we can stay dressed this time, eh?"

Bugger. The image of her sprawled on the floor with her bits and pieces exposed and then me, being me, ending up on top of her, was nearly my undoing.

"I'm sure you're coming down with something. You've gone all red again."

Double buggeration.

೫ೲ

One coffee turned into two, and it was bloody wonderful. Amy was so entertaining, so attentive...so full of life. And for the hour we spent together, I forgot how shite my life was. Unlike our first meeting, I found myself asking questions about her and her life. For the first time in ages, I felt some semblance of involvement, maybe even a modicum of control. And it felt good.

Thirty-four. Single. Full name Amy Marie Fletcher. Single. Part time lecturer of history at the university. Single. Originally from Stratford, or just outside of. Did I mention she was single?

And straight.

I didn't ask her; I just knew. There was no way she was like me. She was just too...too... I don't know how to finish that sentence. I can't identify the classic lezzie look, or even what one sounds like. If I ever had gaydar, it failed me. I usually waited until someone picked up the invisible rays I was sending out into the world, unbeknownst to me. You know, the gay juju vibes.

Therefore, I should change my statement to "I think she was straight." Although I hoped she wasn't.

Before we knew it, I could see the owners of the café clearing their stuff away, readying themselves to close up. Amy, Duds, and I were the only ones left, so I stood to go. I made it a point to thank the owners for letting Duds come in, as I knew that bringing pets inside was usually against the rules, even though he'd been in before.

Back at the car, I hovered half in and half out of the door. I wanted to ask Amy if she would like to meet again, but something held me back—my confidence, I guess, or my lack thereof.

"Do you fancy meeting up again?"

Thank God one of us took the initiative.

"Maybe take Duds to the beach...erm...or something?" Amy said hesitantly.

"He'd love that." Huh? "I mean we'd love that."

She laughed as she fished in her pocket for a pen. "Have you any paper?"

The only thing I had was a receipt from the local pet store, but it served the purpose. In less than a minute she had given me her home number, work number, and mobile, with a comment that I should call her to make arrangements when I had a spare minute.

I had too many spare minutes, that was the problem, but I didn't let that faze me as I slipped the paper into the inside pocket of my jacket.

The smile I sported on the way home is sometimes described as a "shit-eating grin."

I have realised that I go on too long. I should be writing "Climax" or "Dramatic Scene" by now, but I don't think I should rush this tale. Therefore, instead of moving on to the next stage, I'll opt for...

Extended Development

Me being me, I looked at that slip of paper a thousand times. Me being me, I slipped that same piece of paper into the side pocket of my purse, only to sit and stare at said side pocket of my purse for God knows how long before getting out the same slightly worn piece of paper and starting the process all over again.

I wanted to pick up the phone, sluice sexual vibes through the slim black instrument, and fix a time to meet. But, truth be told, I was scared, petrified even. I hadn't even gone out with old friends since the split, and somewhere deep inside me there was an element of fear, fear that I had forgotten how to just "be" with other people.

I know Amy and I had shared a few coffees, and she'd accidentally grabbed my girly bits. I'd seen hers, too, for that matter, but those were all chance encounters, spur of the moment incidents, however nice.

Yes, I remember I purposely went out to see if I could spot her in the park again, but that wasn't the same thing. She might never have turned up. This time it would be a *definite* meet.

And I still didn't know if she was gay. What if I went along and got the wrong message? You know—ignored the little red flags that spout "Back off!" I would feel a right tit, when I was trying to feel the left one, too.

Even if she was on my team, it didn't necessarily mean she would fancy me. What did I have to offer her?

I didn't feel strong enough to deal with any of it— the waiting, the deliberating, the uncertainty, the fact she might be another Sue in sheep's clothing. I think that was it. I wasn't ready for anything that might demand an emotional attachment.

But I liked her, liked her to talk to. Duds liked her, too, and that had to be a sign, hadn't it? Dogs are never wrong. And I had promised myself I would never again ignore the cues from my little man.

"I'm doing this for you, Dudley."

Yeah, right.

છાલ્ક

Saturday. Nine o'clock. Up. Showered. Dressed. Duds fed. Me fed. Picnic made. Stomach in knots.

I had done the deed, called her. Put myself on the line for my child.

Amy had answered after the third ring, sounding out of breath. What was initially supposed to be a quick call lasted fifty-six minutes. I checked. We arranged to go to Wells Next the Sea, a huge beach that allowed dogs in both the winter and summer. And she was picking me up at eleven-thirty.

I know it was only nine, but I was nervous, okay? Ask my bowels. Ask my stomach, if you could get it to stay still long enough, when it wasn't practising a rolling hitch or a sheepshank. At other times I believed I would be better served by getting some time in on tying a noose; my large intestine was free for training purposes.

By the time eleven-fifteen rolled around, I was pale and sweating. The carpet in my living room seemed to have lost its lustre as footprints made by my boots had scuffed all the shag. Duds lay next to the door, his harness on and ball wedged as far as he could get it in his mouth. For once he wasn't yapping and trying to open the door himself. He seemed calm, serene even. Maybe because I was fidgeting like someone who had tried to OD on caffeine, everything else seemed calm in comparison.

When the doorbell chimed, I nearly peed my pants. She was early. Fifteen minutes early. I wasn't ready. Didn't feel ready. Felt exposed and naïve.

My fingers refused to act naturally, and the usual lifting off of the chain took longer because I couldn't seem to grip the bloody thing for long enough to slip it out of its slot and then dip the slender, oblong handle.

She looked beautiful. Her long hair was tied into a loose ponytail, and stray bits played at the sides of her face. Or maybe it was the wind that was brushing past her. Her smile was stiff, and I wondered if she was having second thoughts about our meeting, but then I realised she was nervous, too.

I'm not saying I thought of that straight away. It was her voice that betrayed her—slightly high pitched and with a noticeable quaver at the end of her greeting. Call me old fashioned, but that made me feel more relaxed. Not by a lot, but decidedly more relaxed than I had been feeling a couple of minutes before. My stomach even opted for a simple bowline knot.

Things were looking up. It's a pity the English weather didn't cooperate.

ഔറ

The beach was empty. Not surprising, really, considering the enormous rain clouds scudding towards us at a steady pace. The beach at the end of October was not the best choice of venues to have a day out. We could barely hear each other above the din of the wind.

But we were there together, and that's all that really mattered. That, and the fact Dudley was having the time of his life. He dug so many holes all over the beach, it was likely that future visitors would think there had been a mole invasion. He looked so cute with his backside stuck in the air and his front paws going ten to the dozen, accompanied by little snorting sounds. When he looked up, his face was covered in sand and he honestly looked as if he was grinning.

We walked for miles, or so it seemed. The car park was quite a trek away from the beach in the first place, but at least we were sheltered on the way in. Standing out on the sand, we were totally exposed, in more ways than one.

For some strange reason, I did feel a little at a loss. Maybe because I wasn't too sure what I should call our outing. Was it a date, or just an innocent walk along the beach? And why did it matter? Why couldn't I just accept our time together at face value and enjoy it? Why couldn't I stop asking questions?

Amy was fun, what I could hear of her anyway. She spent time with Duds, quality time— throwing the ball, chasing him, or letting him chase her. I laughed, really laughed, at their antics. I joined in, and in no time I was sweating underneath all of my layers.

It was Fate that decided it was time to move things on a little.

Black clouds gathered over us, until it seemed like night. The wind dropped. Kaput. Gone. And the scene changed from a crappy English day to something out of a Stephen King novel. Even the seagulls had buggered off, and their squawking was painfully absent. The air was full of tension, and if I had brought the proverbial knife with me, I bet I could have spliced through the collecting pockets of electricity.

Splat. A huge drop of rain hit me right in the face, ice cold and out to shock. Splat. Splat. Splatter. More quickly now, and seeming to increase in size and weight.

"Shit." Our exclamation rang out in unison, and then melted into the growing wetness.

Duds just looked at us, as if to say, "What's the problem?"

"Run!"

And we did. Like greyhounds. Soaked greyhounds, less than twenty seconds later. The problem arose when we realised we didn't have anywhere to go. The beach was just that—a beach. There were no cafés nearby, not even a public toilet where we could shelter. But we kept running, and the sky kept pelting us with gobbets of water.

After a few minutes, Amy began to slow down, then stopped. I caught up with her and just stood in front of her, the rain running down my face in rivulets. Then she did something that surprised me—she took off her coat and covered our heads with it. I couldn't understand why, because we were drenched already, so why didn't she just keep it on and stay warm? I know—ungrateful.

The thing is—have you ever been underneath a coat with someone, especially when you have to huddle together closely to make sure you are both covered? If you have, you will understand how close we were. I could feel her breath on my face, warming my skin. And you will also know it is nearly impossible not to look that person in the face, and that close proximity was nothing short of intimate.

The sound of our breathing was deafening, more like panting. I don't know if it was the exertion of running or...

"Errrrrrrruummmmmmmmmgh."

That broke the spell.

Dudley was between our legs, trying to keep himself from getting blown about by the elements, and he did look a sorrowful sight.

"Here. Bend down."

Amy's words seeped into my head, but I couldn't quite grasp what she meant.

"Like this."

Her left hand settled on my shoulder, and a gentle pressure pushed me downwards. Then the penny dropped. She was trying to get us closer to the ground so Duds would get more shelter, both underneath the coat and from our bodies.

It was like being inside a tent, with the battering of the rain on her coat sounding as if we were being pelted with stones, but the atmosphere inside was quiet, expectant. Amy rested her forearms on her knees so the coat was draped over us. I was holding on to Duds, rubbing his wet back to try to warm him up. I was freezing, soaked and freezing.

"You're shaking."

And I was. But I didn't know whether it was because of the cold, or because I was underneath a coat with Amy. Nerves are funny things sometimes. I just couldn't shake off the feeling of being so close to her and still wanting to be even closer.

It was hard. Hard because I had no idea whether she felt the same way, and hard because I knew it was too soon to be wanting to become involved with someone else. My emotions, everything, were still so raw. I didn't want any interactions with Amy to be a reaction to what had happened with Sue. I was still in the first stages of trying to cope with being me again and getting on with my life. I didn't yet have the strength to start it all over.

"Come here."

She didn't wait for me to comply, just slipped her arms around me and pulled me close. Duds was pressed in between us, so I didn't get the full impact of her body next to mine, and I can honestly say I am glad I didn't. The feel of her arms around me was initially uncomfortable. Stupid, I know, but it was, mainly because I wanted to pull back and run. Thankfully, I didn't, because in just a few seconds I felt like I belonged there, *really* belonged there. It was a feeling of safety I had been lacking for so long, not just the warmth of her, the essence; it was the *everything*. Nothing could hurt me whilst I was in her arms.

It was just Amy, me, and Duds. Nothing else mattered. Being stuck on a beach in the middle of a storm was nothing. Being underneath a coat in her arms was everything. And the scent of wet dog had never smelled so sweet.

The storm lasted all of fifteen minutes. Rain petered away to drizzle, and then to a mist. Wind lashed against our frozen legs and made heavy jeans truly uncomfortable. All I wanted to do was strip off and climb into a vat of steaming, bubbly bath water, to soak and relax. But that was at least an hour and a half away, as we had to get back to the car and then drive back to Norwich.

We were all chilled to the bone, but at Wells Next the Sea, proprietors being anal about health and hygiene refused us entry to cafés to get a much needed coffee and warming. Not because we were wet; this is England, remember. It was on account of Duds: "No dogs allowed."

Not all was lost, though, as The Ark Royal Public House let us all in without protest. Thirty minutes after getting off the beach, Amy and I were tucking into a hearty lunch, drinking coffee, and warming up next to the fire. The landlord even served Duds some meat in gravy, which he devoured in under two minutes. I didn't care that I had prepared a picnic; I was getting warm.

After our plates were empty, we sat in silence, totally at peace with the world. Life seemed perfect. The day seemed perfect. All was once again well and good in Bethany Chambers' world.

"So, tell me about you. I hardly know anything, apart from you've recently split up with someone."

Fuck.

"What was his name?"

Double fuck. Even a fuckity fuck fuck fuck. She must have seen my reaction. You know, the one where all the colour drains from your face and you squirm like you've just messed your pants.

"If it's still painful..."

"No. It's...erm..."

"Hey, no problem. You can tell me when you're ready."

She sounded so sincere, so honest and open. Should I come clean? Should I come out? Should I run? "It's a little more complicated than that."

"Was he married?"

"Erm."

"Never mind. Look, it doesn't matter. Fancy another coffee?"

I nodded, and she was up and at the bar ordering whilst I sat and stewed. Would she be disgusted? Shocked? It's amazing how we respond to people finding out whom we sleep with. I mean—does it change the person they liked as a friend? Unfortunately, yes. Some people can't accept the fact that when you leave them, you have a life that is different from theirs.

She was barely back in her seat when I began. "Sue."

"Excuse me?"

"Her name is Sue. My ex. Sue." I tried not to look at her face, tried not to know if she was reacting in a way I would add to the growing list of insecurities I was collecting. But I couldn't avoid it. I had to know.

"Sue?"

I nodded.

"As in a female Sue?"

I nodded again. "And the fact I said 'her.'"

Amy sat back on her chair, her lips pursed in consternation until they broke apart to reveal a brilliant white smile. "Good. We're not that different after all."

The relief was overwhelming. I didn't want to lose this budding friendship, and I didn't want to lie to her either. Then it dawned on me. She was gay. Amy was gay. The woman sitting in front of me was gay. Gay. Relief was replaced by...erm...relief? I want to say joy, happiness, euphoria, but I won't. Not that I didn't feel those things, but because relief was still the most overpowering emotion racing through me.

"I can't tell you how much better I feel by telling you that." I grinned at her and picked up my cup. "You too, huh? I would never have guessed."

"Why? Don't I look like the typical lesbian?"

It's amazing how a room suddenly goes quiet just as a word like "lesbian" appears in the conversation. I could feel the stares from a couple of people in the pub, and I wanted to say "Why don't you pull a chair up? You'd be able to hear everything then." Instead, I said, "I'm gaydar retarded," and took a sip of my coffee.

"We're not that different after all," she repeated.

The coffee in my mouth spewed into the air and all over Amy, who just sat there, coffee beading on her face. And that made me laugh again.

"Go on. Laugh at my expense."

So I did, head back and emitting throaty laughs until she had to join in. It felt so good. So good. Amy made me feel so bloody, fantastically good.

After we had allowed the relief to come out in the form of a good old laugh—about something that in the light of day, or to anyone else but Amy and me, could not be seen as that funny—we settled into comfortable silence.

Amy apparently decided that ten minutes was long enough to sit and stare silently into the fire. "Do you want to tell me what happened?"

I looked straight into her face, and I knew I would be safe. So I told her. No elaboration, just the facts—clinical, removed. And she listened, sipping her drink and nodding at all the right places. It felt good getting things off my chest, as I had not told a soul about what had happened, really happened. I usually said that Sue and I just drifted apart, thought it was for the best that we split up. I didn't believe people needed to know the nitty gritty...or that they would be interested in my shortcomings.

"You know what you need, don't you?"

A spine? I shook my head.

"Fun. Something totally distracting. Do things you would never usually do." Her face became animated, and I was definite I saw a gleam of the devil dancing behind her gorgeous eyes. "And you know something, Bethany Chambers?"

I shook my head again.

"I'm good at fun."

I bet you are. I couldn't wait to find out.

I know what I'll do now. I'll introduce a chapter heading, although there's no point calling it Chapter One, as I've bypassed that long ago.

Chapter Two(ish)

After that day on the beach, Amy and I spent quality time together. Duds was included on most excursions, but you don't see many dogs at the flicks, except maybe on the screen.

It's redundant to say that the more time I spent in Amy's company, the more I liked her. We "got on" as friends, but nothing more. I was relieved that "nothing more" had developed, as I didn't feel capable of beginning a new relationship so soon after the breakdown of the pseudo relationship I had shared with Sue. I know I shouldn't make comparisons between the two, but until you have been as badly burned as I was, you won't know how totally mind fucking it can be. The sorry thing was that when I was with Sue, I didn't even realise I was becoming fucked up; I just lost my sense of self.

I knew my self-confidence was at an all-time low, off on vacation without the sniff of a postcard, but the more I tried to lift myself out of it... Aw, you know the drill. I'd catch myself looking at Amy, absorbing her, her laugh, her smile, the twinkle in her eyes, and I would feel myself melting and nearly believing I was whole. But then I would remember, remember that I wasn't worthy of her.

Utter crap, I know. It should come with the slogan "I can't believe it's not utterly butterly crap." Or I should come with the slogan, considering I come out with the most imaginative crap conceivable. Even though it had been a few months since Sue had physically left the picture, I was still acting as if she would suddenly crawl out of the woodwork and demand to know why I was doing anything that she had not given me permission to do. Now and again, I would catch myself looking over my shoulder and feeling confused when no one was there. I had lived that way for three and a half years, and in retrospect, it felt like a lifetime.

Yes. Once again, I have gone off on a tangent. I was supposed to be telling you about fun, but as usual, I veered off down Self Pity Street, this time on a skateboard with three wheels. Why a skateboard with three wheels? Well, if it had four, it would have made things a hell of a lot easier, wouldn't it?

So let me go back to Fun, with a capital F to show how important it is.

I won't bore you with all the details of our days out, or evenings at the pub with impressions of Mr Darcy and Elizabeth Bennett that sounded more like Andy and Lou from *Little Britain*. I'll just tell you about the biggie—the weekend away, the last weekend of the season. It was a trip to Blackpool and its Pleasure Beach, a place that can evoke vomit just from the smell of the beef burgers. I went with the beautiful Ms Amy Fletcher, sans Dudley. I know we hadn't known each other for very long, just a few weeks, but when Amy suggested a fun trip to the seaside, I didn't even give it a thought, just said yes, which, as you know, is so unlike me. My way is to deliberate for days, weeks, even months over something like that. So when the answer came out, I think I surprised us both. But not as much as it surprised Duds.

Let's start with the look of absolute rejection on his face, shall we? Set the scene once again. God. That dog can twist my heartstrings around his paw with just a look from his adorable brown eyes. I mean, it's not as if I left him to fend for himself with only a slowly dripping tap for water and a sack of dry biscuits to keep him going. He went to my parents' for the three days, totally kitted out with his overnight bag, bed, toys, and every conceivable thing a spoiled pooch would ever need. My parents dote on him too, and treat him as their furry grandchild, as they have come to terms with the fact they are never getting a real one from me. I knew Duds would be walked extremely well, as my dad had the knack of knackering anyone who said they would go for a walk with him. He was a speed walker, and my mum said it made her feel as if he didn't want to be seen with her, as she was always left half a mile behind.

So, no calling the RSPCA. Dudley had it made.

But when I said goodbye to him for the thousandth time and then went back for the thousand and oneth kiss, my dad hoisted me under the armpits and nearly threw me out of the door.

Amy picked me up on the Friday at two o'clock, and, to tell you the truth, we both must have been mad to go to Blackpool in the middle of November. I mean, in the middle of the summer it was usually pissing down and freezing. And we had the added disadvantage of it being the last weekend before everything began to close up for the winter. But Amy had said we were on a quest for fun, so Blackpool it was.

It wasn't just that we were going to the epitome of British Garishness in all its glory that put me on edge. It was the fact Amy had made all the arrangements for the accommodation, and I didn't know where we would be sleeping—double, single, twin. I didn't know her expectations for the visit. What if she wanted to share a bed? Was I ready for that, even if it meant just sleeping? What if she thought this was the ideal time to make a move? Hark at me and my animal magnetism. As if she would be interested in someone who was as screwed up as I was.

That didn't stop me wondering and worrying all the way to Blackpool. Even when we played "Who can spot the tower first and win 10p," my heart was not in it. All the way along the M55, Amy strained to glimpse the mini-Eiffel tower that symbolised the seaside town. I began saying "Pylon. Pylon. Nope, pylon," without even looking at what she was identifying as the tower. It was the usual mistake everyone made when watching for the tower, but when you actually see it, it doesn't look like a pylon at all, and usually appears from nowhere, a little like *Brigadoon*.

And then, suddenly, there it was, surrounded majestically by gathering grey clouds against the blackening sky, with the fake orange glow that comes with urban life. What an image! I swear, if I'd rolled the window down, I would have smelled the grease from the fish and chip vendors even from five miles away. My stomach was in a dilemma—come up through my throat, or slip through my bowels. Decisions. Decisions.

When we entered Blackpool, we had the interminable job of searching out our guesthouse. No easy feat, as everywhere you looked boasted "The Best Guest House in the North West" and sported bills of fare as "Full English." Nearly an hour after entering the town, we stumbled on the place we would be calling home for the next three days, eloquently named "The Beachcomber." I mean, if you have ever visited Blackpool, you know that if you comb the beach, all you find are turds, used condoms, and tampons, usually in that hierarchy of frequency. It played out like a Scooby Doo chase, where they are running and keep passing the same things over and over again—turd, condom, tampon, turd, condom, tampon. Now and again you might spot a broken bottle or an empty beer can, but there is definitely no sign of buried treasure.

The next thing you have to look out for—a little bit of advice for anyone visiting—is the Blackpool Landlady. A law unto themselves, honestly. They always make out they're doing you a huge favour by letting you stay in their house, while charging you through the teeth to be a guest with them. They all look the same, too. They always look like they are getting ready for a night out on the town—hair in curlers but faces completely decorated, like extras from *The Mikado*. Footwear comes in the form of fluffy mules, pink, usually, and the torso sports an ample bosom that pushes its way out of a top that is two sizes too small.

The usual greeting is "You all right, my lovely? Come far?" as they are stitching you up like a kipper for your stay.

I didn't even listen to the long-winded gibber, as I was worrying myself stupid about what I would see when we opened the door to our room. I can't even honestly tell you what I wanted to see, but when Amy pushed the door back and I saw twin beds, a feeling of disappointment rippled through me.

"It's all right, isn't it?" The question she asked was merely rhetorical, as she threw her holdall on the nearest bed, only to have it bounce in the air and land with a thud on the floor. "Good. Springy mattress."

I laughed the laugh of the relieved. "It's a bit small, isn't it?" "Bit" was an understatement. Swinging a cat would be murder.

"I prefer to call it cosy."

We decided it would be best if we left the Pleasure Beach until the morning and just went for a stroll up the Golden Mile. I should explain what the Golden Mile is, shouldn't I? No. It's not like a Golden Shower, at least that would be warm. The Golden Mile is the three-quarters of a mile of shops, arcades, and lights that run along the seafront. I know it isn't a mile, but the Golden Three-Quarters of a Mile doesn't have the same ring to it.

Shower time was fun, to say the least. At least the box room we had gotten was en suite, so there would be no ducking down the hallways, flashing bits and pieces to all the other tourists doing exactly the same thing. Amy let me use the bathroom first, and I was in and out before she had gathered her toiletries. Her face showed her surprise at my quickness.

"I'm not one for messing about." I grinned, water still trickling down my face.

I sat on the edge of the bed and continued to dry myself off whilst Amy went to have a shower, leaving the door partially open. I know I shouldn't have peeked, but come on! Blood does run through these veins, after all. And it's not as if I was leering at her when she was in the shower. Erm...well...not exactly. I didn't look at her directly, I...erm...well, I could see her reflection in the mirror, which, thanks to the crap heating systems in crappy guestrooms, didn't steam up.

The bathrobe she was wearing when she went into the bathroom was slowly peeled off, and my eyes followed each movement of the material. She had her back to me, and it was flawless. Flawless. My mouth began to water at the expectation of the taste of her. My eyes were glued to the spot, wishing for her to turn around so I could see more. I watched her hang the robe on the hook at the side of the door, and then, as if in slow motion, she turned.

Fuck me.

I felt my jaw sag. The vision in front of me was nothing short of perfection. Per–fec–tion. Her breasts were full and round, and the nipples were slightly erect from the coolness of the bathroom. The skin was creamy and smooth, the same as it was on her back, and I could feel all sense of reason leaving me, could feel myself standing up and being drawn to her. Then she stretched her arms up to pull her hair back, and those wonderful breasts raised up at her command. Her stomach flattened and became taut, the line of her muscles taking my eyes lower and lower and lower until I could see the top of her pubic area. Black and inviting. Beckoning. I could almost taste her.

"Beth!"

Shit.

"Beth! Are you there?"

Double shit. I looked down at my feet, and they were one in front of the other in the act of making their way towards her. My towel had fallen, and I was naked.

Amy's head poked around the door at the very moment of my realisation. Her eyes left my face and glided down my body, hesitating slightly before making their way back. It must have taken all of a second, but I felt as if I'd been fully digested.

"Could..." She cleared her throat. "Could you pass me my towel from the bed?"

I just stood there. Staring.

"Beth?"

"Huh?"

"Towel?"

In my jumbled thoughts, I thought of towel, thought of me and my nakedness, and swooped down to reclaim it and wrap it tightly around myself.

"My towel. Oh, never mind." And she came out of the bathroom in all her feminine glory, breezed past me and picked up her towel, which was about two feet away from me, and then waltzed back into the bathroom.

Meanwhile, I hadn't moved once, except for my eyes, which followed her progress intently, devouring everything, even down to the small gold pendant around her neck.

It wasn't until I heard the click of the bathroom door that I realised what I had done, or hadn't done. The colour raced to my face, and I felt lightheaded. I stumbled to the bed and fell face first onto the candlewick covers, my glowing face buried in the indentations of the fabric. I felt like a right twat, gawping at her like she was a prize heifer or a slab of meat, and not even hiding the fact that I was doing it. What would she be thinking?

Nothing, apparently. She came out of the bathroom thirty minutes later, glowing and full of beans, ready for our walk up the prom. I was decently dressed by then—clothes on, fixed firmly in place. I tried to act normal, but the overwhelming emotion racing through me was one of foolishness. Actually, more like exposure. I had shown her in those few seconds what I wanted: I wanted her. It was so obvious, yet so bloody out of reach.

"Ready?"

Now that was a loaded question.

∞⋈

Hustle and bustle, bustle and hustle. That's what the seafront was like. Gangs of youngsters stalked the streets, sending out clear signals that they ruled the world. The scent of beer, candy floss, and onions clung to the air and completed the scene. The wind was whistling in from the exposed coastline, and the air was freezing cold.

Amy grabbed my arm and nearly frogmarched me past all the street vendors who were touting deals on all the latest materialistic crazes, all at knock-down prices, likely because they were knocked off.

Nearly an hour, and fifteen quid later, Amy had "won" me a teddy from the grabbing machines. Honestly, she could have bought it five times over for the number of twenty pence she had slotted into its greedy, money grabbing mouth. But it was the thought that counted. She had purposely set out to win it for me, and I hated to seem ungrateful.

I looked down at the fluffy puppy in my hands, a black and tan cuddly toy, and knew she had wanted me to have it because it looked like Duds. The beady eyes were the same, especially when he wanted to go for a walk.

"What are you going to call him?"

I looked at the fake fur and a myriad of names sprang to mind, but one kept pushing its way to the fore. "Charlie."

"Charlie? Why on earth Charlie?"

She laughed, and I felt a little foolish. But when I looked over at her, I could see no malice in her face, only a kind of wonder, innocent and curious.

"He just looks like a Charlie, don't you think?" I lifted the toy up close to her face and waggled its head, making it seem animated.

Her laughter rang through the arcade, and people began to look.

It's amazing how something so simple can embolden you and make you act the fool.

"Give us a kiss, lady," I provided on Charlie's behalf. Fuck. Where had that come from?

It wouldn't have been so bad, but I insisted that she kiss him by jamming the whole thing in her face.

She grabbed the toy and yanked it from my hands. "Mwah!"

The slap of her lips on the toy took me by surprise. Then she crushed it to her, and the gutteral moaning sounds emerging from beyond the black and tan tuft made my southern regions wish they were Charlie.

"Satisfied?" she asked, holding him out to me.

I swear to God that dog was smiling. If I'd been in his position, I would have been laughing my pants off.

"It'll do." I think I mumbled it, but knowing my luck, I probably bellowed it so everyone within two miles heard it.

"You've gone red."

Is that all the woman ever noticed about me?

Bugger.

∞⊙∞

The evening ended early, as we were both tired from the journey and our exposure to the bracing sea air. We ended up having a nightcap at the guesthouse and then sloping off to bed under the scrutiny of the landlady and a few other guests. I figured we would be the talk of the evening, even though we were in a twin room. People always find something to talk about, and two women sharing a room seemed to always fascinate people, especially men.

I was once again nervous about taking off my kit in front of Amy, and her getting hers off in front of me. Two things should have calmed me down. One, I could use the bathroom, or she could. Two, hadn't we already seen each other's bits and pieces? In the café. Not the usual place, I know, but hadn't we? And earlier, when we had showered. Too bloody right, we had, but that still didn't stop the anticipation, did it? I mean, we were getting undressed and staying like that all night. Well, apart from sleepwear.

Did she wear anything in bed?

Aw, crap. More things to worry about, as maybe I would do what I had done earlier when she had been in the bathroom and gawk at her as she slept, only this time being caught in the act.

I worried about it all the way up the stairs, all the while I was staring at her arse. There was even an element of worry as I stood behind her while she wiggled the key in the lock to get the door open. I even worried as I grabbed the key off her, tugged on the slim handle and shouldered the door whilst wiggling the key like crazy. It wasn't until the door suddenly shot inwards, taking both her and me with it, that I stopped worrying. I was too busy trying to get up off the floor, which isn't an easy feat when you have someone on your back. Why is it that when I'm around her, I always end up sprawled on the floor? She does too, for that matter.

To add insult to injury, as we were huffing and puffing, trying to disentangle ourselves, a voice drifted into the room. "You would think they could have waited until they shut the door."

The voice sounded put out, and as I looked between my legs, and Amy's, too, I could see the pickle-puss faces of a middle-aged couple standing in our doorway.

"Instead of standing there, you could lend us a hand," Amy choked out, maybe because my elbow was against her throat.

"How dare you!"

The bloke grabbed the handle and slammed our door shut, the vibration of the action seemingly unbalancing our precarious tottering and forcing us back into a heap. We lay there for a couple of minutes, the sound of our ragged breathing the only noise in the dark room. She was still on my back, the whole length of her body against mine, and it felt wonderful.

An agonizing coldness swept over me as she slowly lifted herself up off of me and sat back on her haunches, still quiet. Then a snigger. One from her, then one from me. Then another, and another, until we were both in stitches on the floor.

"Did you...did you see the...the look on that woman's face? 'How dare you!'" Amy laughed loudly, "It was worth the...the carpet burns." Her silhouette moved upwards and towards the door.

The room pulsated with light, and my eyes burned at the onslaught. I swear the landlady had used the brightest bulb that she could lay her hands on, maybe surplus from old lighthouse stock.

Ignoring the extended hand, I struggled to my feet and began brushing the front of my clothes, ridding them of imaginary dust and fluff.

"Don't you think?"

"Eh? Think what?"

"It was worth the burns. Look."

She lifted her sleeve and there it was—an angry red welt running up her forearm. You won't know this, but I have a thing about forearms. Not a fetish, a *thing*. I love the shape of a woman's forearms—the strength, the contours of the muscle, but also the femininity.

Therefore, it was no surprise that my hand reached out to stroke it. My fingers trailed alongside the mark and gingerly caressed the skin around the burn.

"It's a cracker, isn't it?"

I carried on touching her skin.

"Beth?"

Reality came crashing in, and my finger slipped and inadvertently poked the sore part.

"Jesus, Beth! Are you trying to kill me?"

My hand shot away from her, even more scorched than her skin.

"You've—"

"Gone all red. I know." I turned away from her and rummaged around in my bag. "Here. Put some of this on." I held out a tube of Savlon, my eyes not meeting hers.

And that was that. She went into the bathroom. I changed into my nightwear like getting undressed was an Olympic event, and dived under the covers. I don't know why, because as soon as she came out, I had to go and brush my teeth.

When I emerged, she was under her covers, lying on her side, facing my direction. Bugger. I thought I was quick getting my kit off, but that woman took the gold.

Then it was lights off and a muffled "goodnight." Sleep was an age coming, but I was soothed by the steady rhythm of Amy's breathing, and before I knew it, the morning was smiling through the thin curtains, heralding another day of fun. And when I say "fun," I actually mean it. Being with Amy was exactly what I needed.

Chapter Two was rather long, don't you think? I really should break this up. Maybe this could be the overly anticipated development stage, because the way I was feeling there was definitely something developing. But then, it would be all one-sided, wouldn't it? I was no nearer to finding out if Amy liked me in that way. She had given no indication of being interested in anything other than just friendship. And in the beginning, that was all I had wanted—someone I could just be "me" with. You know, be the Beth I used to be. Thoughts of Sue were becoming less frequent, less intimidating, although the memory of her was still lurking there on the sidelines, waiting to send another jolt to my self-esteem.

You may be wondering why I haven't mentioned Sue much since Amy came on the scene. But that's the whole point, isn't it? To a degree, Amy made me forget what had transpired in those three-plus years I spent with Sue. Amy made me want to move forward and become a whole person again.

To use a tired old cliché, I wanted to step into the light and feel the sun on my face once again. I was beginning to believe Amy was the light that was helping me chase away the darkness that had taken residence inside me.

Chapter Three:
The Overly Anticipated
Extended Development Stage

After breakfast—which was accompanied by glares from the middle-aged couple from the previous night and burnt toast, in that order—we piled on more layers and ventured out into the brisk November air. First port of call was the South Beach, or the Pleasure Beach.

What a day! I screamed so much on the rides, I was nearly hoarse by lunchtime. The worst was The Big One. Fuck. That was *big*. And fast, and pants-fillingly frightening. I tried to act cool, but come on! I thought the bastard thing was going to derail. At one time, it was the highest rollercoaster in Europe, and I was on it, screaming like a girl, waiting for death in a very loud way. It was the thunking sound as it attached itself onto the rail that first alerted me that something smelled rank in the State of Denmark, and my underwear, for that matter.

Have you ever been on a rollercoaster and, when it reaches the topmost loop, begun to scream in a crescendoing fashion? It starts like a low moan then rapidly rises into a shrill, banshee wail, tears pissing from your eyes and spit drooling from your mouth. Then they have the audacity to try to sell you a photo of you looking your absolute worst.

And then the woman who you fancy buys the photo as a memento. And she looks relaxed and happy in the picture, like she's reading a book, whilst you look like death is chasing you. She even looked cool and collected although I was gripping her carpet-burned arm. Tightly. Like a parrot on a perch. A squawking parrot that is faced by next-door's cat wearing a bib.

Let's put it this way: It was a while before I went on another ride, and then they were tame ones.

On the way out of the funfair, I spotted a new attraction. I wish I hadn't bothered. It was called the Paseje del Terror. The word "Terror" should have triggered warning bells, but no. I think all my screaming from the Big One had deafened me to the warning jangling that should have been clanging like a fire alarm as I paid the bloke at the counter. I didn't even know what the attraction entailed. If I had, I can guarantee it would have been a brisk walk along the seafront for me.

We had to wait for a few more people to join us, as we were going to be in groups, and I distinctly remember thinking I wanted a wee, but by the time I had registered the imminent bladder problem, we were being ushered inside. And I heard the guide, who was dressed like Dracula, lock the door behind us.

There were about ten of us in a room that was the size of an air raid shelter. There were three groups of people—a group of four, a threesome, Amy and me, plus the Dracula-fetish bloke, who was sans the pointy teeth, obviously for speaking purposes.

"You are now locked in. You can only go forward."

As he was speaking, I heard someone fart, and I hoped it wouldn't smell. No such luck. I gagged, and I lifted my scarf up to cover my nose and mouth whilst others did the same. The only ones who didn't react were Drac and a very tall lad standing to the left of me, glowing with embarrassment.

"You will encounter some very unpleasant sights..."

And smells, mate. Don't forget smells.

"But you must keep going forward. No running, or hitting the people you encounter."

Huh? There were people in there?

"If you don't touch them, they won't touch you." He paused for dramatic effect. "Good luck on your journey, and I hope to see you on the other side."

The other side of what? Was he being spiritual? I was hoping literal was more his scene, but looking at his garb, I was of two minds. A door to the right of us opened with a creak—how quaint—and people rushed through, mainly to get away from the smell of the lad's bowel emission.

In retrospect, I should have stayed with the fart.

Safer.

There was a corridor leading gradually downwards, and Amy grabbed my arm and pulled me along. I could hear screams in the distance, and I knew they were coming from the people who had recently been standing next to us in the anteroom.

Blackness. The bastards turned the lights out on us, and I was frozen to the spot and wishing for the light bulb from the guesthouse. Or a match, although that would have been a bad idea with the smell of methane still lingering in the air.

"Come on. Let's catch them up." Amy's arm was tightening around mine, and we stumbled along the corridor, feeling the walls with our hands.

Click. Blue light shone on Pinhead. Yes, Pinhead, from *Hellraiser*, who was standing right in front of me, his face mere inches away from mine and fucking leering at us.

A scream shot out of my mouth, and a little bit of pee shot into my drawers. I tried to back up but Amy was behind me, screaming loudly in my ear. Her arm was now around me, pulling me close against her, and if I hadn't been so terrified I would have loved it. But that wasn't my focus at that moment. Click again. Lights off. I grabbed her hand and ran, dragging her with me, bumping into the wall but using it as a guide, too.

When Regan, out of *The Exorcist*, screamed at me, I screamed louder. Laughing and screaming—or I should say, laughing, screaming, and peeing—I ended up on the floor, as did Amy, as our legs were so weak by this stage they could no longer hold our weight. We crawled on our hands and knees to the exit of the room, not caring that we both must have looked completely stupid. After leaving the room, we found that instead of continuing to scuttle on all fours, the best plan of action was standing upright and holding each other tightly when things got to be a little too much, and even when they weren't that scary.

But there in the dark, when she had me in her grip, I felt so safe, so contented just to be in her arms, even if it was under the pretext of our being frightened, or in my case, me actually frightened for most of the experience. As she held me, her mouth was mere inches from mine. I could feel her breath skip along my face, ragged and hot, and I wanted to lean in and kiss her mouth. Softly. Kiss her soundly, yet softly. And if it hadn't been for the lights clicking on again and someone looming over her shoulder, there was no doubt that I would have. Instead, I broke away from her and almost fell backwards, only the wall stopping me from hitting the floor.

She looked startled, but I didn't know whether it was a response to the figure's presence or because she knew what I had intended to do. The ache in my chest was an agony that had nothing to do with what was going on around me. No. It had everything to do with the woman standing with her shoulders slightly stooped and her hands dangling by her sides. I didn't know how to react. I didn't know if this was the moment I should tell her that I wanted more than just her friendship. So I did what I thought I should do—I pretended nothing had almost happened.

I could see that she was expectant, that she was holding something behind those eyes, perhaps some kind of question. And then it faded, snuffed itself out as I was standing there, as the actor was standing there waiting for us to scream or run or just react in some way. But all I felt was despondent. I think we would have just kept standing there, like a stalemate, if the lights hadn't clicked off again.

I felt her hand tentatively search out mine and grip my fingers.

"Come on. Let's go." Her voice was quiet, resolved. She tugged my hand, and we were on our way through the blackness once again.

Although the attraction became even scarier, I don't think either Amy's or my heart was in it. Don't get me wrong, we screamed and laughed like before, but it somehow seemed hollow.

A masked Jason blocked our exit. Jason with a chainsaw. The bloke in the couple in front of us calmly said, "That's a handheld Hoover, that is." But he stood very still, just in case, I think, and then he and his wife made a run for it.

Then it was our turn. Each of us attempted to dodge the battery-powered suction device as if it would suck the very soul from within us. I took a chance and nervously moved forward, before deciding I was too chicken shit to keep going. Amy slipped her arms around me, and the contact seemed to give me the gumption to take a step. Which I did. Tentatively. Her arms tightened, and I felt her move close against me before edging me towards the door and into the light. I know I said I wanted to step into the light again, but I meant it metaphorically, not the literal dingy lights of a pub.

I nearly pushed Amy over and raced across the pub looking for the toilet, even though I was sure some of the contents of my bladder was already in my underwear. Thankfully, that was not the case, and the euphoric sense of relief when I sat down was akin to an orgasm. I stared at the ceiling, silently giving thanks that I hadn't actually peed myself and staggered out of the experience steaming at the vee juncture of my jeans.

Not that I wasn't already feeling something along the lines of embarrassment. I mean—I had nearly kissed her. Nearly crossed the line. Nearly made a fool of myself. Again.

I lifted my hands to cover my face and could feel the skin burning my palms. How could I have even thought she would want me to kiss her? Reliving the scene in my head, I felt worse. My stomach was roiling by the time I heard Amy pull the chain and flush her toilet and then begin to wash her hands in the basin just outside my door. Then I heard the hand dryer. Then nothing. Quiet. Still.

I wanted to cry. I wanted to shout, "I'm sorry!" I wanted to curl up and die. But I just sat there.

The door to the loo opened and closed, and I knew she had left, so I sat there even longer. It must have been fifteen minutes I sat there, with my jeans round my knees and my head in my hands, until I realized I had to get up sometime or else I would get piles.

When I walked back into the pub, Amy was sitting near the exit of the Paseje del Terror with two drinks on the table.

"I was just about to come and look for you." She looked worried. "Are you okay? You look pale." I nodded and sat down in front of her. "I knew it was scary, but I didn't think it would frighten the shit out of you." The half-smile was there, and there was a twinkle in her eyes.

"You cheeky bugger."

She threw her head back and laughed, and suddenly the drama I had wrapped around what had almost happened in the Paseje seemed to fade and fizzle. I had to remind myself that Amy was not Sue. She wasn't the kind of person who would drag a situation out and feed on misery; harping on mistakes was not her scene. Amy was the kind of person who moved on.

We had a couple more drinks. I needed them, too, after screaming myself stupid in the Paseje del Terror. The next few hours were spent messing about on the seafront, daring each other to take our shoes off and allow the brown seawater to touch bare skin, even staring at the bungee jump on the pier because we didn't have the balls to actually get on it.

It seemed like an age before I realised we hadn't eaten since the candy floss, burgers, and toffee apples at the funfair. I was starving, so I suggested we grab something to eat.

We were about halfway through the meal when I thought about kissing her again. She was in the middle of telling me about one of the lectures she had given at the university, and she was laughing and talking, looking animated and beautiful, and all I could concentrate on was her mouth. The attraction I felt for her was so strong, I thought it was going to choke me. I had to know how she felt, had to ask if I would ever have a chance with her. It was at the precise moment I opened my mouth that her mobile started singing from somewhere off to the side of us.

She dived down beside her chair and rummaged inside her bag, mouthing, "I'm sorry," before clicking to receive the call. In a split second, her expression turned from concentration to happiness. "Jane! How the devil are you?"

A smile broke over her face, and disappointment clutched at me. I had been so wrapped up in the way I was feeling that I never even stopped to think she might be seeing someone. I knew she was single when I first met her, but with her looks and personality, there would be no way she would have stayed that way for long. She was the ultimate catch, the perfect woman. And I had been so fucking self-absorbed, I hadn't even given it a thought.

By the time I came back to the land of the sentient, I realised I had missed most of the conversation, and I only caught the end of her making arrangements for the following evening. That put paid to that. The growing attraction had definitely been one-sided. The look I thought I'd seen whilst we were inside the terror ride had been a figment of my imagination. It wasn't her anticipating that I was going to kiss her; it was her anticipating that she'd have to tell me she didn't think of me that way, that she was already taken.

"Sorry about that." She grinned at me. "Are you going to eat that?"

I shook my head and forced a smile. Her fork swooped over and nabbed the last roasted potato on my plate, and she lifted it to her mouth and shovelled the whole thing inside, all the while making noises of contentment. When she had finished chewing and was trying to swallow, she tried to splutter out something about dessert, then coffee, but I shook my head.

"To tell you the truth, I'm knackered."

Her head tilted as she looked at me enquiringly.

"Must have been all that screaming and sea air."

She nodded.

"Think I might ring Duds, and then grab an early night."

"Erm...okay." She tipped her glass up and drained the last drops of her wine. "You can use my mobile if you want."

I shook my head as I pulled my own from my pocket and waggled it. "I'll ring him when we get back to the hotel. Or should I say, I'll ring my parents." I grinned, but Jesus it hurt to pretend that everything was okay.

Bedtime was the same as the night before, except for the worrying about seeing each other naked. What was the point? She was already involved with someone; it wasn't as if she would be interested in staring at my body. Amy still undressed in the bathroom, and I was in bed by the time she returned, but there wasn't the anxiety there had been when I thought I might have a chance.

A muffled "good night" crept up from the duvets of both our beds, but I could feel her staring at me in the darkness. I turned over and faced the window, then heard her bed creak as she turned away too. And that's the way the morning found us, lying with our backs toward one another.

Before lunch time, we were on the M55 and heading back to Norfolk. Don't get me wrong, we didn't outwardly say anything that made us leave early. It was because I knew she had to get back to meet "Jane" that I may have guided our actions into doing just that. And it was also because I knew I couldn't keep up the masquerade of being happy for very much longer.

Chapter Four:

Regression Stage. (Bugger)

That was the end of The Overly Anticipated Extended Development Stage. I should really call it "The Anti Development Stage," or even "The Two Steps Forward and Three Back Stage." Could even stretch to "The Feeling Like a Total Twat Stage," as the only thing that had developed was my attraction for Amy, but as you can see, that was going nowhere. I don't think I was emotionally ready for anything to happen anyway, but I can only say that because there was no chance of it *actually* happening. So, it is the Regression Stage. Unfortunately.

Amy dropped me off at my house with the promise to call, and I barely threw my bag inside the doorway before I turned around, got in my car, and went to get the man in my life. At least Duds was pleased to see me. Bless him. When I walked through the door at my parents' house, I honestly thought he would pee on my feet, just like he used to do when he was a pup.

He lay flat on his back, groaning around the bright red ball clamped in his mouth, and I was in the midst of tickling his belly when my mum finished the day off.

"Sue called."

Two words. Short. Simple. To the point. Two words that made my stomach heave. I opted to ignore her pronouncement.

"Oi, luggy, I said Sue called."

I turned and looked at my mum, who was trying to unstick the newspaper from the table, as it was glued to the surface with something my dad had spilt. Like usual.

"And?" I hoped I sounded neutral, indifferent. But mums know, don't they? They know when you are trying to hide something from them, and they act one of two ways. Firstly, they could give you a break and go with the flow. Or they could be like my mum when Sue was concerned.

"Told her to sling her hook. That was the best thing you've ever done, getting rid of her."

I knew it was coming, the lecture, and I knew it wouldn't be long before my dad came through and added his two pence worth.

"She was no good for you, and you know it."

I could see her preparing to sit and arrange herself for sermon mode, and I just couldn't handle it. "Did she say what she wanted?" I turned my attention to Duds, splayed on his back, waiting for me to continue tickling him. Which, of course, I did. It was an antidote to the churning in my intestines.

"Said she needed to get hold of you. Tried your place, but there was no answer."

Mum stopped there, but I sensed there was something more. I could hear her fidgeting in her chair, and I could also hear my dad making his way through the kitchen, his Wellied feet clomping mud on the floor. Still my mum said nothing.

"Hiya, sweetheart." Dad leaned over, kissed my cheek, and then rubbed his stubble over my skin, because he knew it irritated me. His laugh was nothing short of evil. "Did your mum tell you the Wicked Witch has been on the phone?"

I nodded, rubbing my face and scowling.

"Bet she didn't tell you she told her you were away on a dirty weekend, though, did she?"

"You are joking!" My head snapped over to where Mum was sitting, sitting and glowing. "Mum, please tell me you didn't say that."

Still nothing. A lot of wriggling, but no sound.

"Of course she did. And called her a slapper, too." Dad was yanking his Wellies off and didn't even notice the thickness of the air or the need for the proverbial knife that usually accompanies these kinds of situations.

"Mum?"

"She deserved it. And you were."

"Whatever went on between Sue and me was exactly that—between Sue and me." The quickness of my movement from floor to standing jostled Duds from his euphoric haze of Mummy love. Pity I couldn't say I was feeling the same thing at that moment. "And for your information, there isn't, and never will be anything going on between Amy and me."

It was at that moment that the full weight of my unrequited feelings for Amy crashed down on me, and I didn't know whether to run or cry. I did both, calling Dudley to follow.

I could hear my parents trying to catch up, even the staggering movement of my dad trying to put his Wellies back on, my mum's voice breaking as she was trying to apologise, hiccoughed breaths telling me she loved me. But there was no way I could have stayed. And it wasn't just about the Sue scenario. I felt fragile all of a sudden, and being with my parents and the sympathy they would flood all over me would definitely send me over the brink.

Ball ensconced in his mouth, Duds was pacing along the back seat when I slammed the engine into gear and performed a perfect screech out of my parents' road. Through my rear view mirror, I saw him hit the back of the seat, and guilt engulfed me. What was I doing? I could have an accident and lose him, lose the only one who loved me as much as I loved him.

I eased my foot down on the brake and slowed the car to a stop. "Come here, fella." And he was over the gap between the seats and on my lap, kissing my face with licks and nuzzles. "You love me, don't you?"

I was crying, big fat salty tears that he lapped away as I stroked the rough fur on his sides and back. We just sat there, him snuffling and me sniffling, until I thought I couldn't cry any more.

"Do you want to go to the park?" His ears shot up, making his face seem comical. "Come on, then. In the back." And over he popped, nestling down on the blanket I kept in the back seat.

As I placed the car in gear, I knew one thing for certain: I loved my dog and he loved me. And at that moment in time, that's all I needed.

෨෭෬

Walks, as walks tend to do, distract you to a degree from how utterly shit your life is. Opting to avoid

Earlham, I took Duds to Mousehold Heath instead. He loved racing through the trees and up and down the embankments. Squirrels fled as he yapped and chased them into hiding. The sun was going down rapidly, and I knew it wouldn't be long before the familiar paths would look like something from the *Blair Witch Project*.

Images of Amy poked and prodded through my thoughts—images of her laughing and joking, images of her screaming on the Big One, then, worst of all, images of her doing the exact same things with her girlfriend, Jane. A confusion of happiness and sadness whirled around me, and I couldn't decide which one was the strongest. I just knew that I missed her, and for once in my life, I felt lonely. I hadn't felt lonely when Sue had moved out, even though, truth be told, in my screwed-up mind I'd had doubts whether I was doing the right thing. I had not even felt lonely when I still hadn't allowed my friends back in my life. Being on my own had seemed the right way to be.

Duds was absolutely knackered by the time we got back to the car, and his panting kept me company on the drive home. Strange thing was that when I indicated to turn into my road, he bolted up and started growling. I couldn't even see what could have made him react that way, but his vocalization steadily grew into a deep-throated, threatening rumble.

As I stopped the car and turned the engine off, he was over the gap and standing protectively on my knee, his eyes fixed to the alleyway that separated my house from my neighbour's. There was nothing there, but that didn't stop him becoming more agitated and pressing against me as if to stop me leaving the car.

"Come on, Duds. There's nothing there, mate. Look."

He *was* looking, eyes staring into the gap between houses and the hackles at the back of his neck making an uncommon appearance. I didn't know what to do, as I had left his spare lead at my parents' house. What if it was the folks next door checking something, and then Duds went all macho on them? Or it could be Mrs Foster's cat, trying to catch birds in my garden. If I opened the door, Duds would be out and at the feline hunter before I could blink, and at this moment, aggravation was something I didn't need.

I popped him in the back with the order to stay and took my chances out on my own. I did feel a bit unnerved, because it could just as well have been a burglar trying to get into my place, or coming out. Even if it was, I doubted Duds would make much difference, though he would think otherwise and could end up injured. There was no way I was going to let him get hurt on account of a DVD player or computer. Those kinds of things were replaceable; Dudley wasn't.

I didn't skulk around the side, as I wanted whoever—if there was someone there—to have the opportunity to take what they needed and piss off. I could have called the police, but what would I say? "Erm...excuse me, Officer, but my dog is growling at an alleyway. Could you send a squad car, and maybe the SWAT team?" Nah. I decided to go it alone, for the moment anyway.

There I was, marching towards my fate, girded in mud and determination. But when I turned the corner, I can honestly say I realized that the cliché "blood turning to ice" wasn't so cliché.

"What the fuck do you want?"

Sue. I should have guessed it was her by Dudley's reaction. He could sniff her out anywhere, and as you already know, there was no love lost between them.

"And why are you hiding behind my bins?" I stood with my hands on my hips, the stance of a warrior. There was no way I was going to let her intimidate me again. After all, it was her that was hiding behind bins.

"I'm not hiding. I was just writing you a note, and I needed something to lean on."

I looked at her hands, which held neither paper or a pen. So I gave her the raised eyebrow look as if to say, "Yeah, right."

"I haven't got time for games, Sue. What do you want?"

She came towards me, raising her hands in pacification and trying to charm me with her tilted head and cajoling smile, but there was no way any of that crap was going to work. I'd fallen for it before, and look where it had gotten me.

"Can't I just come and see how you are once in a while?"

My face said it all, but she didn't get the message.

"Just a coffee and a chat, that's all I'm asking."

I don't know what made me agree to it. I should have done what my mum did and told her to sling her hook. I can't explain it. Just one of those things, I guess. I had to physically restrain Duds and put him in the spare room before Sue could even come into the house. He wasn't happy. Neither was I, for that matter.

Once she was inside, she acted as if she had never left.

"Why don't you go and put your feet up, and I'll put the kettle on."

Sue was already on her way to the kitchen as she made the offer, but I stopped her with an unvarnished, "No."

Her back went rigid for a split second before she turned to me, her smile fixed firmly in place. "It's no bother." She stepped tentatively towards me, her hand reaching out before she pulled it back, a short bark of laughter leaving her mouth. "I think I can remember where everything is."

I clenched my teeth together, biting back the response I wanted to give her at that moment. In my head, I counted to five before speaking. "I'll do it. You go in to the front room." I tried to smile, but it felt fake on my lips. "I'm sure you can remember where that is, too." I stepped to the side and let her pass, feeling some sense of accomplishment at such a small achievement.

As she went into the front room, I started toward the kitchen. Before I reached it, the flashing light of my answer phone on the hallway table caught my attention, and I clicked the play button. The first two messages were from Sue, purring down the phone in that breathy way of hers about her just wanting to "touch base." But it was the third one that got my attention.

"Hey, Beth. Amy. Just wanted to say I had a fantastic time this weekend, and that you don't snore... too loudly." Then her laugh. "We'll have to do it again soon. I'll ring you in the week. Take care. Bye."

The sudden absence of her voice was deafening, until the silence was broken by Sue's voice, right behind me. I should have known that she never did anything I ever asked her to do.

"Amy, eh? New conquest?"

I turned to face her, and I was glowing, for what reason I don't know. It's not as if anything had happened between Amy and me. Even if it had, it had fuck all to do with Sue.

"Seems like you're getting over me just fine."

"There's nothing going on between Amy and me. We're just friends."

I could tell she didn't believe me. Her expression turned smarmy, and I could feel the flirt vibes radiating from her in waves. I had to conjure up the protective anti-Sue force field that lurked just beneath my surface.

"I'd better make that coffee." And I turned and shot into the kitchen, shutting the door behind me.

Five minutes later, I was back in the front room with two coffees and a deep-seated resolve to tell Sue to fuck off, and she could take her coffee to-go. But I hadn't expected her to be sitting on the sofa, head in hands, crying.

I felt a mix of emotions. So many things had happened between us, so many shit things, but I still didn't want to see her upset. My hands shook as I placed the mugs on the table, and then I sat on the other end of the sofa, totally at a loss as to what to do. I didn't want to touch her, didn't want to give her the wrong impression. So I said the lamest thing one can say: "Are you okay?"

Why is it that when you see someone sobbing, you ask them if they're okay? If they were okay, they wouldn't be sobbing, would they? They'd be grinning, or rolling around laughing, or smiling, even a little bit. I plucked a few tissues from the box on the coffee table and shoved them underneath her chin.

A shaking hand came out and accepted them tentatively, folding them into a mass and using it to cover her face. It was a few moments before her staccato voice came tumbling out. "I just miss you so much, Beth."

And then a minute more of crying, whilst I sat there feeling uncomfortable. What could I say? "I don't miss you. Glad you're out of my life." So I kept silent and stared at the cup of coffee I wanted her to take with her, wishing I had the spine to tell her to do it, in spite of her tears.

"I'd heard you were with someone else, but it was a shock to actually hear her voice."

"Why, Sue? We're not an item anymore."

More tears.

I really wanted to twiddle my thumbs and wait for her to stop, but it seemed out of place, so I restrained myself. It wasn't until a few minutes later that I realised that I should have been feeling guilty, should have been apologising, should have been acting differently from how I was. Because *that* would have been the way I'd have been feeling if Sue and I *were* still an item.

It felt good. I felt good. The whole situation, although uncomfortable, felt good. I held back the smile that was trying to creep onto my mouth. There was no point rubbing it in. Or was there? Too right there was, and I was just about to tell her to take her pitiful, manipulative arse off my sofa and drag it as far away as possible, when the house phone rang, the chimes of it echoing throughout the house.

I should've ignored it, but it was instinctive. My hand was around the slim grey receiver, the button clicked, and I had said "Hello" before I realised what I had done.

"Hi, sis."

Bollocks. It was Will. I know I haven't mentioned my brother much, but I have been too wrapped up in self-pity to think about anyone but myself and my own misery.

"Can I come and see you?"

I looked at Sue, who was once again wiping her face dramatically on the crushed tissues and looking at me quizzically.

"Sure, Will. When?"

"Right now. I'm outside yours as we speak."

"Now! But..."

Sue shook her head and gesticulated frantically, indicating that she wanted us to be alone to talk.

"Sure. That would be great. Sue was just leaving."

Honestly, talk about a turnaround. She was like Lady Macbeth, and could have played the part with no primping. On the one face, she was the fragile, wronged party, then quickly swapped that for the face of a conniving little fu—

"Great. I'm on my way up your path." The phone clicked off just as the doorbell sounded.

"Sorry, Sue. Family business."

She was on her feet and smoothing the front of her blouse with one hand, whilst stroking a finger under one eye to remove a smudge of mascara.

I didn't think I should tell her it just rubbed it in more and made her look like a boxer who had lost the bout. I smiled as I went to let my brother in.

She followed me to the door.

As it opened and he stood there grinning like an idiot, Sue pushed in between us and blocked my view of my brother to whisper conspiratorially, "I'll call you." Then she pushed past him and flounced down the path to the gate.

"Bye, Sue. Lovely to see you," Will called, and then turned to face me, finishing with, "Not."

After a bone-crushing hug, we were in the kitchen and I was making a fresh cuppa. I knew there was a reason behind his visit, and I didn't have to wait long before I found out what it was.

"Been to Mum and Dad's tonight."

He waited, but I didn't say anything.

"They are upset."

I ignored him as I heaped four sugars into his cup.

"Beth? Are you listening to me?"

"Yep." I stirred the milk in slowly.

"Aren't you going to say anything?"

"Nope."

"Mum was crying, Beth." He released a deep sigh as he pulled a chair out from the table.

The squeal of the chair leg on the floor grated my teeth. "And?"

"Oh for fuck's sake. Can't you answer with more than one word?"

"Yes." I tinked the spoon on the side of the cup. "I can."

When I turned, he was sitting with his arms dangling between his legs, looking at me as if I had sprouted an extra head. "I can't believe you. Mum was crying, and you make jokes. Bad ones."

I did feel bad, but I didn't want to give in just yet. Will knew me from old, and saw the crack in my blank-faced veneer.

"She's sorry for upsetting you. Said she didn't know where it came from. Before she knew it, it was out." Slam. His cup of tea was in front of him, a quarter of it now trickling over the table top.

"Look, Will. She shouldn't have said anything to Sue, or anybody else for that matter, about things that have nothing to do with her or Dad." I began to wipe up the mess. "I think I'm old enough to look after myself."

Then I suddenly remembered. "Shit!" And I was gone, out of the room and running.

"What's the matter?

I barely heard him. I had forgotten something much more important than silly family squabbles. I'd forgotten I'd locked Duds in the spare room.

His little face lit up as I opened the door, and he came skidding off the bed and charging to me, making a dramatic bounce just before he was in my arms and licking my face. Telling me off, I think.

"Sorry, mate. Give Mummy some kisses."

Will came behind me and ruffled Duds' head, saying hello and making a fuss. The tiff between us was forgotten as we both lavished attention on the little fur ball in my arms. Duds always stole the show, and that's the way I liked it. Saved anyone really getting a good look at me.

The subject of me upsetting my parents wasn't raised again until Will was just about to leave, and by that time I had calmed down enough to agree that my behaviour had been childish. I even promised to call them as soon as he left. And I did. Like a good girl.

I knew why my mum had said what she had. She loved me. I loved her and my dad, too, but I did sometimes wish that they would treat me more like a responsible adult.

In retrospect, it wasn't what they had said about, and to, Sue—which was actually pretty funny. It was the fact they had made me look at myself and my life, how crap it was, the fact I had feelings for someone and I knew they were one-sided. The fact I never had, or ever would have a chance with Amy. And it stung.

Bedtime was a sombre affair, with me bathing for nearly an hour beforehand. I hadn't even unpacked my bag from my trip to Blackpool, as it would make me think of her. As if I needed reminding.

When I closed my eyes, thoughts of Amy haunted me, and when I opened them, I had the strangest sensation that I could almost see her at the end of the bed. Fuck me. I must have been totally screwed up if I was beginning to hallucinate. Or was it just wishful thinking?

One thing I did know—I needed to get to sleep, because I needed to get up early in the morning. The odd thing was, I didn't know why I had to be up early.

Unnerved? You're not on your own. I was beginning to unnerve myself with my prophetic powers.

Chapter Five:
Could This Be the Climax Stage?

I dreamed of Amy. Images of her poured through my subconscious, despite my efforts to block them out. To say I woke up in the middle of the night feeling horny would be an understatement. My lower half began to wriggle, and I heard a grunt from the bottom of the bed. I couldn't do anything with Duds there; I would feel embarrassed. I know—he is a dog, and I should have just carried on and not bothered about his presence. I could even have lifted him off the bed and put him in his basket. But he looked so contented, his tongue slightly out of his mouth and emitting rasping little snores.

I couldn't shift him so I could fiddle with my lady bits. That would be cruel. Nope, I couldn't. But I could shift myself.

Decision made, I was up and out of the door and into the spare room before Dudley could stretch out his paws.

I lay on the bed, closed my eyes, and thought of her face, her smile, her skin and the softness of it.

Thought about what it would taste like on the tip of my tongue, feel like on the tips of my fingers, and I could feel the arousal building. There was a moment when I felt a pang of guilt for thinking of her that way, but it was fleeting. She would never know. And a girl has to do what a girl has to do.

I slipped off my sleeping trousers and sprawled out, my fingers loitering just a few inches from where I needed them. My other hand snaked its way inside my top and began to swirl slow circles around my left breast. The t-shirt was getting in the way, so I pulled it off.

Naked. Naked and wet. Naked and wet and horny, with one person on my mind. Her eyes—figments of imagination—captivated me. Brown. Rich. Moist. If I assigned them a scent, I would say they would smell like freshly ground roasted coffee. Definitely a stimulant!

My left nipple perked and peaked, and I grasped it gently with my index finger and thumb, all the while imagining it was her fingers. Arousal raced to my groin, and I felt the moisture pool and collect. Gently I slipped a finger between my folds and pushed down. A gasp exploded from my lungs, and my body spasmed. I pulled my finger up, grazing my clit. Another gasp, another spasm. My eyes fluttered closed and open with each movement of my finger, and I slid a second finger down the other side of my folds, trapping the engorged clit between them.

Tug. Pull. Tug. Pull...push. Tug, pull, push. Over and over again, the rhythm steadily increasing in tempo. The sensations were all-consuming, feeding the desire raging through me. My other hand cupped my breast and was pumping the soft flesh with unrestrained motion. I was bordering on delirium, on that deep-rooted ecstasy that growls beneath the surface, waiting impatiently to be freed.

I lifted my knees and spread my legs further apart, releasing the grasp on my breast to slither along damp skin and between my legs. Open and exposed, I was ready to separate and indulge. The cheeks of my arse clenched against the bedcover, and I lifted my hips for access to the bulging bud at my centre. One hand to divide and unlock the entrance to the burrow. Slow and sure, sure and slow. One finger inside, prodding and poking and excavating, then a second. I could feel the walls inside clasping and gripping, tugging the fingers deeper.

Then out.

Then in.

Out and in.

Out and in.

Over and over again, steady thrusts, wet thrusts, squelching thrusts that were increasing to plunges. God, I needed more! Needed to feel pressure on top of me, around me, at the sides, everywhere.

Fingers still buried deep, I grabbed a spare pillow and placed it between my legs. Then another, which lay on my stomach.

It wasn't enough.

I moved the pillow from my stomach and put it between my legs with the first, and my thighs clutched as my fingers pumped. Hips bouncing on the bed were making up the rhythm of the missing piece, the missing person, the missing...

Amy.

I gasped as the flutter of orgasm foretold its incipient arrival. I worked harder. Plunged faster and deeper. Gripped the objects between my legs and rode my hand, her hand, 'til the lights appeared and the sound of my cries hit the walls and echoed back to my convulsing body. Reality blurred and the ache subsided, for the moment.

I dressed quickly, washed my hands, and then silently made my way back to my bedroom. Two beady eyes were staring at me from the middle of the bed. Dudley was sitting bolt upright with his ball between his front paws, glaring, as if to say, "Where the hell have you been?"

The embarrassing thing was that he gave me the impression that he knew what I'd been doing. Must be the same as way one's parents feel—

Stop! I am NOT going down *that* road. My parents do not *do it*. Only did it when Will and I were conceived. Other siblings? Artificial insemination. Jesus. Now I'm thinking about— Forget it. Let's leave that train of thought, shall we? My dinner is swirling around in my stomach.

Where was I? Getting into bed. Right. Throat-clearing cough.

After I clambered under the duvet, Duds sprawled himself across my neck and rubbed his face against mine before he fell back to sleep. It wasn't long before I followed his example, his red ball jamming into my side. But I didn't mind. Felt right somehow.

ॐ

The next morning, my unsupported prophesy of having to get up early actually did come true. And it happened very early indeed.

Duds got it into his head that he would bug the arse off me to get up and take him for a walk. This included little whining noises followed by a thudding on my chest as his ball hit me and rolled off. I can't tell you how many times he did this, and no matter how many times I told him, "In a minute," his persistence made it clear that my minutes were a lot longer than his.

Eventually I gave in. He didn't. Talk about being stalked! He followed me around the house, slipping and slouching onto every piece of furniture so he could keep his eye on me. When I came out of the bathroom, there he was. Waiting. I offered him breakfast. He refused. His eyes noted every movement until he heard the magic word "walk" slip from my lips. He didn't even need the word, as the squirt of my deodorant can was enough to send him into an excited frenzy.

He dived onto one of my slippers and enacted a kill, shaking the poor thing from side to side and then lying on his back, kicking his legs in the air.

We went to Earlham. Don't know why, but that's where we ended up. As soon as I opened the car door, he was off and running, down the green sloping hill leading to the river. I watched his bum jump up and down as he ran, and then as he did a detour to the left towards the café. Little bugger. No wonder he didn't want dry biscuits; he was hoping for a sausage or bit of bacon.

I grabbed his lead and my bag and chased after him, huffing and puffing and swearing to take more exercise. When I arrived at the café, the owner was trying to distract Duds with titbits, but Duds was having none of it. He kept trying to sneak by, his tufty little head looking beyond the man as if he was searching for something.

I offered him his ball; he ignored me. I tried to pull him away from the door; he tugged me back. I ended up putting him on his lead and dragging him. He only got distracted when he was out of sight of the café, but I knew he might still become snappy so I kept him firmly attached to me until I could be sure that he was more interested in his ball than running off to the café again.

We walked for miles, and although it was freezing, I didn't care. It was Monday, but I didn't have to go into the office to pick up any more work, as I was still working on the "Promoting Positive Mental Health" campaign, which was quite apt for my present state of mind. My head was so full of crap, I couldn't begin to wade through it all. Thoughts of Amy were plaguing me. So were thoughts of Sue. They took on the disparate roles of angel and demon, like the ones in Bugs Bunny cartoons when each would hover over a shoulder and give him contrary advice. The viewer would know he should listen to the angel, but they wanted Bugs to take the advice of the demon because it was more fun. And in cartoons, it wasn't real. Everything turned out okay in the end.

I'm sure you can imagine who played which part. Amy looked angelic in white, so pure, and... Fuck. I was getting turned on by my hallucinations. Give me strength.

A feeling of unsettlement slithered through me, and not because I was thinking of my life in terms of a Warner Brothers cartoon. It was the feeling that everything was so unpredictable; life was so bloody unpredictable. It had been over six months since I had split with Sue "I will love you forever" Granger, but it still felt as if she had a hold on me.

The last time I had seen her, I had felt strong and been able to block everything out, but my mind was like the English weather—it never knew what it wanted to do. I had spent the last six months living under the black cloud of a broken relationship, shying away from getting stuck out in the rain, and what for? Saving myself for another rainy day? But wasn't the majority of the three and a half years I'd spent with Sue one storm after another, until it seemed as if I was constantly windswept and half drowned?

There were good times, there had to have been, or else I wouldn't have stayed, would I? But at that moment in time, I couldn't think of one half-decent sunny day, not even a gentle warming breeze.

But we can't predict our futures, can we? That would take all the "fun" out of getting screwed over by the dealers of the Fate cards. I think that was where my problem really lay. I didn't know what my future held, what to expect, and I was wary of getting myself into the same situation as I had before. For the last three and a half years, everything had been done for me. I was told exactly what to do, who to see, what to say, even how to bloody wash up, and now I felt naïve, felt I wasn't quite up to coping in the adult world.

Then it hit me. I *was* coping. Wasn't I? My bills were getting paid every month. I fed, washed, and dressed myself every day and took care of Duds. But it didn't feel real, somehow. It seemed as if my relationship—a term to be used *very* loosely—with Amy was as if I was rebelling against what I had previously believed Fate had in store for me, and that meant a life of misery—either in a relationship with Sue, or just as miserable on my own. But, I think rebelling is the wrong word here. Surviving seems to fit better, or beginning to live, beginning to want more than what I had. Until I found out about Jane, I was enjoying every single moment with Amy, and what I was trying to do now was identify why she wasn't interested in me. Why she was interested in Jane and not me. That was the "beginning to want more than what I had," rather than rebelling, wasn't it?

But, I couldn't just brush Amy's relationship with Jane under the carpet. She wanted Jane and not me, and Fate had won after all. ABBA got it right with their lyrics ... "*the Gods may throw the dice...the loser has to fall...It's simple and it's plain...*" And I was the loser. A loser. So I should just shut up and get used to it.

It's amazing how my thoughts could shift without me even noticing the process. I was thinking about Sue and my relationship, and suddenly—bam, Amy. I shook my head, called for Duds, and then made my way home. Away from all the elements.

෨෭ඏ

The rest of the day passed quickly with me wading through thumbnail after thumbnail of potential ideas and slogans, and before I knew it, Duds was in front of me, his harness hanging from his mouth.

Another walk. Another set of thoughts. Then back home again, shower, then bed. I drifted off to an image of Amy laughing, and I felt the crease of a smile slip onto my mouth. Duds curled up in the crook of my legs and released a contented sigh. And so did I.

Chapter Six:
The Anti Climax — Has to Be, Doesn't It?

I kept myself busy, very busy, even went in to the office a couple of times that week. It felt strange at first, talking to people I had worked with nearly every day for seven years. I felt like a stranger, almost an impostor. My work colleagues treated me in exactly the same way they always had—poked fun, took the piss, showed me the designs they were working on. A feeling of normalcy crept in. I felt normal, whatever normal is.

Duds spent his time with my parents, and I bugged the arse off them with phone calls to check that he was okay. I knew I was obsessing, but in retrospect, I think it was transference. I was only out of the house for a matter of hours, and I now believe he would have liked the time on his own—a bit of peace and quiet. He was perfectly happy staying with my parents when I used to go to work full time, and I didn't ring them ten times a day then.

I'm rattling on again, aren't I? Well spotted. And the reason I'm going off on my very own personal tangent is because Amy hadn't called. No more messages on my answering machine, my mobile, not even a text message. I was text free. I think I went out so I didn't have to sit waiting for the phone to get off his arse and do his job. Then when I came home, I did everything I possibly could to not look at the non-blinking light on the answer phone display.

It wasn't until Saturday morning that the musical sound of my muted friend thrummed through the house again. I was making a coffee, or more accurately, I should say I was tipping coffee grinds all over my work surface when the ringing announced Amy's reappearance. There was a mixed bag of emotions whirling inside me. I was happy to hear her voice, but angry because it had been nearly a week since she'd said she'd call. Finally, I felt an overwhelming sense of sadness and loss. She was with Jane, the same Jane who I'd taken an instant dislike to without even meeting.

My tone evened out to indifference as I just barely replied to her enthusiastic hello.

"Fancy meeting up? I'm already in Norwich." By the sound of her invitation, she hadn't picked up on my lack of eagerness.

I had to bite my tongue so I didn't spit out, "Why don't you ask your girlfriend?" But I restrained myself. "Sorry, Amy. I'm working."

I could feel Duds glaring at me as the lie slipped from between my lips, and I mouthed, "What?" to him, as if he understood.

"Oh. Right. Okay." Amy was either disappointed or hatching a plan. "What about later? We could go to the pictures...or grab something to eat. Or both. My treat."

"I wish I could." That bit was true, but it wasn't for the reason I gave her next. "But I have so much to get through. I have deadlines to meet."

"No worries, Beth. I understand you're busy." Her tone was flat, but then she cleared her throat and her voice lifted as she added, "But soon, yes? We'll do something together soon?"

I felt a right cow. "Sure. That would be great. Speak soon, yeah?"

"Erm, yeah." Amy sounded a little confused, probably because I was shutting down the conversation so quickly. "See you soon, okay?"

"See you, Amy."

As soon as I placed the handset back on its base, regret washed over me. What was I doing? I was jeopardising the first real friendship I had had in years because I couldn't handle the fact she was with someone else. I was blaming her for finding someone other than me, even when I had never given her any indication that I even thought of her that way.

I snatched the phone up and called her back. Busy. That didn't stop me leaving her a message.

"Hey. Erm. What was I thinking? Work is ... erm, work. It will still be there later. What do you fancy doing? Call me back when you get this, okay?"

Inside I felt as if a weight had been lifted from me, like I was actually doing something constructive instead of mooching around feeling sorry for myself.

Fifteen minutes later, she called back, her voice happier than the last time we had spoken. "Glad you changed your mind, Chambers."

I grinned, but I felt it slip away as she continued, "Is it okay if Jane comes with us?"

Bollocks.

"She called just after I had spoken to you, and as you said you were busy..."

What could I do? Say "Oops...sorry. Just noticed a huge pile of paperwork I have to get done before tomorrow." Or even "Why don't just you two go out? You don't want me spoiling your fun."

And I did. Said the latter. "Why don't you just go out with Jane." I laughed emptily. "Three's a crowd and all that."

Her end of the line went extremely quiet for a few seconds, and I thought she was deliberating, but then she said, "I wouldn't hear of it. We will meet you at the Bar Tapas in town. One o'clock."

She must've heard me take a breath to reject her invitation, as she shot out, "No arguments."

After I had said goodbye, with the promise to be on time, I dropped my head into my hands. It was okay to be all-accepting when you didn't have to face the "other woman." Anyone can play the martyr from a distance. But I was meeting them as a couple for the first time, and I was regretting calling Amy back.

Duds was shipped off to my parents, who made more of a fuss of him than they did of me, as usual. They didn't even notice I was positively green about the gills. Dad was slipping on his Wellies and promising my excited pal a long walk. So, I was ignored by all and sundry as I went to meet Amy and her bird. Yes. That does sound a tad bitter, doesn't it.

∞⊙∞

They were already there when I arrived. Amy was facing the door, and stood up and waved dramatically, as if she was on a buoy bobbing in the ocean, waiting for a lifeguard to pick her up. A grin split her face, and she left the table to come and give me a hug. My eyes closed and I just inhaled her scent. It was as if I was breathing her right in.

"It is so good to see you. I'm glad you could make it after all.

I slowly opened my eyes and saw Jane looking at us with a welcoming smile. Unfortunately, she was gorgeous—long dark hair and olive skin, with brown eyes that were complemented by long dark lashes. Her smile was brilliant white, and she looked the picture of health and happiness. No wonder Amy preferred her to me. I certainly would.

"Beth. This is Jane. Jane, Beth."

Jane stood and held out her hand in greeting. I knew my palms were all sweaty, but I couldn't avoid shaking her hand; that would be rude. I quickly swiped my hand down the side of my jeans and prayed she wouldn't notice. Her hand was cool, but not clammy. Just right. A firm, friendly shake accompanied by, "It's lovely to finally meet you."

"Jane can't stay long. She's got to be gone by two."

A cheer welled up inside me, and I knew it seemed childish. I had no chance with Amy whether Jane was there or not. I gulped down my joy and said, "Oh, that's a shame," as one does.

"Yes. I have to meet my future mother-in-law in Jarrolds' Housewares department to pick out pan sets and other wedding presents from our list." She turned to Amy. "I can't see why you get out of this. She's your mother, after all."

Fuck me. They were getting married. This was getting worse and worse. I was totally at a loss for words, I mean—they were getting married, for Christ's sake! And there I was, sitting playing gooseberry when they should be picking out pan sets and duvet covers together with Mother. I didn't know how to react, didn't know whether to join in the conversation and wish them luck, or pick up the menu and try to decipher the Spanish. I decided on coy, but it may have come off as vacant. Maybe it was village idiot, because they were both staring at me, waiting for me to say something.

Apparently I'd missed a question. I'd been too busy thinking of an excuse not to listen to any more of their banter. I gave them the "I'm sorry, could you repeat that?" face, and Jane leaned over the table conspiratorially, but with a degree of humour.

"Do you think that Amy should get out of shopping with *her* mother..." she glared at Amy, who lifted her hands in mock defence, "...*and* her future sister-in-law, because she hates being dragged around all the shops?"

My face said it all. Or maybe it said nothing. I can't even gauge my expression. I felt stunned, like a wet fish had been slapped repeatedly across my cheeks, fins and all.

"Huh?" Fuck. At this rate, they would both think I was dim, dumb, or deaf. I managed, "You're getting married?" No shit, Sherlock. "To Amy's brother?" Elementary, my dear Watson.

"Well, I wouldn't be marrying her sister. She hasn't got one. I'm marrying James, her little brother."

They both laughed, and I just sat there, waiting for my face to melt. It was hot enough. The realisation dawned on Jane after only a minute.

"Did you...me and Amy...together?" She sounded like Yoda. She started laughing again, but Amy just sat back in her chair and smiled at her, one eyebrow raised.

By this stage I was feeling like a total dickhead. Like usual. Both feet in and not even hitting the sides of my mouth. It is amazing how stupid one can feel without actually saying anything *really* stupid. As they say, actions speak louder than words, and lately I had been acting stupid. I had assumed that Amy was dating Jane, assumed she was already with somebody and hadn't told me. And you know what they say about assuming: To assume, you make an ass out of u and me. And I felt like an ass.

"Come on. Let's order." Amy leaned forward and gave me the Special's List, followed by a wink and a smile. "You've gone all red."

You bet I had. Inside I was glowing, and it wasn't from the warmth of the restaurant.

‘⍊’

Lunch was good. It was stimulating to mix with people, to socialise and have fun. It had been too long since I had been out with any of my friends, months at least. Come to think of it, it must have been over a year. Sue would always make a song and dance about who I could and could not see. Mainly, we could see her friends, but I couldn't see mine. So, I stopped seeing everyone. There was less aggravation that way. Shallow, eh? Sometimes I couldn't believe how far I had let things slide, how much of myself I had lost in trying to keep the peace. And what for? So I could end up walking in one day and seeing Sue screwing someone else, that's what for.

I know it takes two people to make a relationship work, and any relationship worth its salt needs attention, needs nurturing. Both parties need to know they are loved. And I was as much to blame as Sue was for allowing things to get as far askew as they had. Thinking about it, I believe that if I had put my foot down and actually grown a spine, things would have been a whole lot different. Maybe Sue and I would have had a chance. Maybe she would still be here, loving me forever, as we'd planned. Or at least, as she had planned.

But it was far too late for "maybes" or "what ifs." Too much had happened. Even the clichéd water under the bridge had flowed past.

At ten past two, Jane stood up to leave. "If I don't go now, I'll be in the doghouse with my future mother-in-law. I don't want to get on the wrong side of her before I even join the family."

"No chance of that happening. I'm sure my mum prefers you to me." Amy stood, and they hugged tightly. If I hadn't known about Jane not being Amy's "other half," I would have been totally fucked off by the gesture. As it was, I was grinning stupidly throughout the exchange.

After Jane and Amy stopped hugging, Jane turned to me and wrapped her arms around me, too, squeezing me to her with just the right amount of pressure to make it feel special.

"It has been lovely meeting you, Beth." Her voice, as well as the words, seemed genuine.

"Same here. Been wonderful." Something I had no idea I would be saying earlier today.

A soft kiss landed on my cheek and then she was gone, and I was left staring at a grinning Amy.

With Jane's departure, I had Amy just where I wanted her. Alone. In a café full of people at lunchtime. Not quite the isolated setting I would have preferred, but it did feel like there were only her and me in the whole place. And it felt wonderful, especially now that I knew she wasn't with Jane.

There might be someone else, though. She might have a girlfriend. Just because one had been taken off the "other half" list didn't mean there wasn't another waiting in the wings, or even at centre stage. Bugger. All I wanted to do was ask her if she was seeing someone or interested in anyone, or whether I had a chance. But I just couldn't pluck up the nerve. It would have been different if I hadn't liked her so bloody much; I would've just asked her and took her answer on the chin. However, if I asked her and she said she did have someone else, I would be back at square one again. For the moment, I preferred to pretend that I did have a chance in hell.

After paying the bill, we decided to have a walk around the market and then catch an early film. Amy's mother and Jane were staying at her house for a few more days, as they had come from Stratford to get some shopping in without their men hanging about.

"You don't have to entertain me you know? Why don't you go and spend some quality time with your family? It's not as if you get to see them often." I didn't want to tell her to leave me, but I thought maybe she was just being nice and didn't know how to tell me she had to go.

"No way. I have had enough of them to last me a lifetime. Shops, shops, and more shops. If it isn't shopping, it is all about the bloody wedding." There was a moment of silence before she continued. "And I want to spend time with you." She paused. "I missed you."

I stopped mauling the dog bed on the stall and turned to look at her. She seemed sincere and open. There was something just below the surface in her expression that made my heart giddy up and rear excitedly. I swallowed a couple of times to clear the lump that had suddenly appeared in my throat, finally mumbling, "I missed you, too."

"Well, that's okay then." She tilted her head and looked at me, the smile creeping out and easing the tension between us.

It was a weird sensation. The tension, I mean. It wasn't like I was worried, more like expectant. I wanted to read more into the smile, the expression, the feeling, but I didn't dare to. So I just turned around and bought the dog bed for Duds without even giving it the thorough examination I usually did. Another multi-coloured accessory that he would sniff at before jumping onto the sofa. He had three already.

We skipped the film. Too much to carry, thanks to me and my aversion techniques. We went to pick Dudley up and take him for a walk, and Amy came in my car as she had walked into town.

When I walked into my parents' house, Duds went crazy, gave me a quick lick, and then was all over Amy like a rash. He had her pinned on the sofa in less than a minute. The funny thing was, she wasn't sitting down, or even attempting to get on the sofa when it happened. The little bugger knocked her clean off her feet.

Have you ever noticed how your parents act when you bring a date home? I know Amy wasn't a date, and I'm sure you've taken someone home who wasn't, but your parents think they are the new love of your life. Talk about embarrassing. They keep grinning, winking, and nodding at you every time the person looks away, mouthing, "She's nice" or "Keep this one." And they suddenly stop when the person looks at them, making it really bloody obvious. This time was no exception.

It took on the flavour of the Spanish Inquisition— Mum asking questions with Dad digging for details. At one point I expected them to ask to see her bank statements, and I was trying every trick in the book to steer Amy and Duds to the door, but to no avail. My parents were on a mission.

Eventually I gave up the idea of escape and accepted another cup of tea and the invitation for Amy and me to look at Dad's garden. It was pretty, although most of the colour was gone. He was explaining how he was preparing for the onset of winter, because one could never be too early, when Mum appeared.

"Beth? Can you come and help me pour the tea?"

I stared at my mum before asking, "You honestly need help pouring the tea from a tea pot?"

My mum's lips straightened in the way I recognised as me being in for it if I pushed my gobby luck. "It's not all about the tea. There's milk to consider too."

I couldn't believe she said it, but I knew better than to contradict her. Instead I followed like a lamb, albeit a lamb who was making questioning gestures behind her mother's back.

As soon as we were in the kitchen, she said, "She's lovely, Beth."

Ah. She thought separating us would weaken us, and I would spill the beans about how fantastically in love I was.

"She thinks the world of you."

I looked at her with surprise. "And how on earth do you make that out?"

"Mums just know."

Cryptic, and also annoying. Especially when she turned and made the tea herself, not even asking me to pass wind, never mind the milk.

I just lounged against the kitchen work surface and watched with admiration sprinkled with laziness. I wanted her to continue, wanted her to explain what she meant by Amy thinking the world of me. Did she mean the "thinking the world of me" like one friend feels for another? Or...

"For God's sake, don't let the girl see you looking like that. You look gormless."

I straightened my face and my shoulders, and rolled my eyes. Amazing how much one changes as they get older. If I'd still been a stroppy teen, I would have rolled my eyes first.

၆၁ၛ

It was too late to take Duds to the park, too dark, as the evenings were upon us so early now. He didn't seem to mind the walk around Amy's neighbourhood. I think he enjoyed finding out who was about by sniffing every single lamppost and gate.

The walk was comfortable. We chatted about what we had been up to during the week.

"I went to Earlham early on Monday." Amy's voice was a little lighter than usual, and I found myself turning to her to see if there was a reason behind it.

She was looking at me as if she was expecting a response, or trying to work out what to say next. A flush seemed to creep up from the pit of me, and I focused my attention on the view ahead, even though it wasn't as beautiful as those brown eyes.

"I ... thought maybe, well, I might be able to catch up with you."

"Oh yeah?" I had no idea why I answered with those two words, so I tried to improve on them by continuing. "Duds and I were there on Monday, but we didn't see you."

A memory from the previous Monday started to emerge in my head, an event that at the time I hadn't thought to be important.

"I had a coffee, but I had an early class and couldn't wait long." She paused. "The rest of the week was spent either working or playing tour host."

I grunted a response. I couldn't concentrate on what she was telling me; all I could think about was Duds' behaviour on Monday. He had raced off and tried to get inside the café. Surely it was a coincidence, as there was no way he could have known she was there. Was there?

Just as the thought meandered through my mind, Dudley turned to me, and he looked for all the world as if he was laughing.

And they call them dumb animals. Makes me wonder which is the more intelligent species.

Chapter Seven:
The Climax

I left Amy with a promise to pick her up at nine-thirty the following morning. She wanted to come out with me and Duds for his early morning run, or as I thought of it, "the pissing off with the ball" walk.

When I climbed into bed that night, I felt like I would never be able to get to sleep. But before I knew it, the alarm was blaring and Duds was reinforcing it with his excited licks.

Up. Showered. Fed. Both of us. Well, Duds declined the shower, using the time to attack my slipper instead.

As I hovered outside Amy's front door, the butterflies in my stomach vied with one another for a front row seat, and I kept lifting my hand to knock, then dropping it again. Eventually the door swung open, and a woman in her late sixties stood there grinning.

"Are you going to knock, or are you going to keep threatening the poor doorknocker?"

My raised hand was inches away from her chest, where the knocker would have been. Well it was—Erm, two of them to be exact. Oh fuck, I was so not going there.

"You've gone all red. Are you all right?"

Bugger. Like mother like daughter. I nodded and she smiled at me, which further confirmed my assessment of her relationship to Amy.

"You must be Beth. I'm Marion, Amy's mother. Come in, dear. You'll catch your death out there."

His ball gripped in his mouth, Dudley waited patiently at my feet, looking like a little angel.

"Aw...bless. You must be Dudley." She bent down and ruffled the hair on his head, whilst he emitted a low gurgling noise of contentment around his ball. "Aren't you a gorgeous little man. Yes you are. Yes you are."

Amy appeared at the end of the hallway, her coat and scarf in her hand. "Mum! For God's sake, let them in."

I smiled at her, and she returned it with knobs on. Dudley howled in excitement and yanked me into the hall, trying to get to her. I nearly bumped into her mother and turned to apologise. She was nodding at her daughter whilst mouthing something. I looked at Amy, who had flushed scarlet.

"I can't let you two girls go out without giving you a cuppa to warm you up," Marion said as she closed the door.

I'm definite that as she passed her daughter, I heard her murmur something along the lines of, "But by the look of you, I doubt you'll need it."

Amy grimaced and shot me an apologetic glance. "Ignore her. She's going senile."

"I heard that, madam."

The laugh burst from me. I couldn't help it. It was just like being at home. I felt like I had come home.

Tea was an illuminating affair, especially along the lines of Amy's relationship with her mother. They were close, and the banter came easily.

Jane joined us after a little while, rubbing the sleep from her eyes and fumbling around the teapot until Marion tutted, took it, and poured her a cup. Duds kept going from one person to the next, hoping one of us would remember that it was walk time. Eventually he lay down in front of the Aga stove, the ball placed protectively between his feet.

We must have been there for nearly an hour before Amy decided enough was enough.

"Okay. Time to brave the elements. Ready, Chambers?"

I grinned and nodded. Dudley immediately understood that his wait for his walk was officially over, and he jumped to his feet and easily captured his ball in his mouth. As I reached the door, Jane caught my arm and stopped me.

"I've been meaning to ask you, Beth. Would you like to come to my wedding in February? We would love to have you." Jane looked back, as did I, to Amy, who was busily trying to button up her coat. I felt strange, like I was intruding. I didn't know what Amy would think about me tagging along to her brother's wedding. Such things were family gatherings, and I was someone she barely knew.

Amy looked up from her task as if she had sensed we were looking at her. "What?"

"Just asking Beth if she fancied coming to the wedding."

"And?" Amy was looking at me expectantly, but I still didn't know what to say. "It would be great to have you there. You could meet my obnoxious little brother."

Jane sent her a feigned glare and linked my arm protectively. "Ignore her. She's just jealous that he can keep a girl." She laughed as Amy stretched two middle fingers at her. "We'd all love to have you there. You can stay at our house, both of you can."

"Okay. Thank you. That'd be great." When I come to think of it, my answer sounded lame. Almost textbook.

"Amy will give you the details, and I'll send you an invite as soon as the bloody printers sort them out."

"Thank you. That's lovely." I didn't really know what else to say. Obviously.

Marion stepped forward and pulled me into a hug. "Lovely to finally meet you, Beth."

Finally?

"Probably see you at Christmas, if you're free."

Then we left, Amy, Duds, and I. Questions and implications about what had happened swirled inside my head, though for the life of me I didn't know why. It wasn't as if there was a hidden message lurking behind the invite or Marion's comment, but something just seemed out of place. Maybe it was because Jane had also said "finally," when I had met her the previous day.

໖)໕

The walk was fun, an emotion I had come to expect when I was around Amy. The air was crisp and cold, making our faces glow, the picture of health and well-being. We went to Mousehold Heath, and the ground was crunchy with frost underfoot. Duds didn't seem to mind its coldness. He spent his time chasing squirrels and his ball, stopping occasionally to make sure we were close by.

When we came to the clearing, we sat down on the bench to catch our breaths, and a panting Dudley settled down at my feet. The view from the top of the hill was amazing, with a perfect view of the cathedral. It was radiant against the grey winter skyline.

Amy was animatedly explaining about the English Civil War of 1642 and the evidence of bullet marks in the nave of the cathedral, mainly in the columns, but I found my gaze drifting from the architecture to look at her instead. She was truly breathtaking. An ache swelled in my chest, but I suppressed the gasp before it escaped. It felt as if my heart was expanding. Warmth seeped into every nook and cranny of my being. I knew my feelings for Amy were moving beyond attraction, knew the feelings I was trying to contain were breaking free, and there was nothing I could do about it.

When she turned to me with a radiant smile, I desperately wanted to lean over and take her face in my hands and kiss her, or even just hold her and look into those beautiful eyes so she could read my feelings without me having to tell her.

I couldn't tell her. I couldn't take her face in my hands. And there was no way on earth I could make the first move and kiss her. No way. I didn't feel able, didn't feel strong enough to handle it if she told me she didn't feel the same way. Most of all, I didn't feel I could risk losing her friendship—not now that I'd found her.

I felt both elation and sadness—elated because I now knew I could move on from what had happened between Sue and me, sad because I knew what I wanted but also knew it was out of my reach.

"Yap!"

"Come on, Beth. Someone wants us to move along."

Yes. And that someone was me.

§)C3

Days turned into weeks, and our friendship blossomed. Amy and I together seemed like the most natural thing in the world, and the times I was without her were beginning to hurt. I felt I was getting stronger—emotionally and mentally, and I was back at the office full time, much to Dudley's displeasure.

Sue had called a few times—both on the phone and at my front door, banging repeatedly, but I'd just let her bang. Every time she made contact, or tried to, a feeling of guilt would creep over me. Don't ask me why; I haven't a clue. There was no way I wanted that woman in my life again, so I couldn't understand why I would feel guilty around her. I wasn't the one who had shagged another woman in our bedroom. Nevertheless, it was a feeling that would wash over me and make me feel vulnerable. And I had spent too long feeling vulnerable where she was concerned. Thankfully, her bids for attention were waning, and I hoped they would eventually flutter, sputter, and disappear altogether.

Before I knew it, Christmas was upon us in all its resplendent, garish glory, and I once again found myself in a bind. What on earth could I buy Amy that wouldn't either be over the top or not enough? I wanted the gift to be special, to tell her how I felt. And yet I also wanted it not to expose me. I wanted... Fuck. I didn't know what I wanted. I hate shopping at the best of times, and this scenario was taking the biscuit. I even tried tricking Amy into telling me what she either wanted or needed, but she didn't take the bait. Eventually I gave up and decided to give her book vouchers. Forever the romantic—that's me.

But I didn't get them. And you know why? My mother. Jesus! When she found out I was planning on buying book vouchers, I honestly thought she was going to disown me, or keel over. It wasn't as if I had told her how I felt about Amy, and it wasn't as if my mum had asked. But as you might be aware—mums just know. That led to a shopping trip to Norwich, with my mum metaphorically holding my hand and dragging me around the shops.

As we walked around, it was hilarious to watch the other mothers with their kids, and I cringed at the memory of my own teenage years. One set of confused parents was calling across the clothing department, asking her daughter if she had enough money to get home if she insisted on staying with her friends. The girl answered in the usual way of the irrational teen, the pitch indicating the mortification she must have been feeling to be molly coddled by old people in front of her peers. *"Noooooo! Leave me alone!"* The parents were trying to supply money, but the girl just stomped away with her friends, leaving the parents standing there. She probably didn't have the money to get home, but to admit that in front of her peers? Not a chance. Like many teenagers, she would rather die than ask her folks for help and show herself up in front of the gangly band standing behind her.

"Brings back memories, eh?" my mum teased.

I grunted in response.

"Although you still have a charming way with words."

I grunted again.

"Or not."

Interminable. That's the word that springs to mind. Shopping in the city centre with Christmas just around the corner was just interminable. Queues and queues greeted us wherever we went, and I was thinking more and more fondly of those lovely book vouchers that would allow me to get home and put my feet up.

And then I saw it, saw *the* present. It was in the window of an out-of-the-way shop, looking like it was waiting for me to buy it.

"That's perfect, luv."

I turned and looked my mum in the face, and we both smiled the same smile, slowly building into a huge grin.

"It is, isn't it?"

Twenty minutes later, me and my mum were heading for a much needed coffee, a carrier bag triumphantly clutched in my hand.

മാരു

The gift wasn't expensive or glamorous, it was just right, and I couldn't wait to see her reaction.

Jane, James, and Amy's parents came down to her place from Stratford for Christmas, and I wouldn't see her until Boxing night. We had decided to exchange presents then, as the rest of the day was to be spent with family. Still, the day didn't go without a phone call and the customary talking to every member of both families.

Unfortunately, the day also didn't go by without contact from Sue. She timed it to perfection—after lunch, washing up done and dusted, parents sleeping through the Queen's speech, Will and his new flame flagrantly absent. The only ones knocking about were me and Duds, and even he was ready for a nap after eating so much turkey.

I usually would've checked who was calling, but thinking it was Amy, I just flipped the lid on my mobile. When I heard Sue's voice, I felt the sprouts I'd eaten for lunch whirling around, trying to escape from her voice. "What do you want, Sue?" My tone was icy.

"I just wanted to wish you all the best." The cynical part of me didn't believe a word she said. "And I was hoping you were enjoying your day."

Sue waited for me to respond, but I said nothing. I just felt pissed off that she was bothering me with a call. I know. Ungrateful.

"So, how are things?"

"Fine." I bit my lip before asking, "Are you having a good day?" I wasn't interested in her response, but I felt it was only manners to return the verbal gesture of seaonal intentions.

"Not bad. Get anything nice?"

I didn't want to chit chat with Sue. I didn't want to talk with a woman I had broken up with about what I did and didn't receive from Santa this year. What I really wanted was to tell her to never bother me again and then hang up the phone, but instead I blurted,

"I have to get gone. My mum needs me to help set up the tea things."

Her surprise emanated through my mobile. The single "Oh" seemed deafening, and was followed by "No worries. I'll catch up with you soon, okay?"

She didn't even wait for my response. Just ended the call without waiting for me to tell her there would be no catching up "soon," or anytime for that matter.

Although the call was short, it was long enough to put a damper on my mood, and when I hung up, it was as if she was still there. And there was me, having thought I was getting better.

A warm wet tongue slicked itself over my knuckles, and I looked down into Dudley's concerned eyes. It always amazes me how dogs know that you are upset. And I was upset. It was as if I was going along pretending everything was okay, and then—bam, a reminder that I was still fucked up. It is one of the weirdest sensations anyone can experience. I kept on telling myself that my future was in my hands, and I had the power to change the way I thought about me and my life. So why did I prefer to beat myself up about things I could ultimately change?

I'm beginning to sound like those old ladies who complain about anything and everything, and I'm getting on my own nerves.

The rest of the day was uneventful, although it did drag a little. This was probably due to my wanting Boxing night to arrive, because that was when I would be seeing Amy.

She arrived at six-twenty-five, and it was six-thirty-two before I succeeded in pulling Dudley off her. He was all over her like custard over apple pie—licking her face, his paws on her chest, kissing her like mad. At that moment, I wished I were him.

Amy's laughter rang through the house, and every time she laughed, the more excited he became. Little bugger.

"And now it's Mummy's turn."

Amy's voice caught me unawares, but not as much as the feeling of her arms going around me. My body stiffened, but she just squeezed me close to her and kissed my cheek.

"Merry Christmas, Beth."

I think I said something similar back, but I was trying to get a whiff of her hair, and before I knew it, she had let me go. I hadn't really had an opportunity to get a grip on her, which, in hindsight, was a blessing. I know if I'd held her properly, it would have been hell and all trouble for me to let go.

"Present time." She opened her bag and pulled out two gifts. "One for you, and one for the main man."

Dudley loves opening presents. He's good at it, too—only eats part of the paper. It took him less than thirty seconds to reveal the brand spanking new red ball, which he gripped in his mouth and then fled the room, probably to hide it in one of his beds. He ignored the chews that had been in the package with his new best friend—the ball, I mean. Amy and I were momentarily forgotten whilst he ran around the house looking for a good hiding place.

"We'll have to wait until he comes back before I give you the present from him," my hand was clutching the gift-wrapped box, "or else he'll sulk. He saved up all his pocket money, too." I held out the gift I had bought for her, my hands shaking slightly. "You'll have to make do with mine for now."

She opened it so carefully, peeling back the gold paper as if it would break. Eventually she had the naked box sitting on her lap, and her fingers toyed with the lid. I was praying that she liked it, as I had a growing apprehension I had missed my mark and just bought her something I would like.

She slowly lifted the lid off, and then separated the tissue paper to reveal the glistening object inside. She dipped her fingers inside and plucked the palm-sized crystal figure from within "Oh, Beth..." She paused, and so did my breathing. "It's beautiful."

The small crystal figure was a border terrier, sitting proudly, a dark red stone in its mouth. "It's Dudley!" Tears sprang to her eyes, and my own pricked against my rapidly fluttering lids. "He's beautiful." The carefulness of her movements depicted the reverence she felt, and I knew she truly liked it. "Even has his ball." A lone tear trickled down her cheek.

"Glad you like it." That's all I could say.

She looked so beautiful sitting there so full of emotion. I'd hoped she would like it, but I had never envisioned she would be so touched by the gift.

We just sat there for a while and watched the lights dance off the crystal, the reflections catching in her eyes. I think that was the moment I knew for certain sure, I was utterly in love with her.

The silence didn't bother us. It felt right. Everything felt right with her, and that's what made things so bloody confusing.

"What am I doing? Here's your gift." She held out a flat, rectangular package and then hurriedly sat back on the sofa.

As I was peeling the paper off, Dudley came trotting back into the room, jumped into the seat next to Amy and snuggled against her leg. His ball must be well and truly hidden; he wouldn't have come back unless it was.

I turned my focus back to unwrapping the package. Amy was watching my every move, and I was hoping I would react in the way she wanted me to. As I spied a wooden frame and a glint of glass, impatience pounced on me and I tore the paper away.

It was Dudley. I mean, a photograph of Dudley, looking all gorgeous and handsome and clean. He sat bolt upright, staring directly at the camera, looking straight into my eyes and hitting me straight in my heart. Nestled at his feet was his ball, chewed and tattered. The photo became blurry as my eyes filled with tears. I looked over the edge of the frame to see two pairs of eyes looking at me with expectation.

"I...I...he's...how..." The words jammed and clambered at the back of my throat—wanting to escape, yet knowing if they did they might reveal more than I was willing to disclose.

Amy's smile blossomed, and Dudley sat up and panted like he was laughing. "A couple of weeks ago, I called your mum and asked her if I could borrow him." She ruffled his hair. "She was a little doubtful, until I told her what it was for."

I wiped the tears from my cheeks and harrumphed understanding. No wonder my mum didn't want me to get book vouchers. She knew the trouble Amy had gone to for my present, knew I would've died of embarrassment when I received this gift.

"It was okay, wasn't it? To borrow him?"

I nodded, then I leaned forward and grabbed her hand. I just had to touch her and let her know how happy I was, because words had deserted me, and all

I could think about was telling her how much it meant to me, how much she meant to me. Without actually telling her *how much* she meant to me.

Her fingers curled around mine and squeezed.

I looked into her eyes, and I saw something there. I didn't know what it was, but her face was getting closer to mine, closer, and oh so much closer.

Bang! Bang! Bang!

No. It wasn't my heart racing, trying to make a break for it. It was the fucking doorknocker nearly being ripped off its little hinge.

Bang! Bang! Bang! Bang!

And along with the doorknocker, reality came banging back into focus, and I took in the scene before me. Amy was actually on the floor, kneeling in front of me. I wasn't aware that I had pulled her off the sofa. Shit!

Scuttling to my feet, I saw Amy sit back on her haunches and look enquiringly at me. She was probably also wondering why she was on the floor, and how I had dragged her there without her knowing. She did look kind of startled. And I could feel the telltale signs of embarrassment creeping up my face in the customary red flush.

Bang! Bang! Bang!

"Okay! I'm coming!" I turned and nearly fled from the room.

I wish I hadn't bothered. Actually, no. I knew I didn't want to make even more of a fool of myself than I already had, but then again, I also didn't want to be standing in an open doorway with Sue. Bollocks.

"You look all flushed. Hope I'm not disturbing anything." But her expression said she hoped she was. "I'm not staying."

So why did she push past me and walk towards the front room? In my book, that's a sign of someone wanting to park his or her arse on the sofa and sit for hours. So, I did what most of us would do—I shrugged and shut the door. I knew Sue would be pissed off when she saw Amy in there. And Dudley.

And Dud...ley.

The sound of Dudley's howl was enough to turn my blood to ice and make me race to the front room.

Amy was trying to soothe him, trying to hold him back. Surprise was plastered on her features, as she had never seen him react to anybody that way. Obviously she didn't know it was Sue.

"Beth?"

"I've got him." As I passed Sue with him, he lunged to take a bite of her, but I pulled him further into me and left Sue and Amy alone whilst I put him in the sunroom. He looked totally devastated when I closed the door, and I felt bad that he saw his banishment as punishment for protecting me.

When I got back, Sue was in her "charm personified" role, but Amy's face was closed. Sue must have introduced herself.

"We're just getting acquainted. Amy, right?"

Amy grunted.

"Beth's told me about how well you two get on—such good friends, aren't you? That's what you said, wasn't it, Beth?"

She is such a shit stirrer. She was obviously trying to get Amy or me to indicate whether anything was going on, so she could put the blockers on it.

"What a lovely photograph of Dudley! I'd love a copy of it."

"Why?"

"Huh?"

"Why on earth would you want a copy of a photo of Dudley? It's not as if you even like each other."

"Now, now, Beth. Don't go getting all argumentative *again*, especially in front of your *friend*."

I looked at Amy, who was decidedly uncomfortable with the situation, and decided that for once Sue was right.

"What do you want, Sue?" From the corner of my eye, I could see Amy collecting her things. "I've got company." I hoped she would take the hint and bugger off—Sue, not Amy. But, as usual, she had arrived wearing her rhino skin clothing, and the hint that I wanted her to leave bounced right off it.

Amy stood, pulling her bag over her shoulder. Crap.

"Just thought you might want a little company. I wasn't going to stay long." A slight pause. "But if your guest is going..."

The fire in my gut flared, and I wanted to tell Sue to fuck off, but that would have just made me look base and common in front of Amy.

"Beth, I have to go. I'm leaving for Stratford in the morning."

I hadn't known she was going away. Panic filled me. Panic? No, not quite the kind of panic one would expect in a situation that was life threatening—even though in a way that seemed quite apt, and yet not. Oh crap. I didn't want Amy to leave. I wanted it to be ten minutes earlier, when she was at my feet and I was on the verge of making a fool of myself.

"You're going away?"

"For New Year's. It's a family tradition—ringing it in on the town square." Her voice faded at the end, as if her attention was drifting off of what she was saying.

Sue was patting the sofa and fluffing the cushions, and I had the urge to grab the nearest one and smother her with it. The base and common thing was becoming more and more appealing.

"I think you'd better go, Sue. I have a guest."

"But—"

"No buts. You'd better leave." I had an unfamiliar sensation at the base of my back. I think it was my spine forming. "Now."

Her hand stopped mid fluff, and she turned to face me. "If I'm not wanted—"

"You're not. And this is no time for dramatics."

Amy looked at me, her face saying she didn't mind leaving, but I was having none of it. There was only one unwanted person in that room, and there was no way I was going to let her take over my life again. Sue looked livid, but I didn't give two hoots.

"Don't forget your bag." I picked it up and thrust it at her. "And shut the door behind you on your way out."

"Still the cold, heartless bitch, Beth? Thought a bit of time on your own might have defrosted you a little." She turned to look at Amy. "Good luck, love. She's as cold in the sack, too." Then she was gone.

Slam.

Definitely gone, if the groaning of the door's hinges were any indication. The bang that reverberated through the room in pounding pulses, throbbing off the walls and pinging off the furniture. Amy and I both cringed at the impact and waited for the ricochet to cease. I didn't want to look at Amy; I didn't want to see the realisation of who I was in her eyes. So, I turned and left the room to retrieve Duds from the sunroom.

He was pleased to see me, that is, I think he would have been if he had stopped for a minute instead of bolting past me into the living room to finish what he had started. I wished I could have finished what Amy and I had started before the Wicked Witch of the West had turned up, or that the tornado had dropped a house on Sue instead.

I waited a couple of minutes before I made a move to go back, thoroughly expecting to hear another slam as Amy left before having to make up an excuse. But there was no slam, just the sound of cooing. Cooing?

By the time I got back, Duds was giving Amy what I like to call a thorough doggy inspection. He was sitting on her knee, and I could tell by her face that he had given it a good old-fashioned washing whilst I wasn't there to pull him off. He was giving her the "beady eye"—the expression where it honestly looks as if he is reading minds. Amy was stroking his back and cooing adoringly into his face—a beautiful woman stroking my beautiful boy in a beautiful way.

Her eyes drifted to mine and she smiled, and I felt my heart pound out "I love you I love you I love you" until the breath released from my mouth into the air.

"Sorry about that. Coffee?"

Shit. The breath caught again as I waited for her to give me the knock back, but she just blessed me with one of her smiles and nodded. My brain tried to get me to relax, but my heart wouldn't listen. Little bugger.

Chapter Eight: The Buggering Up Stage

Sitting in the living room with Amy, I didn't mention the events that almost occurred just before the arrival of pointy-hatted witchy poo. I also skimmed over the part where aforementioned witchy poo had tried to make me look like a dickhead. Amy and I just had a coffee and picked up the conversation about her going to Stratford for New Year's. I tried to be positive and tell her she would have a wonderful time with her family, but the words kept jamming in my throat, and I kept changing the subject. An observer would have thought one of two things: either I had a speech impediment, or I didn't give two shits about her leaving.

But I gave two shits. Not entirely sure that ruled out the speech impediment, though. And Dudley loved all the attention Amy and I were bestowing on him. He kept making grunting noises of contentment.

Not long after, Amy hesitated as she stood in the doorway, and I was sure she was going to ask me something. She looked pensive as she fiddled with the strap of her bag; I fiddled with the hem of my top. All in all, there was a lot of fiddling going on—but no question came.

"See you next week then." She turned to leave, stopped, turned round and hugged me to her.

I was shocked, to say the least, and unfortunately—being a moron—didn't respond quickly enough. She was gone before I had chance to get my bearings.

The growl of her car alerted me I had been standing like a knob head in the doorway for too long. Bugger. I had missed the chance to reciprocate a hug and maybe more, and Amy would be leaving for Stratford first thing in the morning, so there was no chance of me seeing her for nearly a week.

Once again I had buggered things up, so I did what any like-minded girl would do in a situation like that. I got pissed. Not angry pissed, but drunk pissed. Two bottles of wine pissed—one red and one white, for balance of course. Obviously I didn't alternate the colour whilst drinking, not to start with at any rate. And by the time I could have alternated, I was well out of my tree and feeling decidedly sorry for myself. As best I can recall.

I remember putting CDs on and imitating Bridget Jones with Dudley's plastic bone as a microphone, singing (badly) Damien Rice's *The Blower's Daughter*. Unfortunately, I can also remember dancing around like a loony whilst singing the Prodigy's *Voodoo People*—must have been thinking of Sue—not that there are many words in it, which was just as well. I finally passed out with James Blunt's *You're Beautiful*, and my last lucid thought was "Yes. You are" before blackness mercifully enveloped me.

∞∞

Waking up with copious splotches of dribble sticking to my face, and the side of the sofa, was not good. The realisation that the Piss Head Fairy had been in and sandblasted my mouth was not a good one either. There was pain in my arms and legs, as I had slept half on, half off the settee, my arms above my head and my legs curled up underneath me.

Dudley was watching me from his comfortable place on the sofa, his head mere inches away from mine. It was as if he was trying to work me out. As if he had a chance. Even I couldn't do that.

It took me ages to unfurl myself from my agonising position, my head pounding with every movement. Bastard. My limping trek to the bathroom was more like the gait of the elderly, and my hands covered my ears as my brain tried to focus on a prayer to stop the booming brass band that was resonating inside my skull. The refrain "Never again" whispered into my sensitive ear, and at that moment I honestly believed it would be a cold day in hell before another smidgeon of alcohol would pass between my lips.

Showered and dressed, accompanied by a dog that probably wanted a tinkle, I felt more human. Not *all* human, but a little. Duds raced into the garden whilst I prepared coffee, and he didn't even sniff before he had a wee. Bless. I'm such a bad mother. But he wagged his tail and licked my hand as he came rushing back in again, so all was good.

It wasn't until a good hour after my emergence from the land of the comatose that I ventured back into the living room. Christ. It looked as if a bomb had struck. Bottles were strewn on the floor, a glass tipped over. The cushions were squashed nearly flat, and the memory of me standing on the sofa screeching out some crappy song blinked into my head like a bad dream. Finally a noise sneaked into the mess and alerted me that all was not right, a muffled, burring noise. A noise like...like a... Fuck. Like a phone off its cradle.

Frantic searching ensued, pulling up cushions and kicking away the crap on the floor. Nothing. Well, nothing except for the whining noise coming from somewhere in the room. Whoever invented the cordless phone should be shot. Well, not shot, per se, but told they needed to sort out the "I'm lost" feature.

Dudley was no help either. He just stood next to the bin, sniffing intensely. And if the wreckage strewn around me and the feeling in my gut were any indication, the bin would be the last place I would be venturing. That is always the way though, isn't it? The last place you look is the place where the missing item will be found. Obviously. Because you wouldn't carry on looking if you had found it, would you? I fully expected the phone to lift up little imaginary arms and scream "Mummy!" when I looked into the wicker basket and saw it lying on a mound of tissues and wrapping paper.

Why tissues?

Images flashed into my head of me talking incoherently into the phone and crying like a two-bit actress, stumbling over words and repeating myself to the point of absolute annoyance. Snot was streaming, and I was snorting it like a coke addict. Quaint? Methinks not. But whom had I called? Who was I calling and blubbering and snorting at? Dread filled me at the thought that I might have called Amy and sworn undying love. There was only one way to find out. Shaky fingers hovered over the redial button until sheer curiosity got the better of me and I pressed it hard enough to nearly break it.

The ringing sound pulsated in my head, the hangover still gripping me and conjuring images of a full drum kit in full swing. But that wasn't the worst of it. I found that out when I heard a very familiar voice pick up the receiver.

Sue's voice.

Shit, shite, and khak.

I had called Sue and told her I loved her. I could remember it as plain as day: I told her I loved her and wanted to be with her. Aw fuck.

I didn't answer the "Who is it?" I was too busy being mortified. Slamming the disconnect button with an adamant thumb, I shot to my feet and staggered backwards, the phone in my hand.

Then the little bleeder started ringing.

I knew it would be Sue calling me back, and there was no way I felt well enough to carry forward my stupidity of the night before, however good I was at being stupid.

It stopped. Then started again. Stopped. Then started.

I stared at the phone, willing the phone company to cut off my service at that precise moment. I had to make a decision, and fast. So I did the only thing I could think of—threw the phone onto the settee, where it vibrated and cried like an abandoned baby. Stuff the metaphorical baby arms reaching out to me. There was no way Mummy was picking up this bundle of disaster.

I had to get out of my house and hide, hide big time. Hide in a place where no one would ever find me and Duds. By the time I re-emerged from my sanctuary, hopefully Sue would have taken the hint and realised I was not in love with her and I definitely did not want her back. That crap had come from a drunken woman doing a very good impression of being suicidal, not from me.

Quickly, I packed a bag—well, stuffed items into a holdall, to be more precise, collected stuff for my furry pal, and was out of the door in less than fifteen minutes. The phone rang eight times in that short period. The more distance I put between it and me, the better.

Once inside the car, I was stumped. Where on earth could I go, with a pooch to boot? I couldn't go to a hotel; they didn't allow dogs. Couldn't go to my parents' or Will's, as Sue would show up there. I wracked my brains, then wracked them some more. Then shook them. But they refused to cooperate. Bloody neurons. Never around when you need them. But I needed to get away.

Earlham Park was deserted, but I also knew I couldn't sleep in the park. My days sleeping under the stars were well and truly over, especially with all those squirrels around. But sitting in the park gave me time to think. Who could I plant myself on? Someone Sue would never think of calling. Someone she didn't like. That didn't narrow it down at all, because Sue didn't like anyone, especially if I liked them.

Then it came to me, like one of those lovely epiphany doo dahs: Fi and Sarah. She hated them. Probably because they were witty and clever and funny, and *my* friends, not hers. And also because they had told her in no uncertain terms that she was a psycho.

A grin split my face, and some of the weight lifted from my shoulders. Fi always made me feel welcome, and I had ignored her for too long. Mainly because I was a limp, spineless git, but there was an element of not wanting to have to explain my breakup and everything leading up to, and after, me finding Sue with her pants down. I had disregarded my friends and their feelings in consideration of my own, and I did feel a bit of a shit about using them now. But I would make it up to them. I would stop hiding away and embrace my friendship duties.

Knocking on their door with a knackered dog and a holdall two days after Christmas, praying they hadn't gone away, enabled me to see how far I had come. Or not, as the case may be.

When Fi answered her door, her face said "Fuck me!" Not literally, of course, but the good old way of showing amazement. But she actually said, "Beth! *Fuck me!* It's Beth!"

Talk about her exhibiting her surprise on more than one level.

As usual, they were lovely. And it didn't seem any longer than eight months since I had last seen them both. I didn't even have to ask if it was okay if Duds and I forced ourselves upon them; Fi just offered, with no expectation of explanation. It's amazing how we take our friends for granted, expecting them to always be there for our mistakes and letdowns.

Watching Fi and Sarah rally round, sorting out clean bedding and the like, a mixture of emotions wrapped around me. I felt safe, which was good, but

I also felt like a bastard. I had allowed someone else to dictate whom I could or could not see, allowed someone to tell me what I could and could not do. But the worst thing was—I realised that it wasn't Sue's fault; it was mine. All mine. How I could have let her take control and allowed myself to hurt others in the process was not such a huge mystery. I had allowed it to happen because I had been weak and spineless, and preferred the easy option rather than standing up for what I knew was right.

I had used and abused my friendships as much as I blamed Sue for using and abusing my relationship with her. This realization struck me like a punch in the gut. My sharp intake of air was audible enough to make Fi stop punching the pillows and look at me, her hazel eyes showing concern.

"What's up?" She dropped the pillow, assessed the scene for a moment, and then ambled over to where I was seated and draped an arm around my shoulder. "Care to share?"

I shook my head, knowing that if I tried to speak, I would just blubber and make an even bigger fool of myself than I had over the last few years.

"Sarah! Sarah!"

Sarah came into the room, breathless and smiling. "What now, Master?" She looked at each of us—me sitting on the chair and Fi on the arm beside me. "What's the matter?"

I shook my head.

Sarah knelt in front of me. "Yes, there is. Anything we can do?"

I felt the concern flowing from her, her blue eyes warm, and inviting me to open up and take a chance.

A single tear slipped past my defences and down my cheek. A second followed, then the rest of them tumbled unchecked.

Fi and Sarah didn't say anything, just stayed with me, comforted me with touches and hushes. That made me cry harder, because it was another reminder of how badly I had treated them.

After what seemed like hours, but in fact was mere minutes, I stuttered out "I...I... p...post...ed...your...ca...card."

They looked at each other, confusion evident. "We know, hon. It's on the mantelpiece."

See? Friends. I spoke like an idiot, mentioning bloody Christmas cards when I was in "Wailing Woman" mode. But that wasn't what I meant. What I meant was, I had posted their card rather than bothering to bring it round. Some friend I had turned out to be.

Eventually I managed to tell them why I was blubbering like a baby.

"I feel like a shit. A real shit." Through my tears I saw Fi and Sarah exchange puzzled looks. "I just dumped you. Ignored you. Treated you like you didn't matter."

"No, Beth. It wasn't you. Sue made you do that."

Sarah tried to make me feel better, but I knew where the blame lay. "No. Sue didn't make me do anything. I could have stood up to her. Could have told her that I wanted to see you two."

Fi took my hand in hers, her fingers squeezing mine gently. "We understand, Beth. The situation was not as cut and dried as you 'standing up' to Sue and telling her you wanted to see us. She manipulated you, made you feel as if you were not showing her how much you loved her if you did something you wanted to do."

I would have loved to be able to accept that as the reason, but I had started to realise it was my fault. I had been the one who had forsaken my friends. I was the one who had forsaken myself.

A deep, heavy sigh shuddered through me. Reaching out, I grabbed Sarah's hand with my free one and lifted, in turn, their hands to my lips, leaving a kiss on their knuckles.

"I promise you now, it won't happen again. Relationships come and go, but true friends will stick together whatever comes."

"Friendship is like peeing your pants—everyone can see it, but only you can feel the true warmth."

"Oh my God, Fi!" Sarah glared at her partner. "I can't believe you've just said that."

Fiona started laughing, and so did I. Sarah just stared at us for a moment before joining in.

It may not have been the most delicate way of expressing friendship, but Fiona was right. Friendship was like peeing in your pants and allowing the warmth to spread. Although if you don't take care of the pee, it becomes cold, uncomfortable, and smelly, and then people start avoiding you. Metaphorically speaking, I hadn't taken care of my pissy pants, but now I was going to change those sodden drawers and make sure the clean pair was well taken care of. That does sound rather awkward, doesn't it? Talk about extending a metaphor.

Enough said.

The rest of the evening was spent catching up on news and remembering times past. Fi was one of my oldest friends; I had met her at uni. She originally came from Wales, but I always teased her that I didn't hold that against her. The enigmatic Sarah was a Pilates teacher. That's where Fi had fallen head over heels for the auburn-haired beauty almost six years ago. Their relationship was solid, and the banter they had was easy and natural. I wanted that. I wanted to be in a relationship that was like theirs—so giving.

I refused a glass of wine with dinner. Just the thought of raising a glass to my lips was enough to make my stomach roil in dramatic protest.

Dudley loved the attention and spent the evening moving from one lap to another. He was lapping it up, literally, and rolling over onto his back to expose his winky, like the attention seeker he was.

On the outside I seemed to be more settled, I seemed to have reached some kind of closure, but when I lay in bed, just me and Duds, I let the cleansing begin. Tears streamed down my face, trying to wash away the mistakes I had made. Some mistakes were too big to wash away with just one try, and still others loomed that I would have to put right. First, I had to make things right with Sue. I had to tell her that I didn't love her and didn't want her back. Easier said than done, but I had to do it, as it wasn't fair to her to leave things as they were. Then and only then could I rectify the situation with Amy. I had to tell her how I felt, the lot—the nitty gritty and beyond. And I had to tell her with no expectations of her falling into my arms and swearing undying love.

Then I thought of her, her brown eyes that glistened and were always full of expression, her laugh—what a laugh—so musical, so delicate, so contagious. My smile didn't last very long, because I also thought about the "unrequited love" aspect of our relationship. I loved her. I knew it as well as I knew I had to breathe to live, but I also knew she didn't think of me that way.

And that made me start crying again.

∞∞

I called my parents the next morning so they wouldn't phone the police or put my picture on the side of a milk carton. I also pre-empted the visit or call from Sue, or at least I tried to. Too late. My dad happily told me she had already called and didn't sound happy, especially when my mum graciously told her to sling her hook once and for all.

What could I say? My parents were never going to do what I asked them to, especially where Sue was concerned. So I moved past the angry "why don't you stay out of my business" stage and tried to end the call.

"Look, Mum, I'll be in touch, okay?"

"When? And where are you?"

"Does it really matter? I'm safe and happy. That's what you've always wanted for me, isn't it?"

I knew I had her with that one. I didn't want to be so vague with my parents, but my mum found it too hard not to let things "slip," as she so delicately phrased it.

"You're becoming too secretive, lady." I heard her sigh in that injured way only mothers can pull off. "You're right, though. As long as you're healthy and happy, I'm happy. I love you, Beth. You do know that, don't you?"

A lump formed in my throat, and I had to swallow a couple of times before I could respond.

"Of course I do, Mum. I love you too. And Dad."

"Take care, and call me tomorrow. Promise?"

I grinned and nodded at the receiver. "I promise. Love you."

≈≈≈

Fi and Sarah were great, even when I told them about my drunken verbal escapade on Boxing night. They just laughed, although Fi did call me, and I quote, "a daft twat". Bless.

I was a daft twat, too. I mean, I had called my arch nemesis and told her I loved her. It's like Batman calling the Joker and asking him round for a shag. It's not done. Come to think about it, Sue actually did have a look of the Joker about her, although she wore less make-up. Uncanny.

It wasn't until the third day that I spilled my guts about Amy. Not all of it. Just told them that we got on and stuff. It was the "stuff" part Fi and Sarah were interested in, but I wouldn't budge. I wanted to, God, did I, but I didn't dare. Because, you see, if you say something aloud, it becomes real, doesn't it? And if it became real, there would be a chance I could fuck it up. So, I decided to keep my mental meanderings inside my head, just to be on the safe side.

≈≈≈

Yes. It's still the buggering up stage, if you were wondering. As if you could have doubts about it.

But that isn't the reason I have entitled this section with the aforementioned name. Not by a long shot. Therefore, I need to move things along a tad. Can you feel me winding up the wheels of Fate? The figurative clock? Otherwise I will just drone on and on about me me me me, as if I haven't already. Am I forgiven? You know, for focusing on the past and balancing precariously on "what ifs"?

Let's get moving, shall we? On your mark...get set...

I was standing outside my house, Dudley snug on his lead and me rattling my key in the door. It was New Year's Day, as I had brought the New Year in with Fi, Sarah, and a crowd of friends down at the local. It was fun, but there was definitely something missing.

But not for long. I had no sooner opened the lock than I heard a car pull up behind me. Yep. You guessed it. Amy.

Shit. God, I wanted to see her, missed her so much, but this was too soon.

And then another car pulled to the kerb. Sue.

Double shit and big fat hairy bollocks.

I thought of racing into the house and locking the door, barring it with furniture, and then escaping out the back way. This was not good. My initial reaction to Amy stemmed from feeling a little exposed; my reaction to Sue was the knowledge that all was going to be revealed, big time, in front of Amy—me swearing undying love to Sue, the lot.

Awww sausages.

Dudley was pulling on his lead, torn between the two women, completely confused whether to wag his tail or bare his teeth. So he did both.

I felt a little like he did. Well, they do say you turn into your pets. Or is it the other way round? Enough of that. Now where was I? Oh yes—just about to die of embarrassment.

New Year's resolutions flew out the window as I shoved Dudley through the door. I had enough on my plate without him adding to the dramatics. I had to break the news to Sue, in front of Amy, that I hadn't meant all those things I said to her on Boxing night, that we were not meant to be together after all.

It was the way Sue stormed up my path that alerted me that not all was well. When she grabbed me by the scarf and dragged me close to her face, I thought, "Here we go. She's gonna fucking kiss me now, in front of Amy."

However, the spit hitting my face and the volume with which the accompanying words came out made me take stock of the situation. Correct me if I'm wrong, but does this seem to be a loving reunion to you? Thought not. It didn't to me, either. Especially when she threatened to punch my lights out. Then she kind of disappeared, rapidly, like she had been yanked away by an unseen hand.

"Get your greasy motherfucking, wanking hands off her."

Huh? That wasn't me. Come to think about it, it wasn't Sue, either.

"Touch her again, and I'll rip your head off. Got it?"

Amy? Professor at the uni Amy? Speaking like me?

Amy was right up in Sue's face, her eyes flashing and her lip curling devilishly. "Can't you get it into your thick skull? She wants nothing to do with you."

Uh oh. Here it comes. This is the part where Sue tells her what I said.

The thought was stopped mid flow, mainly by Sue's reaction. She didn't thump Amy or crawl off with her tail slapping her stomach. She grabbed Amy's fingers and peeled them back like a ripe banana.

"*Take...*" one finger loosened, "*your...*" two, "*hands...*" three—my math is getting better—"*off me.*" Sue flicked Amy's hand away, but it didn't stop them squaring up to each other like a couple of dogs at the park. Dudley would've loved it.

"Suppose it was your idea, was it? Getting her to call me?"

"Beth has a mind of her own, not that *you* would know that."

Crap. There was going to be an all-out bout of fisticuffs at this rate, and I was as much use as an ashtray on a motorbike.

"Funny that she decides to call me after she's been with you all night. Did you listen in? Did you like her telling me what she thought of me?"

I cringed.

"Is that how you get your rocks off?" Sue spat.

Amy just glared at her, her face saying everything that words would struggle to define.

I looked from one to the other, expecting to be dragged into the conversation at any moment.

"As for you, you spineless..."

See? I should read people's horoscopes.

"... piece of shit. You waited until I was gone before you could be arsed to tell me what you really thought of me."

"But..." I was confused. Why would she be acting like this if I had told her I loved her? I thought she wanted to get back with me, so this reaction was over the top, even for her. So I told her. "This reaction is rather over the top, even for you."

"Over the top? Over the *fucking* top!"

The whole street must have heard it. I could see curtains twitching, and Dudley started scratching at the door to get out.

"You call me in the middle of the night to tell me how much I screwed up your life, and you think *this* is over the top?"

Huh? That's not what I remembered of the phone call. My version was an imitation of Bette Davis on smack, sans the drama lessons.

"You couldn't even be bothered to tell me off when you were sober."

She lurched towards me, and Amy stepped in between us. Sue tried to struggle around her, I could hear the scrabbling of feet, but she didn't get very far.

"*And* you call *again* the next day, like the coward that you are and won't answer your phone when I call you back."

"I didn't—"

"Oh yes, you did, Beth. I checked the caller's number, and it was yours. I *think* I remember your number."

"I'm not. I—"

"You know what your problem is, Beth Chambers?"

Cut off again. Bloody women. They're serious candidates for goat's disease—forever butting in. I didn't even make an effort to reply; I knew she would only interrupt me.

"You need to get over yourself. Take some bloody responsibility for your life."

She shoved Amy away from her and smoothed the front of her coat. Then she made eye contact, cold grey eyes boring straight through me. The silence in the air was razor sharp, but not as sharp as her words.

"You play the victim well, Beth, and you hurt so many others along the way. I loved you, and you didn't think enough of me to say to my face that you, and I quote, 'would rather eat your own shit' than get back with me."

It would have been bad enough, even if Amy hadn't laughed, turned, and given me the thumbs up. I could have gotten over the embarrassment of being a vulgar drunk, but now I had an approving audience. I mean, how do you follow that statement?

"I'm sorry, Sue. I—"

"No." Sue glared at Amy, who was trying to hide her mirth behind her hand. "*I'm* sorry. Sorry I've wasted over four years waiting for you to realise people act differently...we are not all the same." She turned her wrath on Amy. "And *you*," the words flew from her mouth like a knife thrower was delivering them, a look of scorn and hatred clear on her face, "are welcome to her. Good luck."

Then she was gone. No broomstick, just her car screeching out of my road like the hounds of hell were chasing her.

The quiet surrounding us was painful. The images of a showdown at High Noon flitted inside my mind, accompanied by the whistling tune of a lone gunslinger. If I had seen tumbleweeds rolling down the centre of the road, I wouldn't have batted an eyelid.

"I take it you called her then?"

The thing that was confusing me was, if I had phoned Sue and said all those nasty things, who on earth had I poured my heart out to?

"Shall we go inside?"

Oh crap. Buggering up stage complete, Captain. How on earth would I get myself out of this one?

⊗⃝⊘

Funny thing was, Amy didn't act any differently towards me. She made a fuss of the overly excited Dudley, who was sitting behind the door so closely, we had to push him out of the way when we opened it. Then she plucked my holdall out of my hands and tossed it into the hallway.

"Make me a brew, Beth. I'm spitting feathers." She grinned at me. "Well, come on, woman, I've been on the road all morning. Haven't even been home yet."

Thoughts were whizzing around my head, too many things to pin one down. Was Sue right? Was I so far into myself that all I thought about was how I was feeling? Did I play the victim? I knew I should have taken responsibility for how I allowed myself to feel and react, but did I use Sue as much as I believed she had used me? Was I a relationship fucker-upper, too far up my own arse to actually make a relationship work? But I had tried, hadn't I?

See? Loads of bloody questions. And more if I could actually be bothered to tell them all, but I doubt you would want to know what was spinning around in my fucked up head.

And there was Amy. Even if she ever should think of me in that way, could I put her through the curse of Beth Chambers? *Get over yourself! Sue was right. You are a self-centred little fu—*

"Come on, girl. Brew. Now."

I snapped out of my musings about "poor me" and saw Amy standing there, looking at me quizzically. Funny thing was, Dudley was giving me the same look.

"Ignore Sue." Amy came closer, taking my hands into her own and gently pulling me into the house. "She's bitter and out to hurt you." Her face tilted, and she looked up at me, her eyes soft and tender. "This is her style, remember? To make you feel bad about who you are and unworthy of a relationship."

She pulled me against her, and my head slipped onto her shoulder, clicking in place as if it was always meant to be there. Her breath tickled my ear and made me shudder, the tingles racing down my spine to my toes, and back upwards again.

Slowly, she pulled back and looked into my eyes. She was beautiful, so beautiful, and the sob collecting in my throat wanted to scream it out. "By the way..."

I looked at her expectantly, of what, God only knew.

"Happy New Year."

And then she brushed her lips over my cheek, and my eyelids fluttered at the touch. Another kiss on my nose, then on my eyelids—so gentle, so perfect, it was as if she was the only one who could kiss me like that and elicit that reaction. I wanted to take her mouth and devour it. I wanted to kiss her, fall into her and lie on her chest, forever next to her heart, knowing that I would be safe.

But you know me by now, don't you? Spontaneity was not my bag, however hard my hormones fought to "just do it." I wished I were wearing Nike trainers, as I believed they would help me summon the gumption to disregard possible consequences. At least that's what their adverts imply.

"I have to tell you something, Amy."

Was that my voice? Was I just about to spill my proverbial guts and tell the woman how I felt? She just stood there, looking beautiful, and my stomach was thudding onto my diaphragm as if it was a trampoline.

"I... I..." My spine was forming—the pain, the agony of mending bones. "I ...I..."

But mending years of feeling worthless needed more than Plaster of Paris and a few gentle kisses. Much more. There was no way I was ready to be with someone else, that I knew as well as I knew the clichéd back of my hand.

Amy was waiting for me to continue, so I swallowed my pride, my hesitancy, and my love, and spluttered, "I haven't any milk."

Her brow furrowed, the statement hitting her like a baseball bat, then the eyebrows slowly drifted apart and a grin chopped her face in two. "Well..." she released me, "I suppose I'll have to take what comes, then."

Just like me, I suppose. But this time, I had to be with someone for the right reasons, not just because it was handed to me, like when I first got with Sue. The feelings I had for Amy were so different, so perfectly different from anything I had ever experienced before. And if I played it wrong, made her wait too long, maybe I would lose her—something I definitely didn't want to happen. But I also couldn't face things going wrong again, couldn't face losing someone who had become such a crucial part of my life because I wasn't the person they thought I was. If waiting a bit meant losing Amy, so be it. Then it wasn't meant to be.

I sent Amy into the living room whilst I put the kettle on. I had no sooner entered the kitchen than I heard Amy shouting for me to come quickly. The panic in her voice turned my blood cold, and when I got there she was standing in the doorway, her face ashen.

"Beth... Jeez, I don't know how to tell you this."

What? Tell me what? I tried to push past her into the room, but she held me fast.

"I think you'd better call the police."

"What's happened? Let me see." I pushed past her. The room was a mess. *My* mess from Boxing night.

"You've been burgled." She slipped her arms around my waist and pulled me against her.

Honest to God, it did look as if I had been burgled. Cushions were everywhere, rubbish tipped over the floor, glasses and bottles strewn around.

"Bastards. Who could do this, eh?" she said with a comforting squeeze

"Erm."

"Can you see if anything's been taken? The TV is still there, and the stereo." She released my waist and began to walk around the room. "Do you think they were looking for something?"

Yeah. The phone.

"Do you keep cash in the house?"

I couldn't just stand there and let her believe I had been robbed. Erm...could I? "Well...erm." Flaccid hands flapped in front of me as I tried to explain what had actually happened as she picked the phone off the settee and begun to punch in numbers. "Amy?"

Intently listening to the speaker on the other end, she held up her hand as if to say, "Don't worry. I'll deal with this." Her long fingers started to weave through her hair as she spoke.

"I'd like to report a robbery, please."

Shit! No! "Shit! No!" See? Sometimes your words can mirror your thoughts.

Amy thought I was meaning I had spotted something awful and covered the mouthpiece to mouth, "It's okay. We'll sort this out."

I raced forward and grabbed her phone hand, pulling it down. "It was me."

She looked at me as if I had lost my marbles, so I repeated it and added a little extra clarity.

"It was me, when I was pissed. I didn't have time to clear up."

Confusion raced fleetingly across her face, and then she threw her head back and laughed...then laughed again, whilst I was dying of embarrassment.

"Sorry, Officer. My mistake." She listened to the speaker, nodding, but all the while she was grinning at me as I started tidying up. "Okay. Thanks again." And then her full attention was back on me. "Beth?"

I turned from picking up the sofa cushions and looked at her, mumbling a "what" in response.

"You've gone all red."

"Exertion. All this bending over."

"Well, lady, there's only one thing I want you to do now."

I wish.

"I want you..." she walked toward me.

All the moisture in my mouth disappeared.

"...to..."

The cushion I was holding slipped out of my grasp. All my muscles tensed and relaxed.

"...make..."

I knew where the moisture had gone!

"...me a brew."

My heart stopped pounding against my ribcage like a trapped daddy long legs wearing hobnailed boots. I could hear Dudley banging his dish against the floor, alerting me it was time for him to be fed and watered. I promptly made that my excuse to flee, all the while giggling like a teenager after a packet of wine gums.

In the kitchen, Dudley just stared at me, his eyes demanding me to get my act together and take care of him. He didn't have all day; he had sniffing to do, had to check the perimeters to make sure his archenemy had pissed off. For effect, he clanked his dish with his paw one more time and glared. Bless.

He was happily munching away before I remembered why I had come into the kitchen in the first place. Making a total arse out of yourself does that sometimes—makes you forget what you were doing.

As I clicked the kettle on to boil, I leaned against the counter. It wasn't my imagination, was it? She was flirting with me, wasn't she? The thought made me go warm, or rather hot, all over. Maybe I hadn't buggered it up after all.

Her voice broke into my reverie, and I turned to see her standing in the doorway, arms loaded with bottles and glasses.

"And after you eventually make me a coffee, we can chat about your call on Boxing night."

She set the glasses on the side of the sink, placed the bottles next to the rest of my recycling, and went back to the living room. Whilst I stood there crapping myself.

Buggering up stage was still in action. Phase one hundred and twenty-two now in place.

I trudged back into the living room like a woman condemned. My discovery about Amy maybe flirting with me was forgotten, as I concentrated on what was about to happen. She was going to put me in my place, tell me, like Sue, to get over myself, she wasn't interested. Probably point out that I had to get juiced up before I called her, too.

"'Bout time. A woman could die of thirst in this house." She leaned over and grabbed the steaming mug from my hands, yelping a dramatic "ouch" at the heat.

The smile on her face was so enchanting, that I forgot to be worried...for a split second.

"You were really out of it Boxing night, weren't you?"

You know that sinking feeling in your gut, the one that makes you want to puke and also makes you go freezing cold yet hot? Well, that's nothing compared to how I was feeling. It was as if I was standing on a stage, naked, with people jeering and laughing... maybe even throwing rotten fruit.

I tentatively sat on the couch opposite her, gripping my mug so tightly that the heat scalded my fingers. "Yeah. Sorry about that." What else to say? "I had a little too much to drink; can't remember what I said exactly." Nice one, Chambers. Now she is going to think you don't love her and were only saying it because you were pissed.

"I could barely understand what you were saying on the message, either."

Huh? Message?

"I must've been in the shower. I didn't even know you'd called until the next morning."

I didn't speak to her. I'd rambled on like a Shakespearean spare part to a bloody answering machine! That would mean it was all on tape. Aw fuck.

"You just kept on apologising for Sue's interruption and threatening to call her." She laughed. "Which, by the look of things, went down beautifully."

I stared, gob open.

"Then you said you had something to tell me, but the machine cut you off before you had the chance."

So, I must have told British Telecom I was in love with them. No wonder they didn't cut me off.

"When I called you the next day, the line was busy. Then when I tried again, no one answered."

It was Amy, not Sue, who had called. Crap. If only I had spoken to her, then the entire hide-and-seek scenario would have been unnecessary.

"Left you a couple of messages, too. But considering you didn't turn up, I take it you either didn't fancy a trip to Stratford, or you weren't here."

She'd invited me to Stratford! And because I was spineless, I had missed the chance to bring in the New Year with her.

"You didn't say you were going away. Anywhere nice?"

How could I respond to that? On the one hand, I was relieved she hadn't heard me spew out how much I thought of her when I was pissed and incoherent, but on the other, she still didn't know how I felt about her. And then there had been the chance to be with her, but because I'd been such a chicken, I had flown the coop in order to avoid facing potential consequences. As per usual.

I had to stop fleeing the scene without getting all the details. It wasn't doing myself or anyone else any favours, just complicating matters. From now on, my New Year's resolution was going to be: "The buck stops here." I had to deal with the things life threw at me, whether I liked it or not. It was all part of the learning curve, and without facing my responsibilities and learning from my mistakes, how on earth could I be prepared for the next time I got myself in a mess? Not that I was thinking I would be getting myself into a mess in the future, but it is best to be prepared.

"So, what was it you wanted to tell me, then?"

Did I say the buck stops here?

"Uh...it was nothing. Fancy another?" I stood, leaned over, and grabbed her half-full cup. "Maybe I have some coffee whitener in the cupboard. Two ticks." Then I flapped into the kitchen like the chicken I was.

Cut me some slack. Rome wasn't built in a day. I was a novice at this taking responsibility malarkey, but I will, with time, get my act together. Promise.

Chapter Nine:
The "Can't be Arsed Thinking Up a Heading" Stage

That was two months ago. Doesn't time fly when you miss out great big chunks of your life? Poetic license. Or it would be if I were a poet, but I'm not. But it's my story, and you'll have to like it or lump it. Or you could do both—like it *and* lump it, your call. You are the reader, after all, and I leave that decision entirely up to you.

Now the month was February, and it was the Thursday before Jane's wedding to Amy's brother, James. I packed my bag, and in it, I put... I love that game. But this is not the time. I was packed. Dudley was at my parents' for the few days I would be away, bless his furry paws.

Though it was forty-five minutes before Amy was to pick me up, I was already sitting on my suitcase, waiting for her. We had decided to go down to Stratford a little early, as the weather prospects were not looking good. To say Jane and James were going to have a white wedding would be an understatement. Snow was billowing its frosty way across the North

Sea from Siberia, and we didn't want to get stuck on a road somewhere, turning into ice pops.

As I sat there fiddling with the strap on my handbag, images from the last two months paraded through my mind. Amy and I had really bonded, and every time I saw her, I loved her more. It was weird, really. Every day I thought I couldn't love her more, and then bam! It just got stronger. Nothing had happened between us, but every day I hoped and prayed that this would be the day I would tell her how I felt about her. I know I said I would start taking some responsibility for my life and my happiness, but I seemed to always find some excuse not to go through with it, just in case. I didn't want her to think she was a rebound fling or a stab at making myself feel desired or desirable again; I wanted it to be right. I also wanted to feel in control enough to handle whatever that giant step might hold for me. I needed to know that this relationship was not going to break me apart like the one I'd had with Sue; I felt too fragile to risk it. I know that's not the way you should look at love, but it was what I needed at the moment.

The sound of a car crunching to a halt outside my door alerted me that it was time to get my arse into gear. I pulled my coat more snugly round me, picked up my case, and struggled out the door.

She was waiting just outside, the smile on her face like a burst of sunshine in the cold temperatures of Norwich. "Here. Give me that whilst you lock up.' And off she staggered with my few days' worth of clothes that would make any travelling woman proud. Well, you have to be ready for anything, don't you?"

As I watched her struggling to lift the case into the boot of her car, I thought of how I had over-prepared.

Not my luggage, but my life since Sue, maybe even before, if I'm honest. I always avoided any kind of upset, lest I hurt someone, or myself, in the process. But where had that left me? And could I really prepare for life anyway? Big thoughts, eh? Cheery little soul that I was, I decided that I'd better not have a chat with the bride or groom, or they would probably call off their wedding.

"Come on, dreamer, before the snow starts."

Keys firmly in my handbag, another check that the door was shut and locked, and I was sitting beside her in the warmth of her car.

She glanced over at me as she started the engine. "You'd better take your coat off. We are going to be on the road for at least four hours. That's if the weather holds."

I slipped my coat off and secured my seat belt. Four hours wasn't nearly long enough to be alone with this woman.

80C3

We weren't fortunate enough to avoid the weather. The first snowflake plopped onto the windscreen of Amy's car as we joined the A11 in Norwich, about fifteen minutes into our drive. The flakes came thicker and faster, and the wipers had their work cut out for them trying to clear the windscreen. Every time Amy had to brake, our hearts were in our mouths—the back end of the car wanted to go one way, as the front end was going the other.

It wouldn't have been so bad, but there were far too many wankers out there believing they were invincible, and I didn't want to be added to the numbers plastered on the police signs along the side of the road. Road kill just isn't my bag, seeing it or being it. Thankfully, Amy felt the same way, and finally she said enough was enough. I think it was the fact we couldn't see the outline of the road, or perhaps that we had spent more time coming back down off the embankment than actually travelling on the A14. She declared that the next exit was going to be our exit.

So, just under four hours after we left Norwich, we were checking into a Travelodge just outside of Cambridge, a journey that should have taken us an hour at the most. And we were absolutely knackered to boot. It was barely early evening, but four hours of staring at the vast whiteness, heart in your mouth, kind of drains you.

Before going inside, I took some toiletries from my bag, and so did Amy. That's all we needed for the time being. It seemed as if there was no point dragging suitcases inside, especially because we were both so tired. We would only have to drag them back in the morning.

After booking a room, Amy asked the woman on the reception desk if there was any chance of ordering food.

"Sorry, Miss. Although this branch of Travelodge does have a restaurant, we have had to close early because of the weather. You know, make sure people got home okay."

"Oh." I didn't have the energy to say anything more than that one sound.

"But the service station usually has sandwiches and snacks. I think that is still open." The woman came from behind the counter and walked past us to the entrance. She opened the door and stuck her head outside, her neck craning.

Amy and I looked each other, our eyebrows seeming to shrug along with our shoulders.

"You're in luck." The receptionist's attention was back with us. "Looks like it is still open, but I don't know for how long."

"Thank you. We'll go now." My stomach rumbled, and Amy chuckled.

"No. You go get the bath running and I'll pop to the service station and see if I can rustle us up something to eat."

I didn't argue. I just wanted to get my cold arse into hot water and maybe have something to eat afterwards.

"See you in a few." Amy turned back to the woman, who was back behind her counter. "Thank you, erm... Charlene."

Charlene smiled and nodded. "Glad to be of service. Enjoy your stay."

Amy tapped her pocket. "Purse? Check." I nodded as if I was helping. "Take my smellies to the room will you?" She passed me her toiletries.

I nodded. "Good luck."

Amy had just turned to go to the service station. "I'm just nipping across the car park. I doubt I need luck."

"Yeah. And Oates said he was only popping outside and might be a while. Look what happened to him."

Amy laughed, her body moving closer to mine. "I think the expedition to the South Pole is a little bit different to me crossing a concrete parking lot in Cambridge, don't you?"

I grinned, my hand twitching to lift up and touch her cheek. She was so close to me that it would not have been out of place for me to stroke her face.

But then I remembered that it would, in fact, be out of place to caress her skin.

Amy was still looking at me as if she was expecting me to continue ribbing her. But, the fun in doing that had been replaced by the knowledge that I had nearly exposed to her how much I wanted her.

Brown eyes half closed, and she peered into my face. "You're knackered, aren't you. Go. Get gone and run that bath. I won't be long."

She left me standing in the lobby staring after her. I stood for no more than a minute, but probably would have stayed there longer staring at the door if Charlene hadn't asked me if I was okay.

"I'm fine. Thank you." I scuttled off down the labyrinth of corridors until I reached our assigned room.

Room 121 looked like an oasis—warm, quiet, cosy. Not the typical description of an oasis, but that's what it felt like to me. I went straight into the bathroom and turned on the taps, dropped in some bath foam and swirled the water to life in the shape of huge, comforting bubbles. I was freezing, and the heat from the bathtub made me feel even sleepier than I had been at the reception desk.

I clicked the latch so Amy could get back in, stripped, and submerged myself in the still running water. It was, in a word, bliss. The aching of my joints was a pleasant reminder I was still alive, and the water caressed places that needed caressing. I turned the water off and laid back, my eyes closing in absolute pleasure. This was the life.

The door opened and closed, and a breath of cold air stabbed into the room. Amy was back, and judging by the sounds coming from the next room, she had been successful in her role as hunter/gatherer. I heard her click the kettle on to make us a hot drink, and that's all I remember until I felt a hand gently shaking me awake.

"Beth. Come on, love. Bed."

I opened my eyes to see Amy leaning over me, and I couldn't quite grasp why I felt wet.

"Lucky you didn't drown."

Then it came to me—I was naked, lying in the bath, with the woman of my dreams leaning over me.

Here's a tip for you, free of charge, which is all the better. Never react like a floundering fish when there is someone fully clothed standing right above you. Reason? They get wet, the floor gets slippery, and then they fall on their arse. To expand on this tip—never shoot out of the bath to help aforementioned person without thinking things through. Reason again? The floor is wet, you are wet and rushing, therefore the outcome is always the same—you fall flat on your arse, too. But unlike the clothed person, you are flashing your lady bits to anyone who has a mind to catch a glimpse, and if you've ever seen someone naked fall, it is not a pretty sight. Believe me, it is not a pretty sight at all.

My mind flashed back to the time we met in the park. Remember? The time in the café. This time it was only me doing the exposing, though, and I didn't have Dudley with me to help change the atmosphere into something lighthearted. I was above Amy, naked, her face mere inches away from mine, and I felt exposed. Not just literally exposed, but figuratively, too. I honestly believed she could see how much I wanted her, feel how much I wanted her, as the bath water was not the only thing wet about me at that moment. There was no way she could possibly know that, but sometimes reason doesn't come into it.

Amy swallowed rapidly, and her lips moved as if to say something. The heat from her body was seeping into my own and I wanted more, and yet I didn't. Do you know what I mean? This wasn't right, wasn't the way I wanted it to be, me making a half cocked—excuse the phrase—attempt at a pass at her. It was so trite, so not me. So, I pulled back and lifted myself from on top of her, stretching to grab a towel and cover myself.

"I guess I woke you."

From more than just sleep, that I can guarantee. I stood and wrapped the towel firmly around myself. "Must have nodded off. Sorry about that." I offered her my hand and she grabbed it, pulling herself to standing in one swift movement.

"I did call out—a couple of times, actually." Her face was flushed, and she looked uncomfortable. "Knocked, too. You didn't answer. And it was so quiet in here, I came in to make sure you were okay."

I stepped around her and grabbed my toothbrush in an effort to make things seem normal again.

"I'll go and make the drinks now. And..." She paused, and I knew she was in the doorway. "You should wait to brush your teeth. You haven't eaten yet."

"I can always brush them again." It was cold and cutting, and no sooner was it out than I regretted it.

I was looking at her reflection in the mirror, toothbrush static. Her expression initially showed surprise and then uncertainty, finally settling into resolution. She didn't answer, just left the room to me and my humiliation.

The minty taste of the toothpaste made me gag, or maybe it was just my reaction to what had happened. I knew I shouldn't have snapped at her; it wasn't her fault I had made an ass out of myself again. I went into the other room, where I found her stirring the mugs, her head lowered as if she was concentrating on the task. I knew her better than that. I knew I had hurt her, and not just by falling on her.

"Amy." I waited for her to shoot a quick glimpse over her shoulder in acknowledgement before I continued. "Sorry for snapping at you. I'm just tired and ratty."

A hesitant smile edged round her lips.

"And embarrassed." I grinned at her in hopes she would give me one back. "Is that for me?" Edging closer to her and encroaching on her space, I leaned in and grabbed the steaming cup of hot chocolate. "You know me so well, Ms Fletcher."

The smile she gave me would have blinded someone with sensitive eyes.

"Thought it would warm you up." Her voice held an element of contained excitement, "And I also got you some chocolate, cos I know you're a bugger for the sweet stuff when you're due on your period." Her face went scarlet, billiard ball red! "I...erm..."

"You've been keeping tabs on me, eh?"

Unbelievably, she went a shade darker, her eyes flicking everywhere but at my face.

But the laugh gurgling up inside me tore out, and I laughed long and hard whilst she stood there and glowed.

"Maybe that's why I'm so ratty then. Thanks for reminding me."

"I'm just going to grab a bath. Won't be long."

And she was gone, leaving me alone to sip my drink and smile smugly to myself.

The bed was comfy, soft yet firm—a perfect combination. It wasn't long before contentment glided through me. My eyelids felt heavy, like they were weighted down with stones, and I wanted to snuggle under the covers. There were two things that prevented me from yielding to the allure of rest. The first was that I hadn't made up the couch, which seconded as a bed, and the second, my sleep shirt was in the boot of my car. I had remembered toiletries, but forgot about getting ready for bed. All I had was the towel wrapped around me and the clothes I'd worn that day.

I promised myself I would just close my eyes for a few minutes and then I would slip my t-shirt on. Promises, promises, promises. I have no idea how long I had been asleep when I felt the bed next to me move slightly. All I had the strength to do was to scrabble under the covers and fall asleep again.

Dawn was breaking when next I opened my bleary eyes, although I could only see the shapes and shadows of the early light, as I was firmly buried in something soft and warm. Amy. Propriety told me to move away, take my face from the curve of her neck, unfurl my hands from around her waist, my leg from over hers, move out of her grasp. But I didn't want to. Simple as that. I felt safe, so bloody safe, and secure and protected. Being in her arms felt so absolutely, positively right, there was nowhere else I wanted to be.

Sighing in her sleep, Amy pulled me closer. Her lips kissed the top of my head, her breath warm on my skin. The tightening in my gut precipitated the tightening of my hold on her. I needed her. God, I needed her so much. Not just sexually, no. I needed to have all of her—all...of...her. Being in her arms made the world seem bearable, made my life seem bearable and gave it meaning. I knew I had fallen in love with Amy, but I had been scared to do anything about it, to let her know how I felt. At that instant, I knew I couldn't hide it anymore; I had to tell her how I felt and accept the consequences.

Her hand slipped down my back until it rested at the curve of my buttocks. Long tendrils of fire sizzled along my skin and burrowed deeper and deeper, into the very heart of me. Amy's fingertips began to swirl over my needy flesh, each whirl creating a new shower of sparks that slithered and danced across every inch of my body.

I suddenly realised the towel I had been wearing had opened, and I was cleaving to her totally naked, and, by the feel of her skin, she was naked too.

I should have stopped. Pulled away. Gotten up. Dressed. I should have done anything but hold on to her and press myself tighter against her in guilty need, a need to have her, even if it was only for this moment. To accept that maybe it wouldn't be forever, but to be contented with the here and now.

Culpable fingers stroked her collarbone, enchanted by the softness of her skin. They traced the line of the bone and dipped into the recess of her neck, my eyes fixated. Those fortunate fingers lingered in the nuances of her throat and delighted in dipping down...dipping lower and tracing along the centre of her chest.

When I followed their path with my eyes, I could see the curve and swell of her breast enticing me, beguiling me, begging me to circle and caress the joy of her. And I would have, too, if she hadn't shifted and pulled me closer, trapping my hand over her breast in the process. I couldn't free my hand, however hard I tried, not that I tried very hard. Her nipple budded in my palm, and I gloried in the sensation, not wanting it to end. I did feel a little pervy, though. It wasn't as if she had said I could touch her, but then again, she hadn't said I couldn't. Sound logic, I think. A balanced argument.

Temptation was there and agonisingly difficult to ignore. My fingers were spread eagled over her breast, and I had the urge to slide them together and gently knead the pliant flesh. It was so difficult, so bloody difficult not to do it. She would never know, would she? It wasn't as if I would be doing anything really bad, was it? Just making the most of a gift from the gods. I mean, it was a gift placed right in the palm of my hand, and I would be a fool not to accept it, wouldn't I?

No. I would be a fool if I did. It was bad, and I felt ashamed that I had momentarily been willing to take advantage of someone I professed to love whilst she didn't know anything about it.

But her breast was so soft, so ready, so in the palm of my hand, begging me to touch it with more focus and dedication.

What the fuck was I doing? I was turning into some somnolent fiddler, or ready to be. And what if she caught me red handed? Or *something* handed? How would I explain that? I would lose her friendship for certain. And that was not worth the momentary pleasure.

It's okay to get all moralistic and on my high horse about what I had or hadn't nearly done, but the truth of the matter was I was about to fumble like a schoolgirl, an inexperienced schoolgirl who had suddenly been introduced to the world and didn't have a clue what to do. That is just not done. But the buggering part was that it didn't change the fact that my hand was still bloody trapped. What if she woke up and caught me gripping her tit? Would she believe me when I said "nothing was going on, you just rolled onto my hand?" Would she? Hell as like. I wouldn't believe it either, especially if her face were as crimson as mine, with "I'm guilty" written across my forehead.

I was saved, as she mumbled something in her sleep and pushed backwards a little, freeing my hand. The loss of contact left me longing for her to turn back again, but I knew that if she did, it would be my undoing.

There was only one thing for it. I had to extricate myself from her so it didn't happen again. The next time, I would have no control over my reactions. With my back to her, I grabbed the towel and wrapped it around me, thinking it would have been easier to just get up and put something on. But to tell the truth, I couldn't be arsed. That, and the fact my pyjamas were still in the boot of the car.

I thought I would never get back to sleep. Thought I would lie there for hours until it was a reasonable time to get up, and try to ignore the fact I had been in her arms for a little while, try to forget the feel of her skin, the smell of her hair, the softness of her breast. Try to ignore the feeling of total contentment I had when I was with her, and the complete sense of fulfilment. Little did I know that in less than five minutes I would be asleep, dreaming of a time when I could touch her limitlessly.

When I next woke, I felt someone spooning up the back of me, a long graceful arm draped over my stomach, breath at the back of my neck. I wanted to pull the arm around me and snuggle down for a little while longer, maybe to try and keep the dream alive, but I knew better. However long I lay there, I would want to stay longer, and this was only prolonging the inevitable. I gently took her fingers in hand to move them off my stomach, but they curled around mine, holding me in place.

"Good morning, Beth."

The voice was soft and sleepy, but its vibrations raced down my spine and kicked all my nerves awake.

"Sleep well?"

She squeezed my fingers, and I closed my eyes and relished the moment. "Not bad. You?" I have to admit, my voice squeaked.

She stiffened, so I stiffened, too, thinking she was going to say something about my late night meanderings, but she turned it into a stretch and yawn, releasing my fingers in the process.

"Not bad."

I relaxed a little, as relaxed as a person can be when they know the person behind them is naked.

"Had a funny dream, though."

Her voice was stronger, more awake, and given what she had just said, I was instantly alert. "Oh yeah. What about?" I didn't want to know. Why did I ask?

"You were in it. You were holding on to me."

Shit.

"Strange. It felt so real."

"Probably because you were sleeping deeply. We all have odd dreams if we sleep deeply."

There was a pause as she digested that. "I thought if you slept deeply, you didn't dream, or couldn't remember it as well."

As she spoke, I got out of bed, securing the towel around me again. Bloody thing had gone walkies after I had fallen asleep.

Looking back to the bed, I was disappointed to see she had pulled the covers back over her and all I could see were her shoulders. Being a lady, I didn't say anything. She looked so beautiful lying there— dark hair fanned over the pillow, one hand separating the strands even further, her eyes sparkling and alive, her lips moving.

Her lips moving? Crap. She was talking to me, and I had missed it. "What?"

She stopped fiddling with her hair and frowned at me.

"Sorry. I was thinking about breakfast." Yeah, right. Eating, yes. Breakfast, no.

"I said, Hungry Horace, that it felt so real—the dream.'

I cocked my head as if to tell her I already knew that bit. There was no way I could get out of it now. I was trapped in the fabrication of my own making—hoist on my own petard, as my History teacher used to say.

"And you were in my dream, Beth. You were drowning, and I had to save you."

You already have.

"I jumped in and pulled you out of the water. You had to hang on to my neck and grip the front of my top."

I think my gulp was audible, but I couldn't be sure.

"It was as if I could actually feel your hands on me."

I wondered whether I should just curl up and die, or wait to see if there was something more that would embarrass me further.

"And when I woke up, you were just turning over onto your side. I wanted to speak to you, but I knew you were asleep."

Thank God she had woken up after I had released her breast. That would have taken a lot of explaining.

I picked up the empty mugs and started toward the bathroom, stopping near the door to turn back to her. "Probably the incident in the bathroom last night, you know, brought back the memories of the day we first met."

Brown eyes squinted in thought and then grew wide again, the smile breaking across her face like a rush of life. "I hadn't thought of that. You're right. I was probably remembering about that day, the day in the river."

She looked comfortable with the explanation, and I scurried away to rinse the cups in the sink before making morning tea.

As water gushed over the crockery, I thought back to the day Amy and I had met at Earlham Park. She had saved me that day. Just by appearing, she had made me feel that there were things about life that weren't all bad, that life was, in fact, worth living, and for that, I would be forever grateful. She came into the water to rescue me, but it wasn't the water I needed saving from. It was myself. Amy showed me there was another way to look at life, although I didn't know at the time what that way was. She planted the seed that made me try again, made me want to try a relationship again.

The reflection in the bathroom mirror showed a healthier me. Hair a mess, sleepy eyed, but better— stronger, growing in confidence.

Yes, Amy did save me. But could she love me? Only time would tell. And the way I was feeling, I doubted it would be much longer before I knew, one way or the other.

෨෬

Through mouthfuls of Rice Krispies, Amy told me that she had called her folks the previous night and explained the situation.

"I meant to tell you last night, but by the time I got out of the bath, you were flat out." Her spoon rang as it swirled around the base of the bowl to scoop up the dregs of milk. "I'll give James a call to let him know we are on our way again. Don't want them sending out a search party." She laughed as she stood and held out her hand. I stared at her, wondering what she wanted. "Bowl." I looked down at my half eaten cereal. "Just me for seconds then," she said.

I stared at her as she moved back to the breakfast counter, her movements sleek and graceful. A sensory memory of me holding her breast in my hand flitted inside my head, and the blush overtook me at lightning speed as my mouth dropped open in shock.

"Come on, dreamer. Eat up."

Her word choice made me flush even darker, and I expected her to comment, per usual.

Facing my cornflakes, I dug the spoon into the soggy mess and brought a heap of the orange goo to my mouth, shovelling it in like I was half starved.

"That's a good girl. Now eat it all up. It'll put hair on your chest."

At the mention of "chest," I thought I was going to choke. The mass of cereal seemed to clog together in solidarity. Thankfully, some well-paced swallows reduced the threat of her having to perform the Heimlich on me.

Although the roads were far from perfect, they were nowhere near as bad as they had been the night before. Once-white fluff had turned into brown slush, and the commuter traffic was in full flow. The radio informed us the reprieve from the weather would be short-lived. More snow was expected by evening, so we pelted toward our destination as quickly as possible.

Three and a half hours later, we pulled into the driveway of James and Jane's bungalow in Seaford, which was just outside of Pinvin, about fifteen miles from Stratford. Amy's parents, her brother, and his future wife greeted us at the door. It was the first time I had met Amy's dad and brother, but they looked like peas in a pod. Frank, Amy's father, held out his hand, and I swear to God, I have never in my life seen hands so big. They were like shovels. He could probably use them to dig our way out later when the forecasted snow arrived.

"You must be Beth."

His grip was firm and my hand was swallowed up inside his, making it look as if he was shaking a stick. I stared at it, admonished myself for staring, then stared again. I gave myself an imaginary kick up the backside and grinned stupidly at him.

"What am I doing?" He laughed. "No hand shaking for you, young lady. Come here, you."

The bear hug he treated me to had my ribcage aching for release, although I felt well and truly welcome. Marion hovered in the background and then went through exactly the same routine, though her hands were decidedly smaller. James and Jane didn't bother with handshakes, they just lunged straight into the hugging stage. All in all, I felt very much at home.

In the less than five minutes we were outside whilst introductions were made, the heat I had grown accustomed to in the car evaporated. Once inside, coats were discarded and we were led to the front room, where an open fired blazed in the hearth. It was bliss.

"I'll just get your bags." James smiled at me and nodded at Amy to follow.

I didn't mind being left alone with the rest of the family. What could possibly go wrong?

Amy's dad came and sat beside me. "So, you stayed at a Travelodge, did you?" Jane and Marion sat at the dining room table, sifting through last minute paperwork and grinning supportively. "Must have been bad weather then?"

I nodded. There was a slight pause, and I looked at him, waiting for another question. I didn't have to wait long.

"Marion tells me you're a graphic designer. Pay much?"

"Frank! Leave the girl alone," Marion's voice sounded shocked, but it also held an edge of mirth. "Make yourself useful. Go make a cuppa or something."

"I'm only being friendly." He turned back to me "Aren't I, love?"

I smiled at him and nodded.

"See? You've embarrassed the girl."

I could hear Amy's voice somewhere in the hallway, talking heatedly with her brother.

Frank looked towards the door and shrugged. "Just like old times, eh? Them two would argue who shi—"

"Frank!"

Marion's admonition stopped him, but I knew how the sentence ended, and I sniggered. This definitely felt like home, as I remembered the times Will and I had argued over nothing.

James came through into the lounge, his face flushed; Amy followed, even more flushed. No one asked what they had been talking about, apparently accepting that they always had to have a squabble of some description.

Frank didn't seem to notice that his children seemed antsy. "I own a boat refurbishment company. Nothing huge, but it pays the bills." He leaned forward, as if taking me into his confidence. "But I wouldn't mind getting the word out to more than the locals. Doing up boats is a dying art, you know. Could be a lot of work out there that I'm missing."

"Or people that are missing your skills." I smiled.

Frank laughed and turned to Amy. "I like this one. She's a charmer."

Amy gave him a strained smile and nodded. "That she is." Her eyes met mine briefly before she quickly looked away.

"So," Frank's attention was back on me, "any tips about how to reach all these people who are missing out on my genius?"

To be honest, my mind went completely blank. Usually I would have had no problem regurgitating ideas that had been tried and tested, but at the moment, I was more interested in what had transpired on the other side of the room.

"Let me have a think about it, yes? We can work together on getting some ideas down on paper after the wedding."

He nodded enthusiastically, his smile broad. Frank reached over and patted my knee with his huge hand, making my leg seem like a five year old's in comparison. "That'll be perfect. Don't want to steal the limelight from the bride, eh? You know what women are like about weddings." He tilted his head and stared at me. "Sorry, love. You're a woman, aren't you."

I laughed. "I believe I am."

"Not that you don't look like a woman. You are very womanly. And ... I ... Aw bugger."

"Bloody hell, Frank, leave the poor girl alone." Marion's voice held a note of annoyed amusement.

I laughed again. "Don't worry, Frank. I know what you mean." I didn't, but I didn't want to make him feel even more embarrassed, or, worse still, try to explain to me why he had forgotten I was female.

"Glad you do, love. I haven't a clue what I'm saying."

"That sums you up, love," Marion said from her place at the dining room table, her eyes never leaving the paperwork. Jane was looking past me, to the doorway, her face showing complete confusion.

I turned and looked at the other side of the room to where Amy was standing. James was gesturing to Jane to follow him outside, and this was being reinforced by Amy's furtive beckoning. They looked like a mime troupe who had no idea they were being watched. What was going on?

"I'll just get things sorted for tea." And then Jane was gone, followed by her future hubby and his sister.

More heated whisperings from the hallway were punctuated by a louder, "Well, I thought you would have gotten your act together by now," which was followed by an extremely loud shushing from James and Amy. Marion stopped her fiddling at the table and gathered her notebook and pencil, then came to sit on the other side of me. I felt like a Fletcher sandwich, both of them grinning in a way that was making me slightly uncomfortable. I was not too sure why they were sporting smiles when their children were bickering in the hallway.

"Ignore them, love," Marion said. "You can help me check through this list. You read it out, I'll see if I've done it."

It had gone quiet in the hallway, and I knew the trio had taken their discussion to the kitchen. All I could do was accept the offer of being occupied whilst the drama was in full swing.

Ten minutes later, I had been neither use nor ornament. They were all back in the room, a tray of tea and biscuits carried unsteadily by Amy, who kept glaring at James and Jane. Oddly enough, they didn't seem to mind. On the contrary, they seemed to be finding something quite amusing. Tea poured and cup firmly ensconced in my hand, I settled back and listened to the talk about the upcoming wedding, chiming in now and again.

A couple of times I caught Frank nodding and mouthing something at Amy, and her face flushed brightly. I also spotted Jane and James nudging each other and giggling. Sometimes, however hard you try, you still feel on the outside of things. Not that I was concerned, just intrigued, mainly because the usually confident Amy seemed to have regressed fifteen years. On more than one occasion, I honestly expected her to storm off to her room. She exhibited behaviours that were a blend of contentment and discomfort, and it struck me that the last time I had acted that way around my own parents was the day I had introduced them to Amy and they had assumed she was the new lady in my life.

Bollocks. That's what the arguing had been about. They had believed I was her girlfriend, and she was putting them in the picture that there was no way on this God's earth that she would ever want to be tagged with me.

It was agony to sit and smile, absolute agony. I had arrived at a juncture in my life where I realised I had to tell Amy how I felt, and just as I got there, I found out there was no point embarrassing myself. Though it wasn't actually the embarrassment I was worried about; it was the realisation that she didn't want me as anything other than a friend.

I stood, a little too quickly, bringing the conversation to a halt "Sorry. I... I...need..." The words were elusive, jamming in my throat.

"Bathroom, love?" Marion stood up next to me and linked my arm. "I'll show you." Outside the room, she stopped and turned me to face her. "You okay, Beth? The colour has completely drained from your face."

I nodded, but I could tell she didn't believe me.

"Is it something about Amy?"

No answer. I couldn't. I wouldn't. I shouldn't, but I needed to tell someone. Needed to crack the pressure valve that was bottling up all these emotions before I exploded.

No.

"Just feel a little sick, because of the trip and stuff. Don't worry, Marion, I'll be fine."

Her eyes were squinting, as if she was trying to read my mind, but how on earth could someone read my mind, when I didn't know what was going on in there myself?

She didn't say anything, just took my hand and led me to the door of the bathroom. As I was going in, she placed her hand on my shoulder, making me turn to face her. "When you're ready, eh? I'm here when you're ready."

A sad smile slipped onto my face, and I nodded slowly before I closed the door.

A look into the mirror confirmed that I did look pale. No wonder Marion had been worried. I leaned in closer and took a good, long look at myself. Even white skinned, with my hair a mess, the main thing was I still looked better—stronger, and growing in confidence. It shouldn't matter that she didn't love me; it didn't change the way I felt about her. Sad, but true. And I knew that although my love might not be reciprocated, one way or another, I would still tell Amy how I felt, and stuff the consequences.

I felt both terrified and excited. And I swore to my reflection that after the wedding I would do it, tell her how I felt—no strings. And unlike the previous time I'd said that, this time I really meant it.

Chapter Nine and a Half

Nothing was said when I got back into the living room, but Frank and Marion had shifted to the other sofa and Amy was sitting by my spot in their stead. Looking worried when I came back through the door, Amy patted the couch in invitation. Everyone was talking about different things, as families tend to do. You know—when one person starts a conversation and another person begins another, and then it all devolves into confused chatter. Confusing, but very comforting.

"You okay?" She leaned towards me, and I could smell her perfume. Her eyes were gentle, glistening slightly. "I was worried about you." She stroked the back of my hand.

Electricity raced up my arms and ended at the tips of my nips.

"Please tell me if you want to talk about anything." Another stroke, this time with the tips of her fingers. "I mean *anything*, okay?"

I could only nod mutely. I was sure my tongue was swelling, along with other parts of my anatomy.

She took a deep breath, then said in a rush, "I've got something I need to tell you. It's a bit embarrassing, really."

I looked at her, waiting for her to continue. The chatter in the room stopped, and for the first time I could hear the clock on the mantelpiece. It sounded like Big Ben. She gripped my hand, squeezed it, and then relinquished her grasp. I heard murmured excuses coming from behind me as the others got up and made their way to the door. Before long, it was just Amy and me. Bugger. This must be bad. What did they think I was going to do, have the screaming ab dabs or something?

"Erm...there's been a misunderstanding."

Jesus. She already knows, and she's trying to let me down gently.

"Jane and James, well they...erm..."

She grimaced. *Grimaced!*

"They kind of got the wrong end of the stick."

I'm afraid I made it more difficult for her, because I didn't say anything, just waited.

"They...erm...have put us in the same room."

I cocked my head, as if I didn't understand. I understood all right—she didn't want to sleep with me. Last night had been enough to put her off.

"Not that I don't want to— I mean— Erm. Shit. Mind..."

Yeah, right.

"I'm more than happy to sleep with you... Erm... Crap." Her face was crimson. "What I'm trying to say, and not very well is—would you mind sleeping with me?" Blood red. She went blood red. "No, not like— Well, I...see...there's only three bedrooms, and— Bugger. I'm making a mess of this, aren't I?"

I nodded, grinned, and then held my hands up to her face, pretending to warm them over the heat of her cheeks. She looked so adorable as she sat and glowed.

"Jane assumed that...I...we...erm...were like... together. And I told her we were friends, and that's all."

I should have been disappointed by what she was saying, but there was something behind her eyes that I couldn't quite grasp. It gave me a boost of sorts. It wasn't what she said, more like what she didn't say. Probably I'd read it all wrong and it was just wishful thinking, but for the moment I wanted to go with what her expression was saying to me.

"Jane's mother will be here in a short while, and they've given her the third room."

"No worries." I made sure I had eye contact before continuing. "I think I could manage sharing a room with you again."

She grinned and exhaled the breath she'd been holding.

"Just," I added, erasing the remaining tension.

So there it was—drama over nothing. Story of my life, really. I love to make mountains out of molehills. It would be best if I waited to tell her that I loved her, as that tidbit of information might make her nervous as to my intentions when we were sharing the same bed tonight. No one likes to get under the sheets with someone they know fancies them when they don't feel the same. Too awkward. But I would tell her. That resolution was still in place—two months late, but there all the same.

As we had to be up early the next day, we all had an early night. Frank, Marion, and James left not long after eight, wanting to be home and settled whilst they could still get there. Jane's mum, Vera, arrived about seven, appropriately excited about her little girl tying the knot the next day.

I spent most of the night just watching Amy sleep, as besotted people do. She looked for all the world like an angel—so peaceful, so beautiful, so within my reach yet so not. And this time I kept my hands to myself. I didn't want a repeat of what had happened in the hotel. Unless I actually got the guts to confess to her how I was feeling beforehand.

Amy looked a vision when she walked out of the bedroom the next day. She wore a sleeveless crimson dress and her hair was gathered at the back, loose strands caressing her cheeks. For a split second I felt a pang of jealousy, then it was gone, and I was left being gobsmacked. In all the time I had known her, I had never seen her dressed up like this. Not that many people walk about in a bridesmaid's dress whilst walking a dog or going on the Big One. Amy looked so ladylike, she actually reminded me of a character from a Victorian romance.

"I'm fucking freezing."

Or maybe not.

"Good job I've got a shawl, although I doubt it will be of any use out there."

It was a shame to see her cover those glorious shoulders, but I understood that standing outside at minus four degrees would be a little nippy in a sleeveless frock. Aw well. At least I could stare all I wanted at the reception later.

Oh yeah, to be fair, the bride looked nice too.

৪৩৫৩

The reception was heaving with people, and the heat in the room bordered on stifling. After the speeches, it was time to get the party started. Jane and James wouldn't be there the entire evening, as they were off on honeymoon to Cuba, and their flight left Heathrow in the early hours of the morning. It wasn't until late that I found out that Vera would be staying over with one of her relatives who lived closer to the hotel, a cousin, I think. There were so many relatives there that I actually lost count of all the people I was introduced to, and I'd be buggered if I could remember a quarter of their names.

As the evening wore on, the atmosphere became thicker, fuller. I can't describe it beyond than that. It was charged with something that at the time I didn't recognise, and a part of me became nervous. Don't ask me why, I just did. Nothing out of the ordinary had happened, for a wedding, that is. Just the usual. The kids had been taken home, as they had tired themselves out dancing and running round the dance floor like headless chickens high on sugar, and only the adults remained. I had a few dances with a couple of cousins from Amy's side of the family. Nice blokes. Looked a little like her, too. But they weren't her.

It was just before ten that I spotted Amy talking to a woman who apparently had arrived late, as she was standing near the door and just then taking off her coat. I know; I should work for MI5. They were laughing and hugging each other, repeatedly hugging each other. Then they kissed. On the mouth. Not a long kiss, but a kiss on the lips just the same. I watched as Amy pulled back from the bint, holding her at arm's length and looking her up and down, her face showing incredulity. Then they hugged each other again.

I should have felt the usual disappointment and "poor me," but all I felt was anger. I wanted to go over and smack the woman in the face, and maybe piss on Amy's shoes like a dog. I wanted to go over and make my presence known, introduce myself, let Amy know I was still there; maybe throw a spanner in the works.

Bitter? Twisted? You bet. I didn't want anything coming between Amy and me tonight, as I wanted to tell her how I felt when we got back to the bungalow. I could do it tonight, as I knew we would have the place to ourselves and spare beds to sleep in if it all went pear shaped. And if it did go tits up, I could get a taxi to the train station first thing in the morning, so as not to make Amy feel uncomfortable on our journey home. All I hoped was that it wouldn't ruin our friendship. That, I did not want to lose.

I didn't have to get up and go over, because within moments Amy was standing in front of me with the woman latching on like a limpet. "Beth?" She thrust the woman closer to me. "This is Rachel."

I brought up the Chambers smile from deep within, stuck out my hand in greeting, and didn't visibly flinch when she gripped it hard enough to crimp my fingers.

"I've heard so much about you, Beth."

I've heard bugger all about you.

"Amy tells me you and she are good friends."

She turned to give Amy one of those looks, you know the ones, they go along the lines of "Look how clever I am," bordering on arrogance.

The urge to wipe the smugness off her face was almost consuming me, and I had to clench my hands into fists underneath the table while I forced the anger aside.

"I just had to come and meet the woman who makes Amy go all girly. Isn't that right, Amy?"

Amy's throat was pulsing, and I knew she was swallowing rapidly.

"You've just broken up with someone, haven't you? Shame. No chance of you getting back together?"

"Rachel!"

"I was just wondering. No offence meant, Beth."

Yeah. Right.

"None taken. No worries. Sorry, what was your name again?"

Her face was a picture—absolute classic. It was worth biting my tongue and not telling her to shove her "concerned" questions right where the sun didn't shine.

"I'm thirsty."

Talk about blanking my question.

"Come on, Amy. Buy me a drink."

Amy still looked startled, and Rachel tried to grab her hand to lead her away.

"In a minute, Rachel. You go and queue, and I'll be along in shortly."

Rachel looked disappointed, turned and glared at me, and then stalked off.

She was attractive, I'll give her that, but what lurked underneath her skin was far from beautiful—

says me who wanted to smack her one even before we were introduced.

"Ignore her, Beth." Amy sat down in the chair opposite me. "She's a little possessive."

I wanted to ask if she was seeing Rachel, but Amy beat me to it.

"I used to go out with her a couple of years ago, but it didn't work out."

Best news I'd heard all day.

"She was extremely controlling, tending to be aggressive to anyone I even merely talked to."

I'm sure Amy heard me gulp, because she gave me a funny look.

"She was a bit like how Sue used to be with you."

Realisation dawned, thudded into my head actually. No wonder Amy had been so understanding about Sue and how I had dealt, or not dealt, with her. She had been on the receiving end of something similar.

She looked away, and I could tell she was thinking. When she looked back, she looked resolved. "Beth?" Her voice was low, and I heard a little quaver in that single word. "I need to tell you something tonight, to explain something, really."

Thoughts sifted through my head. Did she want to tell me about Rachel? But the look on her face told me it was something more than that.

"I have to tell you how I—"

"Are you coming to get me a drink, or what?" Rachel had come back from the bar, and she didn't look a happy bunny. "One of your cousins just felt me up."

I wanted to laugh out loud, dispel the tension and also piss Rachel off, but I did neither. I was a good girl, for a change. "He's probably drunk." I couldn't resist.

I heard Amy snort, but Rachel just shot me daggers. I wanted to add "Or desperate," but that would have been going a little too far. It was funny how I had taken an instant dislike to the woman, when I didn't even know her. What I had seen of her made me glad that we would never have to act like bosom buddies, maybe because she reminded me of Sue, and you know how I feel about that subject.

Amy gave me a look of apology, stood up to go with Rachel, stopped and leaned over to me. "Don't forget." Warm breath tickled the side of my face. "Tonight." Then she was gone.

I could just make out her profile as she waited at the bar to get served. A couple of times she looked my way and her eyes bored into mine, no smile, nothing. I could tell she was deep in thought both times; about what, I couldn't guess. Thinking about what she was going to say to me later gave me the jitters, but I was more concerned about what I had resolved to say to her. Whatever happened, I would be telling her how I felt when we got back to the house.

James and Jane left just after eleven amongst cheers and good wishes, and it wasn't long before Amy and I were in a taxi and on our way home. The atmosphere was thick with expectation, but neither of us said a word. My stomach was churning, but it couldn't outdo the pounding in my chest. My heart was well aware it was going to be centre stage in a matter of minutes, and I think it was warming itself up.

Chapter Ten

Once inside the house, I could feel my mettle failing. The words were spinning around in my head, but did not make any sense. I didn't know where to begin, how to broach the subject. I didn't want to just blurt it out, and all the preparation I had been doing mentally had fled, leaving me with a vacuous space where my brain used to be.

I had to collect myself before I told her. I had to do this right. I didn't want to cock things up, didn't want to blurt and then regret. I wanted to have a decent chance at telling her how I felt.

Amy went straight into the living room, and I stopped in the doorway and just watched her clicking on the lamps. Her shoulders shimmered and gleamed in the soft light, and I could smell her perfume as strongly as if she were standing in front of me.

"Just nipping to the loo." And I was gone. Door locked, my back against it, my breathing heavy and erratic. "Calm down, for God's sake. *Calm...down.*" I knelt down, my knees nearing my face, and attempted to regularise my breathing. "Just tell her." My heart was in overdrive. "Just...tell...her."

Then it came to me. It was Amy. Amy. Amy. Just tell her.

Before I knew it, I was out of the door and standing in front of her. Her face showed surprise and her lips pursed in question. Words wouldn't come, couldn't assemble themselves into any kind of intelligible order. I couldn't tell her, couldn't just say the bloody words that rattled inside my head, the words I so desperately wanted to say.

So, I kissed her. Cupped her face and pulled her to me and kissed her. Held that beautiful face in my hands and kissed her as if my life depended on it. Pulled her to me and kissed her mouth, her sensuous mouth, the mouth I had so long yearned to explore. Her lips stayed closed, but I continued to kiss her, knowing that if I stopped, that would be the end of it.

Miraculously, she began to respond, her lips parting, her tongue tracing the curve of my mouth. Her hands slipped around my waist, creating a trail of longing in their wake. As she pulled me into her, she parted my legs with her thigh and pressed against the throbbing pool of want collecting there for her alone.

The gasp that left my mouth entered hers, and my fingers trailed down her face, defining the contours of perfection.

Her lips left mine, and she pulled back to look into my face. "Beth."

One whispered word. I placed my finger over her lips. I didn't want to discuss what was happening between us; I just wanted to continue kissing her, wanted her to continue kissing me.

As if she heard my wish and granted it, her lips parted, luscious lips parted and my finger slipped inside to be gently suckled, the sensation rippling in waves down my body. Her firm thigh continued to press and rub, and I could feel the wetness seeping through my underwear. My fingers traced along her jawbone and round to where her hair was clipped back. With one click, her hair cascaded around her face and framed the beauty that was Amy.

Need overcame everything else, and I lifted my mouth to claim hers again. Lips of velvet...soft, pliable velvet. Velvet that tasted of lipstick and promise. Tongues became more enquiring, coming out to dip and dance in the joy of the moment. Hands became clasping, searching, and didn't find purchase on one single thing that could quench the desire rippling and reverberating through me.

Amy pulled away, and the sudden cool air on my face emphasised the absence of the heat of her mouth. "Beth." Almost a groan. "Please..."

I leaned in to kiss her again but she moved her face, her eyes pleading for me to stop. Had I misread her reaction? Had I forced her to kiss me, giving her no option but to comply as I thrust myself on her? But she hadn't pushed me away; she was still grasping me as if I would flee if she let me go. Her thigh was entrenched between my legs.

"Amy?" My voice crackled and split. "What's wrong?" I didn't want her to answer; I just wanted to carry on in ignorance, and pretend that this was meant to be.

Brown eyes looked deeply into my own, searching, demanding, exacting a something from me, a something I didn't know. "Please tell me..."

Tell her what? I could feel the vibrations racing through her as she held me, pulsating waves as she pleaded without words.

The light came. Bright blinding light. The light that makes it clear you have been a fool.

"I love you." Three little words, three syllables, eight letters, but for some people they are the hardest words, or syllables, or letters to say.

Her hands gripped my shoulders and pulled me into a fierce hug, crushing my face against her breast. A sob ripped from Amy's throat and came to rest in my hair.

"*God*...Beth. I..." Another sob "I love you so much... so much." She cupped my face and lifted it up level with her own. "I've loved you forever."

I could have let the phrasing remind me of Sue and her false promises, but this wasn't a false promise. She said she *had* loved me forever, not that she was going to. And forever could mean different things to different people, as had become entirely too apparent with my ex. With Amy, even forever would never be long enough.

Her forehead rested against mine, and her eyes captured my gaze. "I love you, Beth." Then she kissed me, so tenderly that I could have wept tears of happiness, but instead I kissed her back. Firmer. Dedicated. Oblivious to everything around me, apart from the glorious woman in my embrace. I could feel wetness running down my face, and I wasn't sure whether I was crying or it was Amy, or both of us. Kisses and caresses became comforting, stroking, pacifying, anticipation heightening to the point it was almost too much for us to bear.

My knees gave way and I wanted to pull her down to the ground with me, but I knew that wasn't what either of us wanted—our first time to be on the living room carpet.

"Amy..." another kiss. "Amy...we..." another mouth-watering kiss. "We need..."

She kept kissing me—deep, sensuous and devouring, until I nearly forgot what I was going to say. The feelings that were throbbing through me needed no words, no explanation. All they needed was her. I was finding it increasingly difficult to formulate a sentence, and all I could conjure from the bank of words and phrases in my head was, "Bed."

Amy slipped her leg from between my thighs and stepped back, the smile on her face inviting and accepting.

My heart fluttered, or was that my stomach? Stuff the sideshow of organs. Who cared? I was going into the bedroom with the woman I loved.

Extending a hand in invitation, she lifted an eyebrow and her lips parted in a sensual smile. "I thought you'd never ask."

She was a vision, an absolute vision of everything I had ever wanted, and more besides. Placing my hand in hers, I felt my future click into place. This was where I should be, where I wanted to be, where I needed to be to feel complete again.

஋௵௸

The bedroom was dark, but there was no need for lights; the moonlight slipped though the crack in the curtains and silhouetted her frame. I didn't need a light to guide me to where she was; I could sense her.

Long fingers grazed my cheeks and buried themselves in my hair, and she gently eased me forward and into her—her mouth tantalisingly close, her breath sweet and warm. Lips—warm, moist, and tender—brushed against mine, and a rush of sensation raced southwards. I had never felt so alive, so alert, so totally entranced with anything or anyone before in my life.

In that instant, I wanted to take her, consume her and love her, devour all of her. I grasped Amy's hips and pulled her to me, claiming her mouth as reward for the patience I'd attempted.

Clothes were a barrier. I needed to touch her skin, glide reverent fingers over soft, pliable flesh, dip between her legs and sample the delights of her. Kisses became more ardent, hands began to fumble and discover. I gasped as her hand possessed my breast and kneaded it. My hips swayed backwards and forwards, backwards and forwards, chafing my desire. It wasn't enough.

I slipped my hands up her back, grasped the zipper and tugged it downwards, causing her dress to billow at the front. I slowly pushed it down until it pooled at her feet, and she stood in my arms in just her underthings. My fingers slipped over velvet skin as I traced the curves of her waist on my way to her breasts. I broke off the kiss and stepped back, wanting to watch my hands cupping and holding the sensuous curves for the first time. The reality of such a thing is nothing like it has been imagined; it is so much more—so beguiling, so all-consumingly magical. I was spellbound. Her bra fell away suddenly as Amy released the clasp.

Perfect. Absolutely perfect. Full rounded orbs were peaked by dark, erect nipples. I had seen them before, touched them even, but not like this. This was an offering of something sacred, something to be cherished. And cherish them I would, always.

My fingers brushed over the delicate swell of her breast, slowly committing to memory the feel, the sensation, the exhilaration of touching Amy intimately and knowing deep within that this was so right. Nipples perked, as if anticipating my touch. I didn't disappoint. As I rolled the tip betwixt my thumb and forefinger, a soft moan escaped her, and the sound rippled through me. I lowered my head and flicked my tongue over the nub, and revelled in the response as it strained toward my mouth.

"I need to feel you, Beth."

Her voice was raspy, full of need that mirrored my own longing for the moment when we would melt together, skin on skin. I grudgingly relinquished her breast and attempted to unzip my dress from the back. Her hands stopped me.

"Here. Let me."

She turned me around, and I felt the zipper give. My dress fell haphazardly at my feet. My bra was removed next, then my underwear. When I turned back, she was naked and waiting. As she moved towards me, footsteps muffled by the carpet, a shaft of light from the window shimmered across her face and chest. Her eyes were dark and expectant.

Pulling her to me, I closed my eyes and inhaled, luxuriating in the aroma that was her. Mouth covered mouth, tongues sought and searched, hands covered and discovered, until we were lying side by side on the bed.

Fingers traced valleys and dips, curves, and pleasures long hidden. It was gentle, tender, so fulfilling yet agonisingly frustrating to be so close and not have all of her. I needed every square inch, every molecule and particle that made up this vision lying next to me, this woman who washed away my past and embodied my present and future. This woman had made me realise what life had to offer, and gave me the strength to try again. But it was also so much more. I wasn't following blindly anymore; I was taking control.

In the blink of an eye, I was above her, looking down at her lying underneath me. Her hair fanned across the pillow, errant locks resting on her cheeks. I gently brushed them away as I gazed at her face. She was looking at me as if she trusted me completely. What a gift, what an amazing offering from one person to another—trust. The knowledge that she trusted me completely was priceless.

I lowered myself onto her, revelling in the full body contact, her hands clutching my butt and pulling me closer. Her legs parted to allow me to slip in between and push myself into her. Her eyelids fluttered, and she released a breath. So I did it again and again and again. Each time, the pressure she returned increased, making me want to delve deeper inside. But I didn't want to rush it, didn't want the need for a climax to dictate this moment.

I moved one leg over her thigh and slicked my juices up her leg—hot, wet heat on urging flesh. The tempo increased, generated a pulsating need, a desire to assuage the aching which deepened with each contact with her skin. Kisses became ardent, possessed. Breathing was becoming rapid, ragged and heavy. Nothing was enough. However hard I pressed, the throbbing increased, driving me mad with the need to satisfy and be satisfied.

I slipped one hand between us and parted the lips that guarded her entrance. It was slick and wet and wanting, begging me to slip inside and fill her. So I did. One finger eased inside effortlessly, as my hips stayed rhythmic, the top of my leg guiding my hand to the place where earth meets heaven. Inside her I found my Eden, my sanctuary. Another finger, another increase in the tempo. I could feel the tension within me sizzle and burst into pockets of fire.

Making love to the woman who meant everything to me was the most unbelievable experience I have ever had the fortune to experience. Words slipped from my mouth into hers—words of love, words of lust and want, words that spoke of forever. The same words came back in her voice, like an echo. Her hands clasped my ass firmly and pulled me against her, and I wanted to slip inside and live out the rest of my life in such ecstasy.

Faster and faster, synchronicity abandoned as I gripped her thigh and pulled it around my waist, my fingers still buried and searching. I could feel my orgasm building, and I also knew she was close. Juices spilled from me, spilled from her, coating my hand, my wrist. Breathing rasped and caught, and like a still from a movie—snap, with a flash of burning blinding light, my mind captured the memory.

At the instant of our cumming, we cried out each other's name and the snapshot disappeared. I fell forward and buried my face against the curve of her neck, a feeling of wonder and fulfilment undulating through me. Heat enveloped me, my breathing was erratic, but neither of us moved. Until Amy's arms wrapped around me and pulled me close. Safe, secure, but best of all, in her arms.

Minutes passed as we lay there, contented to just *be*. Minutes passed as I fell in love all over again.

"Beth?"

Too comfortable to move, I grunted a response.

"I love you, you know."

My eyes flickered open. I wanted to raise my head, but I couldn't. I felt so at home lying on her chest, feeling her words. But no more words came. And before long, I was asleep.

ℴℴ

Through the night, we woke again and again to resume our explorations, and I committed to memory every nuance, taste, smell, and sound. Our lovemaking was tender and gentle. No inflamed coupling, more like a joining—a finding of each other. When morning came, we were lying in each other's arms, tracing patterns on skin. She held me against her, my head resting on her chest, her fingers running up and down the dip of my spine.

I can honestly say I have never felt so contented in my life, at peace, if you will. I had spent a huge part of my adult life worrying about life and its consequences, mainly due to being in a relationship with Sue where I felt out of place. After her, I had walled my heart away, denying myself the opportunity to sample the joys of being totally and utterly in love. Thoughts of how long I had denied myself this happiness with Amy slipped into my head. Regret twinged through me, dampening the joy of the moment for a split second. But there was no use regretting the past. Regret is a fruitless task that devours time and energy but achieves nothing. I was in the arms of my future, and hopefully would be there for the rest of my life. One thing I knew for sure was, now was not the time to think about what might happen next.

I shifted a little as a memory from last night popped into my head. "Amy?"

She kissed the top of my head. "Mmmm."

"Last night..."

I felt her tense.

"You said you needed to tell me something, needed to explain."

Amy released a breath, her tension seemingly easing slightly.

"What did you want to tell me?"

"Doesn't matter. Old news."

I turned so I was facing her. Brown eyes looked straight into mine, and a twinkle sparked in them. Lips, red and slightly swollen, turned upwards in a secretive smile.

"Come on. Tell. You know you want to."

An all-out grin and, "Nuh uh."

Curiosity bedevilled me. I had an idea what she had wanted to "explain," but I wanted her to say it. I tried to coax a reply from her with words and kisses.

"Nuh uh."

I resorted to tickling, but that just made her squirm and laugh. I contemplated doing the sulking routine. You know, the one where you look really sad and hurt with the "It doesn't matter. I understand" line slipping from your lips like an injured martyr. But to be honest, it really didn't matter. She was right. It was old news.

Who am I trying to kid?

"Okay."

I pulled away slowly, locking eyes with her, making sure she was paying attention as I brought out my sad face. Her expression changed from tormenting to concern, and I knew I had her. "It doesn't matter. I understand." And then I sat up, turned and scooted to the edge of the bed, counted to five before saying, "Would you like a cuppa?" Perfect.

"Drama Queen."

Huh?

And then she was on me, tickling my ribs and pinning me to the bed. "Going to make you pay for that, lady."

I frantically struggled to escape from her tickling, but my strength left me. Laughing, we ended up a tangled heap, a panting, tangled heap.

"Okay, Nosey Parker, I'll tell you."

I felt smug.

"And there's no need to look so bloody smug."

Feigning innocence didn't wash with her.

"Go and make me that cuppa, and then come back to bed." She gently poked me in the chest. "Then I'll explain, okay?"

I snatched a quick kiss before I scuttled from the bed. I believe it was the fastest cup of tea I have ever made. Talk about motivated. She was still straightening the bedcovers when I got back to the room.

Back in bed, cups in hand, she began to tell me everything I wanted to hear. About time, too, but then, I had room to talk—Miss "Procrastinator for the Millennium."

"I think I should start at the very beginning."

I wanted to break out in a Julie Andrews impression with "that's a very good place to start," but I decided that would be bad timing, as I believed she was about to share something personal with me. Singing stupid songs at this stage were not the done thing, especially if I wanted her to know I was taking everything she said seriously.

"Right from the very first time I saw you standing in the river, I knew you were special."

I sat up and looked at her. How could she have thought that when I looked an absolute fright—drawn, sobbing, and soaked to the skin, my mumblings making no sense whatsoever. Not to mention the fact she had to wade into the bloody river to get me out.

Amy cupped my face. "I did, so get over it."

My smile lit up my face.

"I'd been sitting in the café, wondering why on earth I had moved to Norfolk, when in trots the most gorgeous little boy. He came straight over to me and gave me his ball." Her fingers trickled along my face, the sensation rippling to other places. "Eventually I figured out he wanted me to follow him, and the next thing I saw was you, standing up to your waist in water, looking about frantically. I kind of guessed it was because of Dudley. The way he was going crazy told me as much."

"Get to the point."

"Oi. It's my story, I'll tell it how I like." She leaned over and kissed me, and my eyes fluttered closed. "And I'll remind you to keep your gob shut, or else I won't tell you at all."

Opening my eyes, I saw she had placed her cup on the side table and was holding her arms open so I could clamber in. Which, of course, I did, after placing my cup next to hers.

"I tried to get your attention, but you were having none of it. Then when you did see me, your reaction wasn't what I expected. It seemed like so much more than relief. You seemed to crumble, and I just had to get to you."

I remembered it well. Those eyes. The way she had come into the river and held me before helping me back to the bank.

"But it was the tingling sensation I felt when I touched your hand that really surprised me. It triggered something deep inside—a reason to be at the park, beside that river, meeting you at that precise time, if you know what I mean."

God. I knew the feeling well. I seemed to get shocks from her every time she touched me.

"All I knew was, I had to see you again. I couldn't just let you go without talking to you, getting to know you better. I didn't even know if you were gay. Come to think of it, I didn't care."

It sounded as if she had read my mind. I had felt exactly the same way: I wanted to get to know her, but I had denied the reasons why, even to myself.

"I kept going back to Earlham on the off chance I would see you again, but it seemed like I had either missed you or you decided that the park wouldn't be the best place to bring Dudley, you know, after thinking he'd drowned." Amy kissed the top of my head and gave me a squeeze. "Then we met again, and there was no way you were leaving without me at least giving you my phone number...just in case."

I giggled.

"What's so funny?"

"I thought exactly the same thing." I giggled again. Being loved up definitely made me act like a teenager. "Go on. What else?"

"Erm…"

Her face screwed up as she tried to remember where she'd got up to in her story, so I reminded her. "Phone number."

She grinned. "Yeah. You called me and asked if I fancied meeting up with you. I nearly wet myself with excitement. Didn't even know where Wells Next the Sea was when we made the arrangements. Had to look it up and how to get there."

I laughed, and she turned slightly pink.

"And being with you huddled under that coat, in the rain… Jesus. I felt so attracted to you, and I didn't even know you. It was…intimate."

Insid, I was glowing. She was describing all the things I had felt, and it was wonderful to hear.

"Then when I saw you shaking, I didn't know whether you were cold, or you could sense that I wanted to kiss you and you were scared."

"A bit of both, really. Not that I didn't want you to kiss me.

"You didn't feel ready, though, did you?"

I shook my head.

"Thought not. I didn't know what had happened between you and Sue then, but I had a feeling that you were going through a tough time, and I didn't want to complicate anything for you. Especially if you weren't gay. Now that would have taken some explaining."

I turned to look up at her, and I had to kiss that mouth again, just to make sure this wasn't a dream.

The kiss had the potential to carry us away, and I had to tear myself away from her so she could continue stroking my ego.

"Phew, woman, you kiss good."

She moved in for seconds, but I pushed her back, gesturing for her to continue.

"Okay, okay. Later, then?"

I quickly nodded, which made her laugh.

"Where was I?"

"Jeez, Amy, you were just about to tell me you fell in love with me over Sunday dinner. How on earth could you forget?"

"I nearly did."

That stopped my mickey taking.

"The more I got to know you, the more I wanted to know. And when you said you had just come out of a relationship with Sue, I felt elated and deflated at the same time."

"Why?"

'Because it meant you were gay, which was good. But you were also just getting out of an abusive relationship. Not so good. I didn't want you to come to me for the wrong reasons. I wanted you to be with me because you wanted to be with me."

Simple. A child could have worked it out, but I hadn't. Shows how much I know. "Why didn't you ever give me any indication you felt the same as I did? Why just go along pretending you only wanted friendship?"

"Because that's all you ever gave me, Beth. You never showed that you wanted more, and there was no way I would have forced myself on you, not after you had gone through all that with Sue."

I sat up and leaned away so I could see the whole of her. She was propped up on the pillows, her expression almost solemn. "But I did. I did give you signs I wanted more. Like in Blackpool—"

"Ah, Blackpool. Yes, at first you did, and then it seemed as if all you to wanted to do was go home. I thought you'd had enough of me, that I'd done something to offend you."

"It wasn't like that. I thought you and Jane—"

"Were a couple. I know. And I played on that for a bit to see if I could get a response from you, see if I could get you to take the plunge and say something, or show some kind of sign that you were interested in me. But you didn't. You seemed happy enough about me having a girlfriend, and that hurt. It was like the final verification that you didn't think of me in that way."

I frowned, "Didn't you think it odd that I wanted to go home early, especially after you received the call?"

"Nope. You were fine in the restaurant, although you did seem a little short with me on the way back to the hotel."

What to say? What to do? It was true. I had never given her any indication that she meant more to me than just as a friend. And it wasn't just her I had tried to fool. I'd tried it with myself, too. Tried to block out my feelings, pretend they were the result of some rebound thing most dumped people likely went through. Deep in my gut, I knew differently. I was so bloody insecure back then, my self-confidence shot to pieces.

No. That wasn't entirely true. I had tried to overcome the doubts I had about whether I was good enough for Amy, while also trying to loosen the restraints I had put upon myself. The near kiss in the Paseje del Terror...New Year's Eve...the hugs...the constantly wanting her to be with me...but mainly, the near kisses. No one could mistake that for something other than want. So I told her exactly that. She scrunched up her face as if she was thinking.

"True. It could have been you making a move, or even responding to my attraction for you." She leaned forward. "Which, of course, is exactly what I thought was happening."

Her breath brushed over my face and I sat there trying to think of a comeback, but she beat me to it.

"Each time we nearly kissed, I thought it was all my doing, especially Boxing night." She squirmed and sat back. "When I came around, I had the intention of telling you how I felt and that I would wait until you were ready. Then Sue came around as a reminder of everything, and I bottled out."

Trust Sue to put the boot in.

"When I got home, I really wanted to call you, but it wouldn't have been right to tell you how I felt over the phone. I was gutted the next day when I realised I had missed your call, because I wanted to invite you here to tell you on New Year's Eve."

Bollocks. Big fat hairy ones.

"But I couldn't get hold of you."

I know! Rub it in!

"Beth?" She hesitated. "Can I ask you something?"

Believing that vulgar words were the only thing I could give utterance to, thereby limiting me to body language, I nodded.

"If I had, you know, had the bottle to ask you, would you have wanted me?"

Now there was a question. I had wanted her. God, had I! But had I been ready to start a new relationship then? Was that even what she was asking? I was so screwed up back then, it wouldn't have been fair to drag her into my quagmire. All the dramatics with Sue had left me doubting my judgment. It wasn't that I didn't believe that Amy was the person I wanted to be with; it was more a case of not being able to trust that anyone would want to be with me. Like Groucho Marx said, he didn't want to be a member of any club that would accept him as a member.

As I snapped out of my reverie and focused on Amy again, I could see her eyes glistening. She thought I hadn't wanted her back then. Shit. Me and my mental meanderings.

"Good job I didn't then." She attempted a laugh, but it came out as a sob.

"No, baby, no. That's not it. God..." I reached out and wrapped my arms around her, pulling her close. "That's not what I was thinking." I kissed her hair and nuzzled my face into the curly brown locks. "I was just thinking back to how I was then in comparison to now." Not a good start, I know, but I was new to this. "I was all over the place, emotionally, that is."

Another sob shook the both of us.

"Shush, baby. I meant I *wanted* to be with you, and still do..."

She shook in my arms, and I knew I was cocking things up big time.

"Amy?" Except for a couple of snuffling sounds, nothing else emerged from below my chin. "Amy? Look at me."

She lifted her head, and I could see traces of tears on her face.

"Can I just say one thing?"

She nodded.

"I fell in love with you long before that."

The kiss she rewarded me with indicated I had said the right thing, for once. This sweet talking stuff wasn't so hard after all, so I thought I would have another crack at the whip. "I was attracted to you from the start, and it was so hard not to just blurt out and tell you. But I had to get my life into some kind of order first. It would have been a mistake to act on my feelings for you. I felt fragile and broken back then. I didn't want to screw things up. Understand?"

Amy wiped her eyes and gave me a smile that could have softened concrete.

"You meant too much to me for it all to go tits up."

I know. The phrasing could have been better, but the sentiment was sincere. Moreover, I don't think she noticed the words, only the fact that I didn't want to lose her. Her face lit up, and she melted right in front of my eyes.

I lay down flat and pulled her to me, needing to feel close, to let her know that it was all about now, not then. We snuggled and kissed for a while before I thought about returning to the rest of our coming together story. That was what had started this conversation, after all—my need to know what she had wanted to explain the night before, at the reception.

As much as I wanted to get to the end of the story, I set it aside for the moment. Food was now a priority, and so was a shower. Not necessarily in that order.

I had to keep my strength up and smell nice for my woman.

My woman.

All mine.

How perfectly fantastic was that?

୨୦୯ଌ

I smelled good. G-O-O-D. And so did Amy. But nothing smelled better than the bacon, especially to two hungry women. Being with Amy had awakened my appetite on more than one level, and I demolished my breakfast-cum-lunch with the grace and manners of a starving beast. I even nicked the last piece of toast, snatched it right from underneath her extended fingertips, which earned me a feigned glare. I bit into the toast, chewed, and then showed her the contents of my mouth.

"Charming. Do you treat all your women to such a delicate display?"

"Only the sexy ones."

She blushed as she picked up her coffee cup and cradled it between her hands. I could tell she wanted to ask me something by the way she kept pursing her lips. Instead she took a sip of coffee and just stared at me.

I leaned forward and tapped the end of her nose.

"Do you always poke your women?"

"Only the sexy ones." I paused to reflect. "And it depends what you mean by poke." Honestly, I could have reheated lava on her face. It seemed weird that she would be blushing because I had said she was sexy, although I could understand the poking comment being a tad coarse. We had spent the night discovering each other, but she was still shy about alluding to sex.

Time for payback. She always commented on how red I'd go when there was a double entendre to be had. Now it was my turn. "You've gone all red." Of course, she shook her head, which made me persist. "Why've you gone red?"

"I haven't. It's not... Ah...bugger." Placing the cup on the table, she straightened her back and looked me squarely in the face. Her next query surprised me. "Do you think I'm sexy, Beth?" Her voice bordering on timid, as if she was uncertain as to what my response would be.

Was she blind? How could she question how absolutely gorgeous she was? My open mouth evidenced my disbelief. "Why on earth would you doubt how sexy you are? You are, without a doubt, the sexiest woman I have ever met."

There was no answer.

"Amy? Is there something you want to tell me?"

She moved to pick up her cup again, stopped, and then patted her hair. It did not escape my attention that her hand was shaking.

Startled by the change in her, I reached out and grasped her fingers, pulling her hand towards me. "Hey, what's up?"

Amy shook her head, and it looked as if she was trying not to cry.

I got up from the table and made my way round to her side, not letting go of her hand for an instant. Kneeling next to her, I made sure she was looking straight at me. "Honey? You can tell me anything, you know. Anything. It won't change how I feel about you."

Brown eyes filled.

Behind the pooling tears, I could see a battle of sorts taking place. I wasn't absolutely sure why she would be worried about telling me about anything, but I also knew that insecurity about the smallest of things can seem huge if a person believes it to be. I also had a feeling that she was worried about how I would react, although she hadn't said so. I wanted to help her, not because she had always been there for me, but because I hated to think something was hurting her in any way.

Her face took on the resolve of someone who was going to do something unpleasant. "Let's go into the living room. I'll tell you there."

Worry jazzed every nerve in my body. What if she was going to say there was some reason she didn't want to be with me after all? Would I throw a fit, upsetting her more? That couldn't be it, could it? Nah. It couldn't be. We felt so good together, so right. And why on earth would I be thinking she didn't want to be with me, after all we had been through to get to this stage? More importantly, why was I thinking about my own selfish agenda when Amy was upset?

Amy sat on the sofa, but I decided to sit at her feet; it felt fitting somehow. I think it was the dog owner instinct—if you put yourself lower, then they feel like they have the advantage.

"When I was with Rachel..." She took a deep breath.

Fuck. Why hadn't I seen it coming? She had mentioned that Rachel had been very much like Sue.

"In some respects, she was very much like Sue, but then again not, if you know what I mean."

I nodded, not really sure what she meant but wanting to give her support.

"Sue made you feel useless, didn't she?"

Wanting to keep my mouth shut and not interrupt the flow of her admission, I nodded again.

"Same as Rachel. But hers, well, she..." She plucked at my fingers, resting on her knee. "Erm... she concentrated on more personal things, like the way I looked. Her favourite barb was that no one but her would ever want me."

"Fucking bitch. Sorry."

"No need to apologise. You're right, she was a bitch. A clever, manipulative bitch. I'm not saying she was like that from the start, not by a long stretch of the imagination. She was positively charming when we first met."

Aren't they all? My mind flashed to when I first met Sue. She had been charm personified.

"It was a few months later that I was beginning to think that us being together was a mistake. I think she picked up the vibes and didn't want me to leave."

"Funny way of showing it. Sorry, Amy. I won't interrupt again."

She smiled at me and pulled my hand into hers, crushing it briefly before relaxing her grasp.

"It started with the little things, like pointing out grey hairs. I used to laugh it off. After all, we all get older. I'm not vain, you know."

I kissed her fingertips and then settled our hands back onto her lap.

"Then it became a little more targeted. 'You're putting on weight, look at the wrinkles around your eyes, why don't you ever dress up anymore, sometimes I'm ashamed to be seen out with you.' I felt more and more like a mess. And I was beginning to feel as haggard as she made me out to be. I used to keep asking people about those things, you know, doubting myself, but they just said I was imagining it."

I was beginning to see why she had asked me if I thought she was sexy.

"It didn't end there. She, well, she started saying things in the bedroom when we were— You know. And the things she said really began to get to me. One time after she had done what she wanted to do with me, she said she felt sick, and that there was no way anyone else would ever want me." She stopped, and her face closed up.

Rachel was worse than Sue, and I never thought I would say that about anybody else.

Imagine saying that to someone. Imagine it. Imagine a time when you felt so exposed and vulnerable, to have that said to you—that you made them feel sick and no one but them would ever want you. That woman needed shooting. However, this was not the time to think of how I could get back at Rachel. Amy needed to get it all off her chest, and then I could plot my revenge.

So I sat at her feet and waited. I knew there was something else she wanted to share, but if she couldn't say it, I wasn't going to force her. I could never understand those therapists who believed that vocalizing something empowers you. Sometimes it just plain hurts to dig it all up. But then again, that's the way some people deal with things. So I bit the bullet.

"Do you want to tell me? Sometimes it helps to get it all out."

Her deep sigh seeped into the air and disappeared. "Saying them now won't help. The thing is, I think it's more a case of my pride being hurt than anything else."

"What about how *you* were hurting? She was only saying those things to make you feel inadequate, so that you might believe she was the only one who would ever love you."

She shrugged.

"Answer me this, did you think no one else would ever want you?"

Slowly her head nodded.

"See? It worked. She had you where she wanted you, and the more she played on your sense of worth, the more chance she had of making sure you wouldn't leave her or find someone else."

The room vibrated silence. I knew she was thinking about what I'd said.

"You're the first person I've told."

I gave her a look of surprise, as I thought she might have confided in Jane at least. But then my look changed to one of question.

"I felt like such an idiot for putting up with her crap for so long. One day I just thought 'enough is enough,' packed a bag, and left. Stayed with James for a while, and then got the job offer from the uni in Norwich."

"Did she try to get you back?"

"In her own way, I suppose. Kept on calling, trying to get me to meet her by saying we should talk things over like adults. I didn't want to see her. It took a lot of self-persuasion for me to leave, and for a long time I thought I'd made the wrong decision. Seeing her would have been too much then. It's only now that I can see her and not feel a thing." She leaned back on the sofa.

I let her just rest a while, knowing how much her revelations must have taken out of her. It's not a good feeling, putting the lowest point of your life on display, especially when you feel like a fool. Been there and wore the t-shirt like a crucifix for too long myself. After about five minutes, I started to ask her a question.

"We were together for nearly three years."

I closed my mouth, thought for a second, and then began to ask her another.

"I finished it two years ago." She returned my grin. "And before you ask, you are my first since. I didn't feel ready until you."

I got up and took both of her hands in mine. At a loss for what to say, I stood there looking like I was about to do or say something. I was wracking my brain, but the little bugger had gone blank.

"Sit next to me."

I hurriedly plonked myself down beside her, releasing her hands to capture her in a hug.

"That's just what I needed."

I smiled into her chest. Me too.

We sat like that for ages before she continued. "So, you see why I asked if you thought I was sexy?"

I surely did. I nodded against her and mumbled a response. It was amazing to think that this woman whom I believed to be so sure of herself, so in control, had experienced the manipulations of someone else. I was beginning to believe that it could happen to anyone, given the right, or wrong, circumstances.

"Amy, you can't blame yourself, you know." That sounded rich coming from my mouth, the woman who had been beating herself up on a daily basis for God knew how long. "I think Rachel, and Sue for that matter, must have felt threatened in some way, as if they had to prove something to themselves. The sad thing is that they used us to do it. It takes all sorts to make the world, and some people only feel better about themselves when they make someone else feel worthless." I was actually making sense. Can you believe it? "We are in control of our own happiness. It's up to us how we deal with the things life throws at us."

I waited a minute to let what I had said sink in, to myself as well, before I finished by saying, "And for the record, you are sex on legs."

Her laugh was a release, I knew that, but it didn't keep me from joining in with her.

"You know, I would never have guessed. You never seemed concerned about me seeing your body." I looked into her face, so open and full of trust. "I mean, we have been naked in front of each other many times, and you seemed confident in yourself."

She sighed, and I waited. Eventually she responded, "That was different. There were no expectations, no having to be aware of myself all of the time. You made me feel relaxed, content with who and what I am." Her fingers stroked my face. "You never judged me or looked at me as if I was a piece of meat. Even that day in the café, when we exposed ourselves to all and sundry, you were too busy dying of shame to do anything but panic. So, I followed your lead and laughed about it. It was at that moment that I knew

it didn't really matter what others thought about me."
She paused. "And every day it gets a little easier, and
I become a little stronger. Do you know what I mean?"

I nodded and kissed her gently.

We settled down on the sofa and cuddled, giving me
the opportunity to digest all she had said. Thoughts
tumbled through my mind, mainly how I had never
suspected Amy had gone through such things. I was
shocked. I don't think it was because I was so wrapped
up in all I had been through with Sue, just that Amy
was a damn sight better at hiding things than I was.
Would I, if I went back over every moment I had spent
with her, recognise the signs? I doubted it. Covering
up was a skill that people in our situations became
extremely good at. Silence was another thing we did
well. Speaking the truth aloud was not something
most people in our position would do. I hadn't really
talked with anybody about what had happened with
Sue, either. I understood why Amy hadn't shared
her story with anyone else. Sadly, I guess that's why
people get away with treating others so badly—no one
wants to admit to having been made to look a fool.

That's the reason I'm telling you now. Remember,
you are not alone, you are not worthless. And if
anybody tries to make you think you are, it is time
for you to head for the door. Simple when it's said like
that, isn't it? Unfortunately, nothing's ever simple.

Chapter Eleven:
Snow Day

Late in the afternoon, Amy and I decided we needed to get some fresh air, and lots of it. Snow peaked and dipped in the garden, and the country road running beside the house hadn't been disturbed since the snowfall in the early hours of the morning. Everything was stark white, unsullied, like a new palette, very much how I was feeling.

We wrapped and tucked layer upon layer of clothing about us and pulled heavy boots over thick socks to cover our feet. Hats, gloves, and coats were donned, and we were ready to brave the outdoors.

Outside, it was warmer than we had anticipated. The snow acted like insulation over the cold of the earth, the white mantle absorbing the sun's weak rays and intensifying its warmth. It was refreshing to get outdoors. The air chilled the hairs inside my nostrils, and pockets of steam puffed from our mouths when we spoke and breathed.

Linking arms seemed so natural, as if we had done it thousands of times before, and I gloried in the feeling of being with her. We chatted about life in general and, as the English tend to do, the weather. It didn't matter what we discussed, it was perfect. After a while, we walked along in comfortable silence until Amy said, "Dudley would love this."

I laughed, picturing my little fella racing through the snow, collecting snowballs on his fur. "At least we might have a chance of seeing his ball in all this white."

With my next step, I sank into a hole that was hidden beneath the snow, one leg in and one still on Terra Firma. I thought Amy was going to piss herself with laughter, and the more she tried to help me get out, the deeper I sank. In the end, I just gave up and sat down, the wetness seeping through my jeans.

"Maybe not. He would lose the bugger in this. It'd sink."

"Like you, you mean?"

I'm surprised she managed to get the words out through her laughter. There was only one thing for it. Cold, wet snow right in the face. Splat.

Her surprise was fleeting, and she looked almost comic as she wiped it off with her gloved hand. The comic book image faded, and I swear I saw a flash of evil skitter over her features. I knew I had to get away, and fast, but I was stuck one-legged down the bloody hole.

There was only one thing for it. As she was slowly collecting a mound of snow, I scooped a handful and threw it at her, hoping it would give me the opportunity to scramble and flee. It did...by about three seconds. Before I knew it, I was being yanked back, and a handful of snow was making its way inside my jumper. Fuck, it was cold. Naturally.

I screamed and danced about, trying to get the bastard to come out, and whilst I was performing my tribal dance, another fistful smacked me in the face. Another and another, then another. She was unrelenting with her barrage of snow, but by this stage I was too soaked to care.

In retrospect, it wasn't the smartest move, but I was defending myself. Right? I did what any smart-minded woman would do in such a situation—I launched myself at her, taking her down like a sack of potatoes, gloating in the "oof" she emitted as I knocked the wind from her sails. She was underneath me, panting and grinning, and looking so bloody beautiful.

I honestly believed I had the upper hand. You would, wouldn't you? Especially when she said, "Oh, Beth, you're just so strong." A little stroke to my ego, methinks. I should have known it wouldn't be so easy, should have been prepared. But as I said, in retrospect...

Bam. I was on my back, and she was grinning down at me. It was so quick, I don't think I even felt her move me. One minute I was on top, the next, she had me pinned down with her body, her knees holding my arms by my sides. That didn't bother me. It was the look of devilment on her face that concerned me. I tried to wriggle free, but there was no way I could shift her. My hair was getting wetter, and so was my backside. Not a good combination.

"Oh how the tides turn."

Her voice almost sang the line, and to be perfectly honest, I was becoming a tad uneasy about the outcome, as my immediate future didn't look sunny. As she gathered snow around my sides, I was frantically trying to put two and two together. The answer I came up with was "Run," but that option had disappeared alongside "Let's call it quits, shall we?" The only thing I could do was to accept my fate, relax, and take it on the chin, but I decided I should give escape one last try.

"Okay. You win. Pelt me. I deserve it."

I scrunched up my eyes and waited for the mountain of snow to strike, but if my body was reading things right, her movements were slowing down. Instead of the snow, I felt her lips press against mine, warming my freezing mouth. As she kissed me, heat flashed through me, creating tingling sensations in all the right places. I wanted to wrap my arms about her, but they were still pinned underneath her knees, so I concentrated on her mouth.

Amy pulled away, and after a couple of seconds, my eyes fluttered open to look into hers. Slam. She had used that time to gather the snow in her hands and throw it into my face, rubbing it in for good measure. But she didn't count on the fact that she wouldn't be as balanced as she'd been before the latest onslaught, and I took the opportunity to tip her sideways and launch myself at her.

We were a completely soaked mess when we heard a car approaching, slowly, and we were a tangle of arms and legs when the blue four-by-four rolled to a stop alongside us.

"Hello there, girls. See you're getting along just fine." Frank and Marion were leaning out of their windows, smiles evident on their faces. "We've been trying to get hold of you, thought you might need to have some food brought." Marion whispered something to Frank, and they both started laughing.

Amy and I disentangled ourselves and were trying to arrange ourselves into some kind of order, but we just looked a mess—wet, cold, childish, and definitely embarrassed.

"Fancy a lift back?"

In the back of the car, Amy and I sat in silence like a pair of reprimanded schoolgirls. I wanted to giggle, and I could tell she did, too, but we weren't going to give the grinners in the front any more fodder.

"So, you two getting along okay?" Marion turned around in her seat to face us, the grin nearly splitting her face. "You don't mind if we pop in for a cuppa? It's freezing out there." She looked us up and down. "Which, by the looks of you two, you already know. What on earth made you roll around in the snow?"

"I fell into a hole, and Amy was...helping me out." I could tell neither Frank nor Marion believed me, but I didn't care.

Amy's hand sneaked over to mine and clasped my gloved hand.

"That's what we thought, isn't it, Marion?"

And they started laughing again.

ഇറയ

Back at the bungalow, I went straight into the bathroom and had a quick shower whilst everyone else sorted out something to eat and drink. A very good plan, if I say so myself. When I came out, Amy was waiting with an armful of dry clothes.

"Won't be long, baby."

She gave me a quick kiss before disappearing into the bathroom.

The smell of toasting teacakes drifted from the kitchen, and my feet took me there. It's amazing how hungry you get after being ambushed and freezing your tits off.

Marion was in the process of sorting out plates and teacups, so I offered my services, like the well brought up girl I am.

"Frank's just getting the fire going. We'll eat in there, it's warmer. And by the looks of you and my daughter when we found you, I think you'll need warming up."

"The shower did wonders, thanks." It had, too. I felt as if I was glowing, on more than one level.

"Beth?" She waited until I was facing her before continuing. "Can you answer me something?"

Bugger. Was I going to like this question? I nodded anyway.

"Has my big, dumb daughter actually told you she loves you yet?"

Excitement raced through me as if my body had only just found out about Amy loving me.

"Given the look on your face, I take it that she has. About bloody time, too. She wouldn't tell us, either, just grinned like a Cheshire cat every time we mentioned your name. Figured she had, but thought I'd just check."

Frank came into the room, his face expectant. "Yes or no?"

"Yes. Finally."

He came over to me and gave me a hug, crushing me to him. "Welcome to the family, love." He turned to his wife. "I told you she was the one."

The way he was talking, it sounded as if he thought Amy and I were going to get married. A little premature, given the fact I first kissed her the previous night. I knew my face looked gormless, could tell by the slackness of my jaw and a tendency to dribble.

"Don't worry about him, love. He likes to jump the gun a little, don't you, honey?" Marion ruffled his hair as if he were an errant schoolboy, and as I watched him I could see where Amy got her facial expressions. "What he meant to say is that we are pleased for you both. We've been waiting a long time for Amy to get her act together and find herself a nice girl." She held out a stack of plates and indicated he was to take them through to the living room. Then she snatched them back. "Have you washed your hands?"

He nodded and grinned, turning his hands over for her inspection.

"Take these through, then, and don't forget to come back for the tray."

By the time everything was ready, Amy was out of the shower and glowing with health and heat. Tea consisted of stacks of toasted teacakes, English muffins, and crumpets, all swallowed down with vast quantities of tea. Amazingly, no one mentioned anything about earlier events, as most of the conversation was about the wedding the previous day. James and Jane had called Amy's parents from Cuba to say they had arrived safely and the hotel was fantastic. They also wanted to rub it in about how hot it was there. We agreed that all in all, the wedding had gone well. Even the weather had added that extra touch, the snow blanketing the land with the purity of whiteness, making it all seem fairytale-ish.

Frank and Marion stayed a couple of hours before they said they had to make tracks. Frank asked Amy to help him sort the car out before he set off, leaving me alone with Marion for a few minutes.

"You two make a lovely couple, you know."

I smiled, thankful I had the parental approval.

Marion's face turned thoughtful as she appeared to deliberate over something before speaking again. "She's been through a lot, has Amy. Thinks I don't know, but I'm her mother, after all. I'd have to be blind not to have noticed the change in her...and the change back since you came into the picture." She wrapped her arms around me and pulled me into one of those mother hugs. "Thank you, Beth. Take care of my little girl, won't you?" Her eyes looked into mine earnestly, but then she laughed. "What am I saying? Of course you will. You love her as much as she loves you."

"Yes, I do, Marion. Yes, I do."

She hugged me again before turning and going out to join her husband and daughter.

When I got to the open doorway, Frank and Marion were in the car and Amy was talking to them through the window. She turned, looked, and then beckoned me to join her. As I stood next to her, she slipped her arm around my waist and pulled me closer to plant a kiss on my cheek. Her parents looked how I felt— contented, and also a little relieved.

After they had gone, Amy pulled me into a full body hug and whispered in my ear, "You have made three people very happy today."

"Make that four." I kissed her solidly on the mouth. The kiss deepened, and a fire flared up inside me that steadily began to creep both north and south. Hands started to explore, and I was losing all sense of circumstance. It wasn't until a very cold hand slipped underneath my jumper that I realised we were standing in sub-zero conditions, making out.

"Inside now, lady." I grabbed her hand and nearly dragged her into the house.

We were barely in the door before we were on each other, hands frenzied in their attempt to uncover hidden treasures. I pushed Amy against the wall in the hallway and pinned her there, my leg between her thighs and my hands on her breasts. Kisses were ardent and unreserved. I wanted to delve into the fabric of this beautiful woman who held my heart.

I pushed my thigh more firmly against her, hearing her moan, feeling her squirm to increase the contact. Our tops were discarded, but we still wore our jeans and shoes, and I needed to have her naked, to see her completely open and waiting for me to love her. Her fingers gripped my hips and pulled me in, but the pressure wasn't enough. I grabbed the button to her jeans, fumbling around the metal as she did the same to me, all the while moving towards our bedroom.

Once inside, jeans and shoes were quickly gone and so were any inhibitions. There was no way this joining was going to be tender; we were too far gone for that. Hands gripped hair, and mouths were urgent in their quest for satisfaction. But nothing quenched the need bubbling and boiling and overflowing into kisses and clutches.

As we reached the bed, I guided Amy backwards, holding her hands with my hands, holding her lips with my lips. One other thing I needed to do before we went any further—put the lamp on.

The light wasn't a strong wattage, but it was enough to enable me to see the woman I loved, and let her see how much I loved her—all of her. Amy looked a little hesitant about the light being on, so I knelt down beside the bed and placed my hands on her knees. I looked up into her face and tried to put all of what I felt into my expression. Her eyes changed, and I took it as a sign that she was willing to face her fear.

"I love you, Amy," I murmured as I kissed each knee in turn. "I love you so much." Another string of kisses moved steadily up each thigh and then back down her legs. "You..." kiss "... are" kiss "... the most" kiss "... beautiful woman I have ever seen." I stopped kissing and caught her gaze. "And I want to make love to all of you."

I didn't want to rush her, although I was dying to just take her all into my mouth and keep her safe. I trailed my fingers up the inside of her thighs—up and down, up and down, up...and up...and past the core of her womanhood, leaving her gasping as her hips jerked forward.

I honestly don't know how I controlled myself. I wanted her so badly, and I could see a glimmer of wetness gathering at her centre. I needed to taste her, needed to lavish my tongue in and around her, dip into the sweetness that was her. But I didn't. All thoughts of a primitive coupling were gone. All I wanted to do was love her, love her any way she wanted me to, as long as she let me love her forever.

She brushed her fingers through my hair, twirling the strands then letting them fall back onto my shoulders. All the while, I stroked her thighs, skipping past her growing want, exulting in the reactions my touches were eliciting. Finally she wound her fingers into my locks and pressed my head downwards, towards my goal. But I pulled back, preferring to concentrate my mouth on the tops of her thighs, knowing she was ready for me to sample her delights.

A soft lick. A flick. A stroke. The sounds she was emitting were making me wet. A suckle and twist of the lips. Her hands tightened in my hair, and I could feel her trying to push me into her. I shifted back slightly to whisper, "You are so beautiful, Amy, so utterly beautiful." And then I opened my mouth and took her clit between my lips to suck and roll the tip of my tongue around it.

At her cry, my juices slithered down my thighs. God. I ached with the longing to love her fully, become one with her, anything, as long as she never left me.

The flat of my tongue started at her opening and slipped slowly from base to tip, rewarded by the thrusting of her hips as she tried to rush me. When I reached the top, I made my descent, this time taking longer.

"Please, Beth, please." Her voice was breaking. "I need you inside."

Who was I to refuse? My thumbs parted her lips and exposed her. It was perfect—pink and swollen, glistening like raindrops on rose petals, and budding open like a youthful flower. The tip of my tongue was ready and waiting to enter, salivating at the prospect. I had to pause, just for a moment, so I could commit to memory the perfection laid before me.

She leaned backwards, opening herself further, her feet on my back, her calves pulling me closer. Circling around her entrance was a wonderful agony, and I revelled in the sensation of her juices on my tongue. A little push, a little more, and I slipped inside Her walls clutched at my tongue.

All the way in...hold...and then back out. In. Hold. Out. In... flick...out. And on and on and on, the tempo increasing, following the rhythm dictated by her hips. I loved the sensation of my tongue caressing her from the inside out, loved the sensation of being inside this woman, loved...her.

Her hands were pushing and pulling my head, increasing the impact of each thrust. I was on my knees now, my back arched as I teased her impending orgasm. I could feel it building, taste its imminent arrival.

The scream started as I was buried deep inside, the jolt of it vibrating through her body like an electric charge, and I nearly came with her, but my own release would have to wait. As the aftershocks pulsated her walls, I waited before pulling my tongue from inside her. A gentle kiss, a nuzzle. Her hands were guiding me up towards her face, where I captured her mouth, allowing her to share her most intimate secret.

Her hands were on my back, and fingers dug into pliant flesh, eking out jolts of pleasure from both of us. Slowly her caress moved until it reached my ass, where she pulled me in to feel the wetness seeping from her. Blinding flashes skimmed across my eyes as I became swallowed up in the moment. Grinding and pushing, thrusting and pounding into her. Breaths ragged, kisses unrestrained.

Her hand drifted across my hip and slipped between our bodies, searching out the pulsating spot that craved her touch. The same spot that was slippery and wanting the contact of her fingers to alleviate my longing. Each time I pushed, her fingers glided down and then back up to the tip of my pleasure, the tip that quivered and pulsed as if she had my heart pumping in the palm of her hand. I opened my legs wider, urging her to bury herself inside me, unleashing the yearning she evoked in me, wanting her to enter me deeply and stay.

One lone digit danced and circled, taunting me, and I tried to capture it but it flitted away. I slipped one leg over her thigh and pushed the other against her leg to open us wider. My hand cupped her mound, delighting in the heat and wetness there. My middle finger edged towards its goal, slipping between her folds and positioning itself outside her centre, hoping that me making her wait for me to take her would provoke her enough to enter me.

And she did, as I filled her. Our fingers were captured to the knuckle and moving in and out amidst moans and whimpers, thrusts and pushing bodies. I was in heaven...heaven...heaven. She was inside me as I was buried inside her. Her thigh lifted and pushed against her hand, her finger delving deeper. A grunt escaped me, and she did it again and again and... God...the sensations were mind blowing. I couldn't think of anything but her—her finger, her thigh, the... God. She inserted a second finger inside and I nearly came, but I wanted us to cum together, joined in our ecstasy. It was agony, exquisite agony. The vibrations ricocheted through me and pulsated into her, making the experience all the more intense.

Through my haze I could sense she was on the edge, that she was about to join me. I removed my finger, and her hips searched down the sheet, trying to gain contact again. My thumb rubbed her nub and kept her simmering until I could slide two fingers deeply inside her.

With cries of wonderment and bliss, over she went, and so did I, into the sphere of forgotten worries and inhibitions. Over and over and over. Fingers frantic, hips frenzied, breathing coarse and unashamed. Another explosion and we both came again, squirming and slick with sweat.

After a few moments, she pulled her fingers from inside me. With shaking hands, she cupped my cheeks. "I...love...you." The words were broken into breathy snippets, her eyes glazed and satisfied, reflecting my own.

"I love you, Amy." I kissed her softly. "You are the most beautiful creature I have ever seen."

A lazy, contented smile crept over her face, and she kissed me back, longer, but still tenderly. The kiss slowed and eventually stopped, having completed its mission to soothe the aftershocks of our melding. I moved from on top of her and slipped down to her side. Her arms came around me and pulled me close, and we lay in absolute contentment, our eyelids fluttering closed.

My last conscious thought was one of utter completion. I was in the arms of the most wonderful woman in the world, and she loved me, loved *me*. I never wanted this to end, never wanted anything to ever come between us. I knew that if she were not in my life, there would be no point in living. Dramatic? You bet. I had found my reason to live, and there was no way I was ever going to let her go. Call it dramatics or whatever you like, but I had found perfection and I intended to keep her.

Always.

࿇

The next day we were up early, as we had to get back to Norwich. Amy had a lecture first thing Tuesday morning, and I had to go and collect my little man from my parents. I had called them a couple of times since I'd been away to see how he was, and how they were, too, of course, and he was having a whale of a time.

"Dudley played in the snow all day yesterday," my dad informed me on my most recent call. "Lost his ball in a snowdrift at one point. That was fun."

I laughed at the thought of Dudley scrabbling away at the snow, but also at the memory of when I had said to Amy yesterday that Dudley would have lost his ball and ended up down a hole if he'd have been with us .

"Thanks, Dad. Not only do I always know my lad is safe with you, I know he has fun."

"You know we love having him. Only grandchild we're going to get by the looks of things." I could hear the amusement in his voice. "Or maybe now that..."

I heard my mum shout his name in the background, her tone a humorous warning.

"Never mind, eh, love. See you when you get back." I heard mum speak again. "What?"

"I didn't say anything."

"Not you. Your mother." I heard my mum said something again. "Your mum said to let her know when you get near."

"Will do, Dad. Love to both of you." My face was hurting from grinning.

Although we had risen early, we couldn't leave until afternoon because it took the local council that long to get their arse into gear and clear and grit the roads. There had been no more snow since the previous day, and it was starting to melt. Amy was worried that it would turn into icy patches on the road, as the forecast had guaranteed temperatures of minus five by the evening. So, the sooner we hit the road, the better.

On the way back to Norwich, we called in on Amy's parents to say goodbye. They lived in Bidford on Avon in a gorgeous house situated near the side of the river. The boats belonging to the business were dry moored and covered in tarpaulin to keep off the winter frost.

Frank showed me round his workshop, and we talked over a few ideas for promoting his business whilst Amy had a chat with her mum in the warm. Yes. She was in the warm, while I was outside freezing my butt off. I didn't mind, though. I was enjoying talking with Frank.

"We could start by getting you a website, so people can seek you out more easily. Link it with the telephone directory, and there you go—instant access for potential customers."

"You make it sound so easy, love. I don't have a clue about this internet malarkey." He shook his head. "I have enough trouble sending a text message."

I bit my lip, as laughing at this point would have made Frank feel even less confident that he could do it.

"Don't you worry about that. I'll get it all up and running, and then I'll show you how to maintain the site. Deal?" I stuck my hand out as if to shake on it.

His head cocking to the side, he pursed his lips as he stared at my hand.

"I think you have your work cut out, young lady." His grin was contagious. "As for shaking hands, what have I told you about that?" He reached out and pulled me into a huge hug. "You'll take care of my girl, won't you, Beth?" His voice was low, the tone gentle.

Frank held me slightly away from him, his eyes misting. "She's had a tough time of it. Thinks we don't know, but ah... You know. Parents do."

"She's safe with me, Frank."

He hugged me again.

Moments later, it seemed as if the exchange between Frank and me had never happened.

"Come on. Let's get you warmed up before you have to set off again."

Once inside the house, it was a quick cuppa before getting back on the road, and it was nearly two o'clock before we were making our merry way down the A46. The roads were clear, as far as congestion was concerned. Any significant amount of snow became a memory as we entered Cambridgeshire. At certain points, we were hard pushed to see that there had been any of the white stuff at all.

As usual, Brandon was a nightmare. The little village just outside of Thetford always came to a near standstill around rush hour, so we decided to have a comfort break at a roadside café for half an hour or so and wait for the traffic to thin out.

I know. Too technical. Going on about the journey instead of telling you about the conversation within the car. I thought you might like a refreshing change, give you some insight as to what happened. Okay, I'll move it along. Anyway, toilet break. It must have been all the tea I had been drinking, but by the time I got there, I was bursting to go and had been for the past twenty miles.

By the time I emerged from the loo, Amy was seated next to the window, chin resting on her hand. The smile that greeted me was radiant, as if we hadn't seen each other in years and not the five minutes since we'd gotten out of the car. In a way it reminded me of Dudley. He was always like that. It didn't matter if I had just stepped out of the room, he greeted me like a long lost friend every time I came back in. Funny comparison, I know, but to me it was perfect.

It was five-thirty, and rush hour would still be hectic for another hour or so, so we decided to have a snack to pass the time, as it would save us from sorting out food when we got back home. That started me thinking. What would happen when we got back? Would she stay over? Come in for a while? Arrange to see me again? A smidgeon of panic surfaced and disappeared, then surfaced again. Why didn't I just ask her instead of worrying about it? I wanted to casually ask what her plans were, but... Aw...I don't know.

"What are you doing later? Any plans?"

Trust Amy to get in before me. "Just got to collect Duds, and then I'm free." And this is the part where I got a spine. "Fancy coming back to mine for a bit?" A bit of what, I didn't specify, but I was hoping for a bit of what we had experienced the night before. Obviously. But mainly I just wanted to spend time with her. Even if we were watching paint dry, I would love every second.

She grinned and nodded. "I'd love to."

It made me go all girly inside. Like usual. At that rate, I would be painting my nails pink and wearing stilettos, and in my case, that would not be a good thing.

After we finished our meal, Amy sat back in her chair looking absolutely stuffed. She had eaten her meal and then finished mine off.

"It's the cold. Makes me hungry." She shot me a cheeky grin as she nicked my bread roll.

I reached over and nicked it back. "Just to remind you, love. We have actually been in a lovely warm car for the last three and a half hours, and the other forty-five minutes in a café."

"It's just the thought of being cold then, picky."

God. This woman made me feel so bloody good inside. Even when she was calling me picky, I felt special. Weird, but that's how love gets you, isn't it? What a fantastic experience.

Trust me. There is a reason why I have stopped the tale and am writing about snacks, drinks, and toilet breaks. Would I take you on a wild goose chase? Don't answer that. The reason I stopped here and told you stuff that would bore the arse off a train spotter is because something was revealed in conversation, over dessert actually.

I don't even recall how the conversation started. It was like it started in the middle, and mentally I had to work backwards in order to get back to the point that had piqued my interest. It seemed relevant to my future somehow. It was about something Amy had said on the night of the wedding, her needing to explain something. More specifically, the "I have to tell you how I..." bit.

On the night of the wedding, Amy had she said something about James and Jane, the wedding, and then she mentioned Rachel. Mentioning her ex had gotten my full attention. But then Amy had thanked me. For what? For loving her?

"So, what did you need to tell me?" My spoon rested on the side of my plate, and I noted how Amy's spoon seemed to reach her mouth but not enter. The dessert made its way back to her plate.

She pursed her lips, then bit one nervously. Brown eyes met mine and I smiled at her encouragingly.

"I was so worried about telling you, explaining what had happened to me with Rachel."

Explaining? As in her needing to explain? Tell me, yes, but explain?

"I had to tell you. I couldn't keep it stored up anymore, had to get it off my chest if I thought there would ever be a chance for you and me." A sad smile graced her lips. "But I didn't tell you after all. I had to let you know about me, warts and all."

It was her explaining, after all.

How arrogant. Not her, me. I had believed that night after the wedding she had wanted to tell me how she liked me and how she had wanted to tell me how much she fancied me, even loved me. What I couldn't understand was why she started telling me the things I wanted to hear. You know, what she talked about what she had felt right from our first meeting and stuff.

"But you have done, love. What matters is that we can share our innermost fears and exorcise the demons we have."

I reached over and placed my hand over hers.

"When I first started to tell you, I wanted it to be in some kind of perspective."

I should go in for mind reading. I had just wondered why she had started by telling me what I had wanted to hear.

"I couldn't just launch into the whole Rachel fiasco. I wanted you to know that I was different now from how I was then."

"Why?"

Amy looked at me questioningly.

"Why did you feel you had to put things in perspective? Don't you think I would've known you were different?"

Her face screwed up in consternation. "Just felt it was the right thing to do. Didn't want to take any chances with you, that's all."

I reached across the table and grabbed her hand. "I want to say one thing, and then we will forget about all this." Her fingers dug into my hand. "I love you, Amy Fletcher, warts and all."

Honestly, I thought she was going to lean over and kiss me right there in front of truck drivers and the rest of the population of the café, not that I would have minded. Her body lurched forward and then slammed back into her chair, her hand still gripping mine.

She didn't have to say she loved me. I could see it written on her face. But she said it anyway, and my heart fluttered against my ribcage as it tried to get closer to her.

That was that. Cleared up and mess free, a clean palette, shall we say. From that moment, it was her and me, me and her, and we had our future to build together. It's amazing what five months can do. This time last year, I thought my future was bleak and without purpose, thought I was a worthless piece of shit that would never amount to anything. But look at me now. Or should I say, look at us?

∞∞

The sign for Norwich said it was five miles to the city centre, and by this stage all I wanted to do was get back and have a shower, after playing with my little man for a while. I missed him. I probably missed him more than he missed me, given how my parents spoiled him.

The traffic had eased considerably, and the roads were free of snow, so I knew it would be less than twenty minutes before we would be pulling up outside my parents' front door. I texted my mum to tell her I was on my way.

Putting my phone back into my pocket, I saw Amy looking at me from the corner of her eye. Old habits die hard, I guess. I thought she was wondering whom I'd been texting, just as Sue used to do. "Just texted Mum," I supplied.

"It's good that she knows how to use it. My parents haven't a clue."

I laughed. "She hasn't a clue. When she hears the beep, she'll be looking all over the house, trying to find out where it came from. I've sent her loads of messages, and she hasn't read any of them."

Amy started laughing. "Tight bugger."

"Hey! I've got to get my kicks somehow, haven't I?"

It happened in slow motion, really, as if I was pressing the picture frame skip button on a DVD, slow and jagged. It was her face I noticed before anything else. The curve of her mouth slowly descending, her teeth gritting together, her hand coming over to me. Moving my head to look at what she was seeing seemed to take forever. Blue. A moving mass of blue. A swerving, moving mass of blue, heading for the side of our car.

The velocity of two moving vehicles colliding creates a deafening roar of brakes on tarmac, metal on metal. We were all going sideways. Amy's arm was pushing me back into my seat, but I was sliding sideways with the pull of the impact, and she was following me.

Splintering and crushing, my side of the car was cracking through the barriers at the side of the road, and I could see the concrete pillars guarding the embankment approaching slowly. There was nothing I could do to stop it, nothing that would stop the inevitable crunch and bounce the car would experience when...

Thud. It sounded almost like crinkling, except for the screeching of the metal. My arm rose of its own volition and cradled the side of my head, cushioning the blow against the side window, but the pain shot through my head before the gravitational pull lurched me back towards the driver's seat...and then back to slam against the window again.

As I faded to black, the last thought banging through my head was that I couldn't feel Amy's arm anymore.

Chapter Twelve

In and out of consciousness. It was difficult to wake up. The pain burring through my head was accompanied by the searing aching in my shoulders, arm, and back. I tried to move my legs, but they were jammed underneath something, and panic surged through me.

Turning my head, even slowly, sent a bolt of agony through my skull, making me cry out, but I had to see if Amy was okay. The pain in my head and body was nothing to the anguish of seeing her slumped in her seat, her head lolling askew like a broken doll's. Blood was seeping down her face, thick red ropes of it. It was also coming from her mouth and dripping ceaselessly from her chin onto her leg.

Time stood still. I was too numb to react. I just stared at her...couldn't comprehend why she wasn't looking at me and laughing, couldn't come to terms with why her eyes were closed and redness was marring her beautiful face. Wisps of her hair were sticking to the driver side window, and I could see the spider web breakage of the glass beneath her head.

It started in my gut, the wail, I mean. Started deep inside and ripped through my heart and out through my mouth. I didn't even recognise the scream as coming from me. It was primitive and bestial, hollow in its anguish. My hand reached out to touch Amy, tentatively, so as not to hurt her, fingers reluctantly making contact. Panic overrode everything else until grief took root.

I knew that the blood was a bad sign, that I had to get it back inside her somehow. She needed blood to live, just as I needed her. I cupped her face and tried to gather the warm, wet fluid, tried to push it back inside to make her better, but all I was doing was making it look worse. I didn't know where the blood was coming from, didn't know where I should put it.

Tears streamed down my face, my sobbing unrestrained. I was losing her…I was losing her! I knew she was leaving me here, leaving me here without her. I tried to get my legs free, but I couldn't move them. The pain was trying to stop me, but physical pain was nothing compared to the anguish of losing Amy.

I leaned over her and tried to get her to open her eyes, pulled her eyelids back, shouted at her to wake up…wake up…*wake…up*! Nothing. Her eyeballs were partly rolled back, but I could see her pupils—just. They were buried in the brownness of her eyes, almost invisible in their minuteness.

"Please…Amy… Please…wake up." I started to shake her, but her head flopped around as if it was in danger of falling off her neck. I cupped her face, tried to bring it to me, stopped, and just held it. I could feel the warmth seeping from her. I couldn't get close enough to listen if she was breathing, so I tried to find a pulse on her neck, on her wrist. I couldn't feel the thudding I so desperately wanted to feel.

"Don't…leave…me…please…don't leave me…I… love…you…love you…don't go…don't go…wake up… please…don't leave me now."

Nothing was making sense. Nothing mattered anymore. Amy was dead. Dead. I had found her at last, and she was dead, gone, leaving me to try to live here without her. What was the point of living if she was gone? None. No point whatsoever. I was stroking her face, stroking the blood away, stroking the only thing that mattered in my sad little life. I just wanted to curl up against her chest and die right alongside her.

Resting my head on her body was the first comforting thing I had done since I had regained consciousness in the middle of this nightmare, and I resigned myself to go with her wherever she led me. I pushed my arm around her waist and pulled her close to me. I couldn't quite manage to place my head on her chest, as I couldn't move my legs, but being near her would be enough. It had to be.

As I closed my eyes and waited for the blackness to take me, I told her one last time, "I love you, Amy."

෨෬

Voices alerted me. Flashing lights stung and blinded. Cool air seeped through the driver's door as it opened. I was gripping Amy's shirt, and I felt her body shift towards the gap, taking me with her. Pain seared through my body, except my legs. They were numb. Physically and emotionally, I was a wreck. Spiritually, I was broken. I wished I were dead.

The soothing voice from the doorway tried to cajole me into letting Amy go, but I held on tighter. She was mine, and I wasn't letting anyone else touch her. She was my girl, my girl, my everything, and I didn't want them mauling her. Why couldn't they just leave us alone, together?

"Come on, luv."

The voice was male, but I didn't look at his face. My focus was on the small St Christopher sticking to Amy's throat, the patron saint of travellers.

"Let's get you both out."

The medal was shiny, as if it was illuminated.

"You have to let go. Come on, sweetheart."

I unfurled my fingers from her shirt and raised my hand to gently lift the gold pendant. I was transfixed. The coolness of the metal seemed alien in my hand. Memories of seeing glimpses of it when I first knew Amy scuttled through my head. Memories of the time we had shared spun out of the shining disc.

Hands held my shoulders, but I didn't care. I had this bit of her in my hand, *in my hand*, until it slipped away as they pulled her away from me, leaving me with nothing.

I lunged forward and grabbed at her, my fingers sliding off her jeans. I couldn't reach...couldn't get to her. She was going, leaving me all alone. I was screaming something, but I have no idea whether it made any sense. The words were stumbling, tumbling. I was desperate to get to her, desperate to bring her back.

"Hey. Come on. Shush. You're going to be all right."

I didn't want to be all right; I wanted to be with her.

"We'll have you out of there in no time."

Futility took hold and weighed me down, and I slumped onto the seat, completely drained, tears streaming down my face.

"We're going to have to cut away the side of the car to get you out, but you'll be okay. Do you hurt anywhere?"

I shrugged.

"Can you feel your legs?"

I wanted to be left alone, wanted to tell him to fuck off and leave me alone, but I said nothing. What was the point?

The back door opened, and I felt the movement as someone climbed in. Arms appeared over the seat to touch the back of my neck, circling round to the front, the faceless person examining me for injuries and trying to calm me with soft words.

My attention was solely on the outside of the vehicle, eavesdropping on the disjointed words of those I imagined were the paramedics.

"Driver dead on impact."

Four words. Four words that took away the last vestiges of hope I'd been clinging to.

I had no idea how long it took the fire crew to cut me loose; didn't care. I shut down as soon as I heard Amy was dead, crawled back inside myself and watched me die from the inside out. I could hear the saw cutting through the metal, smell the fumes, hear the shouting of the people working and the voices of the ambulance man and woman who were treating me. None of it made any difference. It all just bounced off me, bounced off the transparent shield erected to deflect their kind words. I didn't want their kind words. I didn't want anything anymore.

The metal came away like foil paper, peeling back like a huge metal banana to release my legs. Not that I could feel anything; I just watched them remove me through half closed eyes. Strong hands steadied themselves under my armpits, and before I had chance to acknowledge what was happening, I was outside on a stretcher.

Looking up into the faces of the people who had extricated me, I saw concern and compassion, both of which I didn't want.

"You were very lucky." It was the woman paramedic. She was attempting to look into my eyes with a small torch. Firm fingers pulled back each lid in turn, and she smiled at me. "It could have been a lot worse."

What! Like how? I had lost the woman I loved, and this stranger was saying it could have been a lot worse?

"You were both very lucky."

Why? Because Amy died on impact? Because she didn't have to wake up to being alone?

"Your friend has been taken on ahead. She'll be fine. The other driver wasn't so lucky."

My eyes opened and I stared at her, believing I had misheard what she had said. There was a peculiar sensation bubbling deep inside me. Was it hope? Or was it a sick dread because I thought she had gotten it wrong. Amy was dead. I had heard them discussing her: "Driver dead on impact." But, I hadn't heard which driver.

By the time the words had truly sunk in, she was turning away, but I grabbed her arm with a strength born of desperation and pulled her back. "Please..." The word cracked. "Which driver died?" Each word grated painfully from my throat as if it was attached to barbed wire.

"The Ford Mondeo. The police believe she'd been drinking."

I should have felt some remorse, some sorrow at the news that someone had died, but I couldn't. Somewhere out there, Amy was alive, and I had to get to her, had to see her with my own eyes and make sure it was the truth.

A feeling of lightness washed through me, supreme lightness of being. Fresh tears welled from my eyes, but this time for a different reason. My girl was alive! I needed to look into those brown eyes again and never stop telling her how much I loved her.

The last lucid thought I had before I passed out was, 'I'm coming, Amy.' This time it wasn't a plea to die, it was a promise to live. I had every reason.

∞⟩⟨∞

The journey in the ambulance took forever. When I came to, I kept asking if I could see Amy, but they told me I would see her as soon as we were both taken care of. Pain in my shoulders, back, and legs—most especially my legs—had come roaring back now it knew I gave a shit. I was sporting a neck brace just in case I had a spinal injury, and I didn't want to look at my legs, even before they cut my jeans off.

The change in my outlook could best be described as manic. Before, when I thought I had lost her, I was so low, but now... Bloody hell. No, I wasn't laughing and screaming with joy; that's not manic. I was hyped up, aggressive in my hunger to know what was going on with Amy. A painkiller was administered on the way to the hospital, I think more to shut me up than anything else. I think the crew heaved a sigh of relief when the doors to the ambulance eventually burst open outside the hospital.

Once inside, I started up again. The corridor echoed her name as we raced along the white vastness to get me to the Accident and Emergency room. It wasn't like *ER*, on the telly, I can tell you. The doctors looked knackered, and the nurses looked like they hadn't been home for days. The cries and whimpers coming from behind closed curtains shut me up for a few minutes, as I listened to see if I could hear Amy.

"Please, Doctor...Nurse...do you know anything about Amy Fletcher?"

Their "no" was curt and professional, and they carried on examining me.

I wasn't being reasonable, I know. They were just doing their job, one patient at a time. Or were they hiding something?

"Car crash. Norwich Road," I nudged.

I saw the flicker of a glance from one to the other.

"Tell me, is she okay?"

"Come on. Let's get you sorted, and then we'll check, okay?" The young Asian nurse smiled, trying to cajole me into working with them. She lifted a needle and aimed it at my left leg.

I tried to shift it out of the way, but the pain shot from my knee and cradled in my gut, and I cried out.

"I don't think it's broken, but an x-ray will pick anything up."

Panic surged. X-ray would take ages, and I needed to know what had happened to Amy, needed to see her. For all I knew, she could be in surgery, could even be dead.

"I'm okay. *Please*, find out. I need to know how she is. *Please*." I hoisted my torso off the table and covered my leg with my hand, stopping the nurse in her tracks. "After you do, I'll be good. I'll let you do anything you want to me."

She looked at the doctor for a signal.

He glanced at me, then nodded at her. "Be quick." Turning back, he smiled, "Can't have my patients worrying themselves to death. Bad for the reputation."

The nurse laughed at his joke before focusing back on me.

"What's her name?" She lifted a notepad up, pen poised.

"Her name is Amy Fletcher. Amy. Fletcher."

"Anything else? When did she come in? What for?"

I gritted my teeth. I'd already told her this. I watched the nurse lift the pen from the pad, and my eyes lifted to meet hers.

"Amy Fletcher. Came in just before me. Car accident on the Norwich Road. She was unconscious. Amy Fletcher." I wanted to add "the love of my life" but I didn't.

"Okay. I'll see what I can do. But ..." she tilted her head, "when I come back, you have to behave and let me do my job. Got it?"

I nodded, the pain crashing through my head. "Yes. Got it."

After the nurse had gone, I felt more content as I lay back onto the pillows to wait for news.

The doctor continued his assessment. "Put your hands against mine and push me backwards."

He lifted his hands in front of me as if we were about to play pat-a-cake. I did as he asked.

"And now do the same with your feet."

For a brief moment I thought he meant I had to push his feet with my feet. The doctor seemed to understand why I looked a tad confused. A soft chuckle escaped him. "No, Miss. Push my hands with your feet."

I did as he asked. My right leg ached a little, but I managed to comply. Lefty had other ideas. As he placed his hand on the heel of my left foot, the pain tore upwards.

"Fuck!"

The doctor grimaced—either in sympathy for what he thought I was experiencing, or at the four letter word that had slipped from my mouth.

"I think you've dislocated your kneecap. Nothing major."

That was easy for him to say. He wasn't on the receiving end.

"We'll take that x-ray to be on the safe side."

I was beginning to shut down. I just wanted it all to be over so I could find Amy.

"Is there anyone you would like us to contact?"

Yes. Amy! How many more times did I have to say it?

The nurse took what seemed like forever. I mean—it wasn't as if she had to go miles. I could see her standing at the desk, talking to the woman seated there. She kept looking over at me as she was talking, and soon both of them were looking, the receptionist shaking her head, her lips still moving.

The way they were acting made me think that something was terribly wrong. Breathing became more difficult as panic settled in again. As I sat up, ready to spring off the bed and drag myself over to them, the nurse came back.

"A woman was admitted nearly two hours ago, and our records show she was admitted as Amy Fletcher."

Was?

"We found ID in her pocket. A driving license."

Was?

"She came around enough to alert us that she was worried about her passenger—you, as it happens."

"Is she...is she..." I couldn't finish the sentence.

"She is in the ICU at the moment, under observation. We think it may be concussion, as she suffered a nasty blow to the head. Only time will tell, I'm afraid."

The nurse looked uncomfortable, but not as uncomfortable as I was feeling. This was not good. Not good at all.

"Is there anyone we can contact? Next of kin?"

That's when I blanked. Next of kin? They only wanted to know that if someone was at death's door. Did they think...

"It's just procedure. We like to inform the families in the case of accidents, especially car accidents."

Did they? Fuck. They thought she was going to die.

"We have to notify your next of kin, as well."

I was beginning to shake—from top to toe, toe to top, inside out and outside in. The ache in my chest was battling with their assurances. I knew reason was going to lose, knew that I was going to lose more than that.

This was not the time, not the time, not *her* time. I thought I had lost her once, and look where that had gotten me, gotten her. I had to respond like an adult, show some spine, control, maturity. And I had to show myself I could deal with all this. There would be time to break down after all this was over.

Swallowing rapidly and trying to moisten my mouth at the same time, I gave them all the information they needed—my parents' numbers, and Frank and Marion's, too. After I was done, I felt drained, yet full of strength, as if I had found the ability to overcome just about anything. I knew I had to face this, get through it somehow. I was vibrating with life and empowerment. It seemed that from somewhere deep inside, I had summoned up the capacity to deal with what was happening, God only knows how, but they do say He moves in mysterious ways.

When they'd finished cleaning me up and informed me of my parents' imminent arrival, I was passed on to the porter, George, who had arrived to take me to X-ray. It took me three corridors to convince him he should stop at the ICU. I had tried a few different ploys to get him to comply, but it seemed all I had needed to do was ask him nicely.

Arriving outside the big double doors in a wheelchair was not a good idea. If I'd been able to walk, I would have waltzed straight in and found Amy, but it's not that easy when you can't move and your leg is sticking out in front of you.

"Leave it to me, love."

George disappeared inside the ward, leaving me sitting outside like an escapee. Minutes later, he re-emerged looking very pleased with himself. "We have five minutes. The matron is on a coffee break. If she catches us, you and me will have matching wheelchairs."

The room was deathly quiet. Most of the patients were asleep; the ones that were awake were lying on their sides watching us with interest. We arrived at a little side room at the end of the corridor, the door partly open and soft light spilling out.

Seeing her lying there looking so helpless, my heart broke. She was flat on her back, attached to a myriad of monitors beeping out the rhythm of her heart.

George pushed my chair alongside her bed and clicked on the brake. "I'll be back in two minutes." He was gone before I had the chance to thank him.

She looked as if she were asleep. Peaceful, if you will. I could see the steady movement of her chest and also hear the beep beep beep of her heartbeat.

Taking her hand in mine felt wonderful. Her fingers were slightly clammy, but there was definitely life in them. I could feel the strength of her lifeblood pumping through her veins. Looking at her there, you would never have thought her the same woman I had been gripping in the wreckage of her car. The blood on her face was gone, the pastiness replaced by blotches of pink. Her lips looked full and red. All I could see of her wound was a poppy of a bruise on her temple, the petals surrounding the stitches in the centre. The rest of her was covered, so I couldn't see if she had any other injuries, but the nurse had said it was the concussion they were worried about.

I knew I was running out of time; George would be back to collect me soon. Then I saw it, glistening in tendrils of the soft overhead light as if surrounded by a halo—St Christopher in all his glory. It was like a sign, a prophecy that everything would be okay. He was reminding me he would take care of this traveller, keep her safe until I could take care of her myself. It was amazing that I hadn't thought of that when we had been back in the car.

Footsteps were approaching, and I gripped her hand and whispered, "I love you, Amy Fletcher."

And do you know what? She gripped my hand right back. Her eyes didn't open, there was no other sign of consciousness, but I felt calm for the first time since the crash.

When George poked his head around the door jamb, I was ready to go. I knew she would be all right. Don't ask me how I knew; I just did.

ᔛᔥ

The x-ray was painless; it was clicking the kneecap back in place that hurt like a bitch. I never, ever want to go through that again. Ever. I also had three cracked ribs, a sprained wrist, and a concussion. Most of my left side was black, green, blue, and purple. Luckily, my right side had only scratches and bruises. All in all, I was extremely fortunate, as they insisted on reminding me.

After I had been cleaned up and bandaged, I was given medication to help with the pain, mainly anti-inflammatories for my knee. Because of the concussion, I would have to spend the night in hospital for observation, as if I would have been going anywhere else. Amy was in hospital, and that's where I intended to stay for the foreseeable future.

I was given a room off the ward, as they would have to wake me up every hour to check my pupils and blood pressure.

"It is better that you are away from everyone else, as we don't want others to be disturbed when we come in to check your vitals."

Personally, I was happy not to have to be on a ward with other people.

When I was settled, a nurse came in to tell me I had visitors.

"Are you up for visitors, or would you rather rest? I think it is your parents and brother." The nurse touched my shoulder and indicated I should lean forward so she could plump the pillows behind my head.

Considering I had been resting for far too long in my opinion, I nodded, glancing at the blue blanket covering my lower body.

"Good job, too, as I think we might have had a rebellion on our hands if you had said no," The nurse eased me back, the pillows supporting me more in a upright position.

"A rebellion?"

"They've been outside for God knows how long, waiting to see you." The nurse swiped her hand over my blanket, removing creases in the woollen material. "There you go. All set. I'll go and get them for you." With a reassuring smile, she was gone.

It seemed that no sooner had the door closed than it opened again and my family bundled in. It was obvious that they had all been crying.

Will was the first to the bed, his eyes bloodshot. "Hey, you. Good to see you alive and kicking, sis." He leaned over and pressed his lips against my forehead.

"Same here, Will. It is all a bit of a shock."

Will snorted, the sound uncannily close to being a sob. "You had us all worried, you know. I told them," he tossed his head towards my parents, "you were too stubborn to let a car accident do any permanent damage." His smile was watery at best.

"You're right there. Not going to let a little thing like an accident ruin my day." As I spoke, I heard a noise from behind Will, like someone stifling a whimper. I tipped my head to look past Will, but Will stepped away to expose my dad standing there, his expression showing he was trying to be strong, but failing miserably.

"Hello there, Dad."

"Don't worry, love. Dudley is fine. He's staying with Will's girlfriend for the night."

My dad's voice was hoarse, and I didn't need to ask why. "I didn't even ask about Dudley." I tried to smile but my face hurt.

"You didn't have to. He's your boy. You were bound to be worried sick about him."

He reached over to take my hand but stopped when he saw the bandage around my wrist. His lips thinned, and I knew he was about to start crying. I placed my good hand on top of his and squeezed in reassurance.

My mum gave my dad a dig in the ribs, and his eyes widened. "Oh, yes! Amy's parents are on their way. Reception told us on the way in and asked us to pass it on to you. Frank and Marion asked them to."

"Did Reception say how Amy was doing?"

"Not really. She's woken a couple of times."

Thank God.

"And her breathing is a little erratic."

My face must have said it all, because he quickly continued, "They said that is common in car accident victims. Stress, I think they said. Reliving what happened."

Mum was hovering behind my dad, a carrier bag clutched in her hands, her knuckles white. Will was pretending he knew what he was reading on the chart at the end of my bed. Only my dad was looking at me.

I must have been paranoid. Well, you would be, wouldn't you? Experiencing something so traumatic as believing the woman you love had died, then was alive, thinking she was dead again, and on and on it goes. That would make anyone suspicious.

"Is she awake now?"

"The last we heard, she was sitting up and they were trying to get her to take some fluids, but her mouth is sore."

I looked at them questioningly.

"She bit her tongue, they think."

That explained all the blood on her chin.

"And chipped her front tooth. They think it was when she was gritting her teeth together. Her bottom set pushed out a little too hard."

Considering they were hesitant about divulging details, they sure as hell knew a lot.

"What else did the doctors tell you?"

"They didn't tell us anything. The porter—George, I think he said his name was—told us to tell you. He couldn't come in because the nurses were here."

Bless him. What a lovely person. He had found out everything he could so I wouldn't worry. I didn't know how I could ever thank him.

It must have been the relief, because before I knew it I had my head in my hands and I was crying. My mum was next to me in a split second, wrapping comforting arms around me as only a mother could.

They all waited for me to finish.

"There, there, sweetheart. We're here now. Nothing is going to hurt you now." Her hands stroked my back, soothing me like only a mother's hands can do.

Minutes ticked by, my sobs easing until they were mere hiccups.

"It was a good job Will was around when we got the news." My dad's voice seemed deep again. "He was waiting to see you after your trip."

I looked over to where Will was standing. His hands were clenched together as if he was trying to control himself for some reason.

I nodded at him, the action asking him if he was okay. He closed his eyes slowly, then just as steadily opened them again. One solitary nod followed, and I knew he was trying to stop himself from crying and I should leave him to himself for a while.

"It was his girlfriend that answered the door. What's her name again, Will?"

Will didn't answer. My dad turned to look at him and started to speak, before realising that his son was having difficulty speaking.

My mum stepped in to continue their story, and she sat down on the bed next to me, her hands searching out mine.

"It's the thing every parent dreads, well, anyone really—seeing two coppers on your doorstep at that time in the evening." My mum blew out a breath, a sad smile touching her lips. "Will was laughing at me for not spotting the text message from you, and that it had been sent over three hours earlier, when the police knocked. I knew, just knew it was about you. I had an odd feeling that all was not well."

The message reminded me of the seconds before the crash, when I saw Amy's expression change from laughter to terror. A lump surfaced in my throat, and I swallowed it down. That's when it occurred to me. My phone. My fucking phone had been in my pocket all the time. Why didn't I get it out and call the police? I could have gotten Amy to hospital so much quicker, but no. I'd lost the plot, gone to pieces, become a quivering psychotic mess, thinking about how I was feeling rather than how I could stop things from getting worse. Story of my fucking life. It had been in my right hand pocket; I could have reached it. Why didn't I just pull the bloody thing out and press 999?

"The police said they were on the scene in minutes. The car behind you stopped and called 999." But it wasn't the same as me doing something, was it? And another...

I stopped mid-thought and mentally admonished myself. There was no use in crying over spilt milk, no point doing my "what ifs" and focusing on my shortcomings. I would have to learn that everything did not boil down to me; things that went wrong were not always my fault. I think that was one of my major problems—believing that if I had acted differently, said things differently, responded differently, everything would have turned out better.

The crux of the matter boiled down to this: I was in no fit state to think rationally when I regained consciousness after the crash. I had a concussion. I was hysterical. Not many people would have thought to phone the police, especially when they believed there was no need.

Drama curbed and over. Amy was sitting up, speaking. That's all that mattered. She was alive, and so was I.

"I've brought you some jimsjams."

Mothers. You've got to love them, haven't you?

ဆပ်ဆ

I was getting pissed off. Every bloody hour—lights in the eyes, blood pressure. They were going to kill me with their attentions and lack of sleep. Mum, Dad, and Will left the room every time the nurse came in, and then slipped back in after she had gone. I told them there was no point in their staying all night, but they wouldn't go.

It was almost three-thirty in the morning when I saw a huge hand slip grab the doorjamb of my room, followed by worried brown eyes. It was Frank, followed by Marion. They both looked a mess, a complete contrast to how I had last seen them.

"Mind if we come in?"

After the introductions and the stilted body language of parents who were worrying about their kids, Marion and Frank came to the side of my bed. "How you feeling, love?"

"Like I've been in a car crash." I meant it to be a joke, a bad one at that. "Sorry, I —"

"No worries. I understand." Marion sat on my bed and took my hands. Seeing me wince, she released the left one with a mumbled, "Sorry, sweetheart." Her face said everything her words didn't.

"Have you seen her?"

She nodded and released a sigh. "She looks a mess. The right side of her face is turning black where she hit her head. Her back hurts, she's got cracked ribs, three broken toes, stitches, and a sprained ankle."

"But is she all right?" *You know what I mean.*

"Apart from all that, and her lisp, she's fine. She asked us to come and see you to make sure you were okay. She's had everyone in the ward running around trying to find out your condition. She said she trusted us to tell her the truth."

I didn't know where to begin, so I just said, "Lisp?"

"She bit her tongue, and it's swollen. That, and there's a chip in her front tooth. Whatever you do, don't mention it. She seems more worried about how she sounds than about all her other injuries put together."

That was a good sign, wasn't it? Talking even though it hurt.

"So, lady, how are you? I have a report to my daughter to compile."

Twenty minutes later, I was alone in my room. Marion and Frank had gone back to "testify," as Frank put it, and my family had said they would meet them in the cafeteria so they could get to know each other better. That left just me and my thoughts, me coming to terms with what could have happened and what actually had.

There were too many thoughts, too bloody many, and my head was hurting. I could feel my eyes drifting closed as the events of the night took their toll.

"Just checking your blood pressure."

Bollocks.

₧)(₢

Six-thirty. There was no way the nurses were going to let me rest, and I was about to crack, so I thought it would be better to keep myself occupied, keep myself alert on account of the concussion. That's what I told Will. I convinced him that it would help my recovery if I could see Amy, even just for a few minutes. Time for a mission—with the help of my brother, a wheelchair, and a keen set of ears.

Brothers are weird. You spend your life growing up with them, believing they are the spawn of Satan, but when you need them, they are always there. Many a time I had to pull him off lads who had called me a dyke, carpet muncher, lady garden licker—oops, that was one of my own, and if they were not so inventive, lesbian. He had sported more black eyes and fat lips than an all-in wrestler. Bless. However, ask him to help dry the dishes, and I was on my own. Ask him to cover for me whilst I sneaked out to meet Karen Draycott...nope.

The worst was the irritating noise he made when he was eating dinner. I knew it was just to get a reaction out of me, which typically did follow shortly, as I punched him between the eyes. Then up to my room for penance for hitting my little brother, who couldn't help having sinus problems. Yeah, right.

But he was here now, pushing me along and looking over his shoulder like an undercover agent. "What if we get caught?"

I looked back at him, giving him the pointed look that said, "Idiot."

"But what if we're discovered?"

"We'll get locked up."

For a split second he believed me, I'm sure of it, and then he "accidentally" bumped my left leg into the doorframe. Obviously I'm too much of a lady to tell you what I called him. It started with a "w" and ended with an "r," and it wasn't waster.

It's quite hard to look inconspicuous as you are ducking into doorways and your leg is still sticking out, but we eventually managed to get to the ICU undetected.

As you can see, I had perked up a bit. Still a little bit hyperactive, but I knew I would calm down after I had seen Amy with my very own eyes, personally made sure that she was on the mend, even if she was asleep when I got there.

Frank was waiting just inside the doorway to the ICU, as Will had arranged. He hadn't told Amy we were coming; I wanted it to be a surprise. It was, judging by the look of incredulity on her face as I rolled into the room. She was sitting up, her legs over the side of the bed, her right foot bandaged and looking stiff. But the best thing was, she was halfway through getting into a pair of her very own jimjams, courtesy of her mother, though they looked like her father's.

Her bruised face slackened, and her eyes grew wide with shock, but her surprise lasted only a few seconds. The grin grew huge, exposing a chipped front tooth, which made her look absolutely adorable, almost like a little girl just getting into bed.

"Bethhh." The lisp was apparent, and she stopped, licked her teeth, and tried again. "How are you feeling?" A hand raised and covered her mouth. "Howth the head?" She tried to get up, but her mother pushed her back onto the bed. "Come clother. Let me thee you."

Will had disappeared. As soon as he had come into the room and seen Amy pulling her arms into bright green paisley-patterned pjs, he was gone. It was up to me and my good hand to wheel myself inside. I tried to aim straight, but wheeling a wheelchair as a novice with only one hand was not an easy feat, as the table, the side of the bed, and a bit of paintwork on the wall could attest.

In the end, Marion got up and pushed me closer to the bed. "I'll leave you two alone for a moment."

Then she was gone, leaving me there to assess Amy's battered face, the pain and suffering she was going through, but best of all, the love I could see in her eyes.

There were no words to convey how I was feeling, and given the lack of dialogue, I think she felt the same way. I lifted my hands to hers, and our fingers interlocked. Stuff the pain in my wrist; it would have been more painful if I didn't touch her. Energy sparked between us; the feeling of complete connection was there in spades. Amazing what can happen in twelve hours. Twelve hours ago, I thought I'd lost her, and look at us now.

We didn't even ask each other how we were feeling, just held on, glad to feel the life racing through our veins, knowing that the outcome could so easily have been a very different story. We could have been like the woman from the other car, or worse still, I could have lived. Everything was expressed as we looked at each other—the questions, the answers, the feeling of completeness.

I tried to lean up and kiss her, but I couldn't reach. She tried to lean down, but her back hurt too badly. With all the grunting and moaning we were doing, any people out in the hallway probably believed we were up to no good.

"I really want to kith you, feel you are real."

I swung my leg from its footrest and tentatively placed it on the floor. Next, I gingerly placed my right foot on the ground, tested it, and slowly rose from my seat to flop onto the bed next to Amy. Seconds later, we were in each other's arms, holding as tightly as we dared, lips touching gently, as I didn't want to hurt her mouth.

To have her in my arms, to feel her breathing... I couldn't put that feeling into words if someone paid me. I had my woman back, and there was no way I would ever let her go. Never. I was in it for the long haul, in sickness and in health.

Chapter Thirteen:

Homecoming

You don't know how tempted I was to call this the "Like it or Limp it Stage." So bloody corny, but I like corny. Corny is cheesy with less protein.

Anyway...

The doctor discharged me late afternoon, as he was pleased with my progress, but I wouldn't go home from the hospital. My mum tried all ways to convince me it would be better if I got home, showered, had a rest, and came back. But would you?

Didn't think so.

Amy had to stay in for another day, minimum. Although her eyes were dilating as they should, there was still some concern over the cracking sounds inside her skull. Dr Deaton—whose signature looked like "Dr. Death," honestly—said it could be the movement of the brain as it realigned itself inside the head, but it was better to be safe than sorry.

Safety it was, then.

Amy was moved from the ICU and onto the ward I was vacating. Just as I came out of my little side room, she was wheeling down the hallway. Her face looked as though she had completed ten rounds in the ring, but I could see she already looked better than she had the night before. George was pushing her, and they were chatting away as if they had known each other forever.

"Hello there, sunshine," George's cheery voice boomed down the corridor. "See this? Only been back on shift for ten minutes, and here I am, pushing your other half."

I beamed at him and hobbled over, using the stick they had given me to make sure I didn't put too much weight on my knee.

"You can't leave using that. I'll whip you down in this wheelchair as soon as she's finished using it."

I frowned and pouted, but George added, "NHS Policy. You walk in and get wheeled out." His laugh rumbled out and bounced off the walls.

I didn't kiss her, as I thought it would shock the older man. I leaned over and caught her gaze before saying, "Good afternoon, honey."

"Nice." George harrumphed. "Poor girl is in a right mess, and you can't even be bothered to kiss her."

Amy and I laughed, and I leaned in a little closer. "Can't disappoint, now can I?" And I tenderly brushed my lips over hers.

"Hiya, thweet—" She stopped and licked her lips, and I could see her lips move around, as if she was concentrating on speaking without the hiss. "... sweetheart." She kissed me again. "It seems as if I have been talking with a lisp forever, and I think it's become a habit."

I placed my hand under her chin and motioned for her to open her mouth. She hesitated for a fraction of a second before opening as wide as she could. Her front right tooth had a chip along the edge, and her gums looked a little swollen, but her tongue looked normal, apart from the huge tooth mark near the front where she had bitten it.

"Let's get you settled then."

Unfortunately, she didn't get the private room. She was taken into the main ward and plonked in the bed next to a woman reading *That's Life* magazine. I honestly believe Amy was the youngest in there by thirty years. She looked positively foetal. I also knew that if I left her alone to fend for herself, she would be babied by the rest of them. How could I leave her? You see the predicament I was in. It wasn't because I wanted to spend every minute of every day with her. That would have been selfish.

The world runs on good intentions. I wanted to stay there with her, gaze at her, tell her I loved her every thirty seconds, get on her tits—metaphorically, she was recovering, after all—but to tell you the truth, I was knackered. I hadn't slept properly, and I had gone through hell in the last twenty-four hours. It was enough to take anyone down, and I was no exception. I think I would have been able to persevere if Amy hadn't kept nodding off. We were both wiped out, and as much as I wanted to be with her, I knew it would be for the best if I went home and got some rest.

Kisses and hugs were exchanged, and I could feel the *People's Friend* and *Chat* magazines being put down like falling dominoes around me. Promising to come back later, and under the care and attention of a grinning George, I was gone, leaving her amongst the sharks.

She survived a car crash. The recovery should be child's play.

කාරු

They kept Amy in hospital for five days. Five days! I spent as much time as I could at the hospital, but I had another person to worry about—Dudley.

Talk about nearly pissing on my feet when he saw me. Will brought him round Tuesday evening, and he raced straight through the house and dived on top of me, his bony little feet jabbing my already sore ribs.

I needn't have bothered struggling in the shower, as he gave me a thorough wash, his tongue moving as if it was attached to his tail. Mewling noises expressed his excitement. The homecoming would have been perfect if only Amy could have been there too. Duds didn't leave my side all night. Even when I shifted my leg to get it more comfortable, his head shot up as if to say, "Where are you going?" and he didn't settle again until he was certain I wasn't going anywhere without him.

Taking him for walks was a job. I had to use a stick for at least two weeks, which wasn't too bad, as Dudley was excellent with or without a lead. The problem arose when I needed to drive anywhere. The doctors said I would be okay to drive after a couple of days' rest, but I didn't have the confidence. You know how it is. I know the best thing to do was to climb back in the saddle, but for the moment I was fine with not driving.

Will saved the day once again. Funny that, isn't it? I go through nearly all my tale without mentioning him much, and then I never shut up about him. Will this, Will that, Will was Weird. But I honestly don't know what I would have done without him. He picked me up in the morning before he went to work and took Duds and me to the park, walked round with us, brought me home, went to work. You can see how this is going. Do I need to go into more detail? Do you want me to get a move on?

Thought so.

I have to clarify one more thing before I carry on back to the hospital. Dudley was just as important to me now I had Amy as when I was on my own. I would hate anyone to think I was neglecting him. He would still sleep on my bed, still kill my slippers, and still be my number one little boy. And I would still love to wake up and tickle his winkle inadvertently.

But I can't deny the five days without Amy left me in limbo. All I did, it seemed, was wait until I could go and visit her. Don't get me wrong, I loved being home with Dudley, but it just felt that a huge part of me was missing. Time before Amy, when I was single and happy to be on my own, seemed pointless now.

Truth be told, cards on the table, this was the thing I had feared most—the absolute dependence on another person, the feeling that I couldn't survive without her...couldn't breathe...function...think straight. That she was the centre of my universe around which my life revolved, the focus of every waking thought and emotion. No, I was not obsessed. For once in my life I had allowed the shields to drop and love to come into my world. And the feeling was exhilaratingly terrifying.

I spent most of my time in a daydream, catching myself blanking out and missing conversations. My dad thought it was due to post traumatic stress from the accident, but there was no pulling the wool over my mum's eyes. Knowing smiles and loads of knee slapping, which went down like a lead balloon, until she decided slapping my thighs would be less painful.

There was no question of making the decision whether to let love in, no sitting and wondering if I could turn it down. It was all out of my hands. I had spent too long being afraid of being hurt, allowing no one to get close enough to know me, close enough to hurt me. But you know what? Life's just too fucking short. Carpe diem. Grab that proverbial bull by the horns and go for the gold, mixing my literary phrases with a bit of Latin thrown in. So, 'tis better to have loved and lost than never to have loved at all. Sorry. It's not Shakespeare, as I promised, but Tennyson. However, the sentiment is the same: love, be loved, accept love in all her glory and in whatever guise she falls into your lap. Treat her as a gift, a reason for life, the hope that humankind can do more than hate and start wars.

Whom am I trying to convince—you or me? I've accepted my fate, so...

Let's get back to the hospital. I know you're dying to know. Here goes.

Every time I visited, Amy looked better and better. The bruising had started to fade, making her seem more like her old self. Her headaches were less frequent, and her back pain was easing because she was forced to rest. On the fourth day, a dentist made an impression of her teeth so he could begin work on the cosmetic repair of the chip in her tooth. I had grown accustomed to the uneven smile and the way her words would whistle through the gap, especially when she wasn't focusing on avoiding that.

I was right about the women on the ward with her. We expected them to be shocked at our relationship, but they didn't bat an eyelid after the first time. Dora—*People's Friend* and sometimes *Take a Break*— was great. She adopted Amy from the moment she finished her tea break crossword and kept giving her the soft-centred chocolates from the stash in her locker. Gwen—*That's Life* and *Hello*— was in the next bed to her; she shared the story of her life with me and Amy on more than one occasion. But it was Sylvie who was the absolute star. Married for fifty-four years to Harold, a retired builder from Dereham. Four kids, ten grandchildren, twenty-two great grandchildren.

Jeez, I sound like a game show host. "Syl-vie... come on down!"

I can't tell you what she did differently from all the others, but she was just so lovely. Stories from her younger days were full of fun and laughter, creating the picture of the Golden Era our parents love to tell us about, but we never listen. Shame really, because we could learn so much.

The memory that sticks with me most vividly was when Amy, Sylvie, and I were in the lounge, soaking in some sunlight through the huge plate glass windows. We were chatting about soap operas. Characters were always jumping between the sheets with every Tom, Dick, or Harriet, with no thought for morality or commitment. That was when she said it.

"I was in love with a woman once."

I thought I had misheard her. You can imagine my reaction. And Amy's. I mean...what do you say, apart from, "Really?"

Sylvie didn't bat an eyelid, said it as if it was an everyday thing. "It was before Harold, though he knows about it."

I was praying she wouldn't go into too much detail.

"I was twenty. It was 1948, and I had just moved to London to work in a typing pool. I spotted her on my very first day, and I thought she was the most beautiful woman in the world." She leaned back in the armchair and closed her eyes as she relived the memory.

Usually I feel extremely uneasy when I am faced with older people talking about sex, love, anything that happens behind the bedroom door. I know, I'm being unreasonable—ageist, to be exact. However, watching Sylvie's expression flit over the memories—It was mesmerising. Her wrinkled face didn't seem as old. It seemed to shed the worry and the life-learned lessons, if only for an instant.

"Jeannette."

Huh? Her voice broke through my thoughts and brought me back to the narrative with a thump.

"Her name was Jeannette, and she didn't know I existed."

She sighed, and old tears shimmered in her eyes.

"I didn't know that women could love each other in that way. Was a country girl all my life, farmer's daughter. I put it down to being lonely, being in the city and not really knowing anyone else." When she paused to take a breath, the sudden silence seemed exposing, and not just for her. "All I knew was that when she was near me, I couldn't breathe, couldn't think straight. My stomach would tie up in knots, and I would start to sweat."

I knew the feeling well. I glanced at Amy, who was gazing intently at Sylvie. *I wonder if you feel that when you are near me.* The question remained unspoken, in my head, but I wanted to ask it and watch Amy's reaction. *Will you love me forever?* The thought flitted in, pushing the previous one out. Sue's promise of loving me forever flooded in, and a bolt of fear shot through me at my vulnerability.

"It was nearly a month before she even spoke to me. Came right up behind me and whispered hello in my ear. All the blood drained from my face, even though I only heard her voice. The strength it took me to turn round and look at her close up... Bloody hell. And to actually say hello back. Had no spit in my mouth." A soft laugh escaped her, and she gripped her knees and shuddered. "Thought all my Christmases and birthdays had come at once. Especially when she asked if I fancied going to the flicks."

Sylvie continued her tale, telling us about her first evening out with Jeannette and how she felt being with her.

My initial shock at her being in love with a woman had completely vanished, and I was kicking myself for being very conservative and narrow minded. I expected people to accept my sexuality, but I was just as bad as they were. It didn't matter how old, what sex, race, or religion you were...normal is as normal does. Love is love, whether it's sexual or platonic, and the sooner people, including myself, start focusing on their own lives and not meddling with others', the sooner the world will begin to sort itself out. Hatred and ignorance are *not* qualities, *not* something to pass on to the next generation. Embracing differences and things we don't understand are the means to understanding and change.

Fortunately, we live in a world that is changing, not very quickly, but changing nevertheless. I'm not saying all the changes are in the right direction, either. Bigotry and prejudice are still alive and kicking. And even within the classifications with which we label ourselves, there are still people who disagree with other people's life choices. The lesbian who identifies herself by the way she acts, dresses, and talks can come in for ridicule from the lesbians who believe a woman should look like a woman. Why would, or should, one person ridicule another just because they don't do things the same, think the same way, like the same type? Scorning others, whatever their preferences, is something many of us do but rarely admit to. Love is love. We love, we feel, and we should be allowed to do so without mockery and judgment. There should be no prototype or "recipe" for the perfect lesbian. There should be no ground rules for who to love, who to feel attracted to. Women who love women are all lesbians—there are no ifs or buts.

I know I'm going off the point here, I should just be reporting Sylvie's story, but I needed to say it to understand it myself, to comprehend why people have to judge and put others to type. Myself included. I automatically assumed Sylvie was a woman who loved her husband and had no life before him and no life other than his. But she wasn't just an old lady full of stories, devoid of passion and longing. Love doesn't cease to exist because of age, creed, or sexuality. Doesn't stop because others don't think of you that way.

Sylvie had been in love with another woman, married a man...but loved a woman. What I needed to know was why? Why had she given up on that happiness she had felt? Because the way she spoke, I knew Jeannette had been the love of her life.

"What happened?"

Sylvie looked at Amy, the one who had asked the question. "I want to blame society, but it was all down to me. I pushed her away."

Amy and I shot each other confused looks.

"I couldn't handle it—the deceit, the hiding how I felt for her. I used to start fights over nothing, used to take it out on her that we couldn't tell the world we were in love." Sadness washed over her face, and a single tear zig zagged through the wrinkles on her face. "She finally left me to marry someone she had grown up with. Left London and went back to Dorset. Last I heard, she had a couple of kids and was training to be a teacher." The vibrant woman disappeared, and all that remained was emptiness. "I went to pieces. Came back to Norfolk and married the first man who asked me." Sylvie sat up straighter in her chair, trying to regain control of her emotions. "I told Harold everything. Didn't want him to live in the dark about my past. I owed him that."

"But did you love him?" The question shot out of my mouth before I had chance to check it.

"Eventually." She sighed. "But not in the same way. She was my first, and I think there's part of me that loves her still. Harold's been a good husband and father. I couldn't wish for anyone better."

Except Jeannette.

"So, girls, I hope you'll take a lesson from this old bird."

We looked at her, gobsmacked.

"Don't let anything get in your way, not even each other. Respect, that's the key. That, along with trust. Without those two, you have nothing. With those, you can take on the world."

How true. Trust and respect. Love cannot stand without those foundations, or else you will eat each other alive with jealousy and cruelty. No love can withstand that, and if you haven't got trust and respect, have you really got love at all? Jesus. I'm beginning to sound like that woman from *Sex in the City*.

Later that day, I met Harold. Anyone with half a brain could see he loved his wife with every fibre of his being, and that confused me even more. By Sylvie's own admission, she had loved someone else, but looking at Harold... Could there be hope after love was lost? Not the all-consuming fire of first love, but love all the same? If Sylvie had stayed with Jeannette, what would have happened to Harold? Would he have met someone else and loved her just as much? What about soul mates, meeting "the one?" Was that just a pipe dream?

A hand landed on my shoulder and pulled me round. Glistening brown eyes answered my question. Soul mates? Definitely.

⊱⊰

Marion and Frank picked Amy up from the hospital on Saturday afternoon, and I'd dropped Dudley with my parents whilst I was getting Amy's house aired and sorted for her return. It was amazing to think it had only been a week ago we had actually shown each other how we felt. Apart from the near fatal car crash, it had been the best week of my life.

Though I wanted to, I didn't stay long, just got her settled. I didn't want to suffocate her with my presence, as I knew she would have a lot to catch up on with her parents.

"You can call me anytime, okay?"

Amy's eyes glimmered with tears, and she responded with short, rapid nods.

"And when I say anytime," I stroked her cheek, my fingers delighting in the contact, "I mean *any*time."

She nodded again, and a small smile appeared.

Brushing my thumbs over her lips, I added, "Even if that anytime is three in the morning, call me. Right?"

Amy laughed, but I could hear the bubble of emotion within it, almost as if she was on the verge of crying.

"Right. Three in the morning, it is." Her smile was fuller now, and this gave me the push to be able to leave her in the capable hands of her parents.

Getting about, especially being able to visit Amy whenever I wanted, was much easier now that I was back to driving, so much better than relying on getting lifts or limping around. The swelling in my knee was gradually going down, and my wrist was on the mend. God bless anti-inflammatories and painkillers!

Instead of going straight round to my parents', I had an urge to pop back home for a little while. Don't ask me why, just felt I had to. I hadn't been in the house five minutes when the doorbell sounded.

Sue stood on the stoop, a bunch of flowers gripped tightly in her hand, her face ashen. "Just heard about the accident and thought I'd pop round and see if you were all right."

I fleetingly thought of slamming the door in her face, but instead I opened it wider and limped off down the hallway towards the kitchen. I heard the front door close and then her footsteps as she followed me.

"Where d'you keep your vases?"

"Under the sink, like always." I stopped and thought about how I was behaving. "Thank you for the flowers, by the way. They're beautiful."

She was bent over, rummaging through all the crap I kept under there, but lifted her gaze to mine. Her smile was radiant. It somehow made her look freer.

"My pleasure. Couldn't come round and not give the patient something bright and shiny to look at. They were out of grapes. I fancied some, too."

For the first time in so bloody long, we both laughed together, with no malice behind it.

I started to relax, to be human around her. Everything I had been through over the last few months, and especially the last week, had taught me so much. Many things in life are reflexive; people's reactions correspond to how you treat them. Things are also relative. Everyone has their own take on events. My memories of what had happened between Sue and me might be very different from her recollections of our relationship. Maybe this was the final thing we strive to do—finalise things, find closure. It was an important step in gaining some control over the way I reacted to things in my life.

"We need to talk, don't we?"

Just pulling the vase free from all the clutter in the cupboard, Sue stopped and stared at the glass container. Slowly, she turned to face me, her eyes full of sadness and hurt. Her nod was slow but deliberate.

"Let's talk then. It's been too long."

Settled in the front room, surrounded by thickening air, I was finding the situation almost surreal. Sue and I were actually having a conversation, a civilised one at that.

"I suppose I owe you an explanation, don't I?"

Sue shrugged. "That's up to you. I would like to know why you treated me so badly, although I'm sure I'm not going to like what you have to say."

I had to bite my lip. Why I had treated *her* badly? I was under the impression it was the other way around.

"You may have thought I treated you badly, Sue. Maybe I did, but you played your part in it too." She started to speak, but I interrupted her. "You want to know? Or are we just going to sit here and blame each other?"

She sighed loudly, her whole body seeming to slump. "Just tell me and get it over with."

I pursed my lips and deliberated where to begin.

"It wasn't always bad between us. Certainly not at the beginning." At my words, Sue sat forward, her face lowered. "But by the end..."

"By the end what?" Her voice was cautious.

"By the end, I didn't feel like me anymore. I felt as if I had lost who I was." I didn't like telling her how I'd felt, but there was no other way. This was part of my recovery. "We were not happy. Everything I did, you didn't like. I couldn't see my friends without you kicking off, couldn't do anything. Couldn't even wash up properly."

I noticed Sue's flinch as I said the last bit. I'd have thought I would feel some kind of elation, some kind of liberation at getting it off my chest and maybe hurting her in the process, but no.

"My life with you eventually made me totally miserable. The only thing good in it was Dudley."

The words didn't have the impact I thought they would. On me, I mean. Telling Sue that she had made my life lifeless was not the be-all and end-all of my coming to terms with what had taken place. There was an element of release there, but I already knew that Sue was not solely to blame. To a degree, what had happened between us also rested at my feet. But I was getting there, getting a grip on my shortcomings, understanding that I had to take control of who I was and who I wanted to be.

She sat in silence and heard me out, her face expressionless. At times it felt as if I was talking to the air, but I knew she was listening, taking it all in.

"But, I also know that it wasn't all your doing. I was to blame, too."

Sue lifted her head, her eyes meeting mine. I felt a stab of guilt when I saw the hurt there.

"I didn't give you what you needed. Didn't love you enough to make things work, or to stand up for us. I could have talked to you about how I was feeling, opened up. But I ..."

Sue leaned forward, her tongue swiping over her lips before she asked, "But you what?"

I grimaced. "I didn't talk to you about how I was feeling, because I didn't want to."

A note of anger coloured her voice as she repeated, "You didn't want to? What the fuck do you mean by that?"

I held my hands up defensively. "I know it sounds cruel, know that—"

"Yes! It does sound cruel. It also sounds like you are purposefully setting out to make me the bad guy here."

Sue jumped to her feet, and I thought she was going to leave me sitting alone with a half uttered confession hanging in the air. Instead, she put her head in her hands and slumped back to the sofa.

The silence in the room seemed unbearably loud, but I waited it out. I wanted her to say something before I continued to rip her apart.

It had only been a couple of minutes, but it seemed much longer before she said, "Go on. Finish."

Instead of continuing, I stared at the top of her head until she lifted her face from her hands and looked straight at me, her eyes darker than I'd ever seen them. "What are you waiting for? Finish it."

Biting my lip, I considered making up something positive about our relationship, but then decided that lying at that precise moment would do nobody any favours. I knew my words would hurt her, but I had spent too long playing the coward. It was time to get things out in the open.

"Relationships consist of two people, two people who want the same thing. Thing is, I didn't want the same things as you. If I had, I wouldn't have let things get to the stage they did without doing something about it."

Silence enveloped us. I expected her to become angry at what I had said, to retaliate with a spiteful remark, but she just looked broken.

"I know." She released a sigh and leaned back onto the sofa. "I could sense it. Even before I moved in, I could feel you slipping away from me. That's why I wanted so badly to move in."

I couldn't understand the logic of that. If she *knew*... "Why?"

"I thought that as soon as we moved in together, things would sort themselves out. I loved you, Beth. Still do."

Shaking hands lifted and wiped her eyes, and I could see the tears glistening on her fingers. I started to interrupt, but she held up a hand.

"Don't worry. I know you don't feel the same. I wasn't saying it to make you feel bad. Just thought I'd let you know."

I closed my mouth and sat back, highlighting the literal and metaphorical distance between us.

"The way I treated you... God. Sometimes I still can't believe the things I did." Her voice quavered, and she swallowed and started again. "It wasn't long after I moved in that I knew things were not going to get any better between us, but I just couldn't admit defeat and walk away. I wanted it too much, wanted *you* too much to just leave." She started to cry.

Initially I felt numb, but then I picked up the box of tissues and offered her one. It was not like the usual crying Sue did, the crying I had thought she did to manipulate and control me. It was deep rooted and thick, as if she had bottled it away for years. The realisation of what I had done was beginning to shape and simmer inside my head. I always thought she had everything sorted, had everything tightly under her control. But just as the way I had lived was an act, so was Sue's. She had performed in a certain way in order to get me to take notice, and my response was to shy away from any form of responsibility, any form of commitment.

I'm saying it wasn't all my fault, or all hers. It was one of those situations that you don't recognise until it's too late. To live this kind of life, or lie, is not the way to go. It all boils down to this: No one should have to go through what I went through, whether or not they believe they deserve it. Because no one deserves it. No one. And the way I treated Sue is something I am not very proud of. All she wanted was my love, and I couldn't give it to her. Part of the blame definitely lies at my feet. I should have grown a spine and told her that it wasn't working, instead of bottling it all up inside me to fester and grow into something like hatred, and worse still, indifference. A relationship needs two people who are both committed to it, so it only takes one to put a spanner in the works. What I was trying to come to terms with now was which of us did the breaking— me or Sue. Or was the culprit our inability to tell one another how we felt? The crux of it all was that I hadn't loved her in the same way as she loved me.

"I was scared of losing you, and the more you slipped away, the more frightened I became." The tissue clutched in Sue's hands was crumpled. "I know I wore you down, even to the way you washed up the dishes. I thought that if I could make you feel as if you couldn't survive without me, then you would stay. The more I pushed, the more you pulled away, and then I would try to rein you back in. I knew I was trying to control you, maybe because I couldn't control myself."

Images flashed into my mind of Sylvie at the hospital confiding in us about her lost love, especially the part where she said she had pushed Jeannette away. Had Jeannette felt the same as me? Sue was like Sylvie—they both responded out of the anger and hurt they felt in order to maintain some semblance of control. What about Rachel and how she had behaved toward Amy? Was she another victim of desperately wanting what she couldn't have?

"I hated you seeing your friends. Hated it."

I shook my head. "Why? I didn't stop you seeing yours." I didn't add that I was happy when she spent time with others, as that gave me a chance to be away from her. That was a nugget of information she could do without.

"You were glad when I spent time with others."

I said nothing, maybe because I honestly thought she had just read my mind.

"I didn't like the fact that they received all your attention," she continued.

"They were my friends. They wanted to be your friends, too."

Sue's laugh showed no amusement. "No. I don't think they did, Beth. Your friends didn't want you to be shackled to someone like me."

"Actually, they didn't say anything about our relationship. Well, not all of them."

I probably should have stopped when I said they hadn't spoken about our relationship. But this was time for honesty, even if it only came in small, well-selected snippets.

"I was extremely insecure. I thought your friends would see past the façade of our relationship and tell you to leave me. That was why I'd wanted you to stop seeing them." She paused as her eyes tracked mine. "I was probably right after all."

"But that was one of the problems, Sue. You never gave me the opportunity to think for myself, to make my own decisions. You thought I could be influenced by what others said, maybe because I was so influenced by you. When I made the decision to end our relationship, it was my choice—no one else's."

She gave a slow nod.

"You didn't trust me enough to think for myself, and didn't respect me enough to allow me the freedom to make my own mistakes." I waited for that to sink in before adding, "Without trust and respect, love can't survive. And neither of us showed either of those to the other."

I told you we could learn much from our elders, even about love.

I left Sue with her thoughts and went into the kitchen to make coffee. I think we both needed it. Whilst the kettle was boiling, I took the time to think of all we had said. Quite a lot of feelings and behaviours had been rehashed in Sue's brief visit, and I was beginning to get things straight in my head. Both of us were to blame, that much was obvious.

But why did people stay in abusive relationships? Did they actually admit to themselves that it was wrong, or did they believe it was what they deserved? I remember a woman I used to work with whose husband used to beat ten bells out of her on a regular basis. The number of times we all told her to get the hell out landed on deaf ears. She told us the only reason he did it was because he loved her too much. Too much! She had an affair, and he had found out about it. Ever since, he'd made sure she was accountable for everything she did, where she went, whom she spoke to. But it was never enough. The last part of what I just told you, we surmised; she never told us, only about the affair. However, she used to panic if she was late, or if her husband called and she was out of the office.

One day, Daniel, a workmate, was sitting on her desk telling her that if she had an affair, then obviously she wasn't happy to start with, and it was time to leave the bastard. It was the first time he had ever sat on her desk, the first time he had ever voiced an opinion about anyone else's life, and, unfortunately for him, it turned out to be the worst time to do it. Her husband came through the door, didn't even ask what was going on, just attacked him. Beat him to a pulp in front of us all.

Daniel was nineteen, nineteen and thin as a rake. The husband was thirty-four and built like a brick wall. It took three men to get him off Daniel, and even as they were dragging him away, he was laying the boot in. He got six-months custodial sentence; Daniel got six broken ribs, a cracked jaw, and a black eye, and lost his front teeth. I realised that day that I couldn't stay with Sue any longer. She had never hit me, and I doubted she ever would, but abuse does not only come at the end of a fist.

That night I met the woman who would take my place in Sue's bed. Two weeks later, I walked into our bedroom and found the excuse to leave. Even in the end, it had taken more than watching some poor bloke get the shit kicked out of him to make me stand up and walk away. Life deals us some very wild cards at times, and it was only now I was realising I could shuffle the deck myself.

When I took the coffee in, Sue started again. "I never hurt Dudley, you know. I swear. Never laid a finger on him."

I squinted at her, thoughts racing again. Thoughts of Dudley cowering, of how he hated her so much.

"Come on, Beth. He wouldn't even let me stroke him without growling. You think he would let me get close enough to harm him?"

That much was true. Duds had never backed down from Sue, always wanted to bite her, even when I was there. So why did he duck when I raised my hand, jump when I slapped the paper on the side of the chair? He had stopped doing it not long after Sue had left, so what had been the reason he'd done it in the first place? It came like a bolt from the blue.

"That fucking paperboy!"

It made sense. I had cancelled Sue's paper about a week after she had gone, and not long after that, Dudley had been fine. "That little bastard!"

I was on the phone in seconds, calling the newsagents and reporting the incident. The owner told me the paperboy who used to deliver in my area had been sacked four months ago for tormenting the dogs on his rounds. There had been loads of complaints about him. In the end, the owner of the newspaper shop had followed him delivering papers and caught him kicking a black Labrador who lived two streets away. *Kicking a dog!* Can you believe it? What sick little fucker would hurt living, breathing thing who couldn't speak up for themselves?

A loaded question, and one, unfortunately, with many answers, all of them names of people who see nothing wrong with such behaviour. The husband who beat the crap out of his wife, for one.

Then I thought of me punching Sue in the face, hearing her nose crunch. I looked at it and noted the slight curve at the bridge.

She saw me looking. "I deserved that, Beth. Not for hitting Dudley, but for all the shit I put you through."

"No. No one deserves that. There are other ways to sort things out without resorting to a fight in the street."

She thought about that and then nodded. "But it's in the past now. Everything's in the past." Sue lifted her cup and took a long pull. "One more thing before I leave you in peace."

I gave her a questioning look.

"I'm sorry I couldn't let it go. Sorry I tried to hurt you in any way I could, like taking your furniture and threatening to go for custody of Dudley. In my screwed up mind, I thought whilst you were hating me, at least you were feeling something. At that point, I was willing to take whatever I could get." In a flash she was standing, the cup back on the table. "Thanks for listening, Beth. Don't worry, I'll leave you alone from now on."

I just sat there.

"Amy seems like a keeper."

How did she...?

"Promise me...no...promise *yourself*, you will take good care of each other."

Before I could say anything, she was gone. Fast, like she had to leave as quickly as possible. There was more I wanted to say, more I wanted to explain, but I guess she felt we had both said enough. It was time to close that chapter of my life and move forward.

Something on the coffee table caught my eye, an envelope with my name on the front. I picked it up and peeled open the paper. Inside was a homemade CD. On the front was written: *Maybe this will help you understand*.

The soulful acoustics of Radiohead's *Creep* filled the room, the words mournful and full of longing. They spoke of the singer's idyllic view of the person he loved, and I sat mesmerised by the lyrics, gaining a better understanding of what Sue must have gone through.

The verse that stood out was agonisingly wanting, and tears trickled down my face—the realisation of what it was like to be in love and not feel worthy. The words that rang a bell said that he didn't care how much it hurt him, he wanted to have control. But the kind of control that Sue wanted was not what we could have both lived with. And who was it hurting? Just me? Just her?

The lyrics that conveyed how badly he wanted the woman in his life to notice when he wasn't there were so key to any relationship. I wanted someone to notice if I wasn't there, too, but in a way that showed love, not ownership. It was recognising the difference that mattered.

Noting how special your loved one is, that "feeling special" part, is vital, but not when you are feeling less special than the one you love. Isn't a partnership built on equality? Sue had been so bloody unhappy, and all the time I was with her I thought she had everything sorted, was sure of whom she was, the same mistake I had made about Amy when I first met her.

To become aware of how wretched someone else is feeling, and to know it is because of your actions, is soul destroying. Sue had gone, but she had left me the reasons for her behaviour in the only way she could. To think she believed herself to be a weirdo, a creep, and to know all she wanted was for me to love her, was a revelation. I should have seen it.

The pain in my chest became intense, and tears began to fall. I'm not special, no more than anybody else. Even now she felt inadequate. Why else would she have given me the CD?

As I said, life and its events are open to interpretation. We need to step outside ourselves occasionally and look at the bigger picture. We might surprise ourselves. It may be that the "we" are like me, or perhaps we are the Sues of this world—it all depends on who is watching. But what we must recognise is that whether you feel the victim or the offender, you might in fact be a little of both.

And for the record, we are all special; we all deserve to loved fully and completely. If we're not, then...

Sermon over.

Chapter Fourteen:

Nearly There Stage

Four months had gone by since the day Sue visited me, and I was still haunted by her message. I knew that I should find a way to help her overcome her feelings of failure and insignificance, but that would come with time. At the moment, things that had happened between us were still too raw.

I told Amy about Sue and what conclusions I had finally drawn. Her response got right down to the crux of it all.

"So, honey, what have you learned from this?"

"It's better to be open and honest with someone than bottling it all up?"

She nodded, her smile encouraging, so different from how Sue would've reacted, and how I would have treated the situation, too. I was not going to blame all that had happened onto Sue. I had been just as guilty, even if it had been out of apathy.

"Also, I can draw a line through it all and get my life back on track."

"I'm really proud of you, you know?"

Amy's words surprised me. "Proud? Why?"

"Because you faced up to it, faced up to Sue and the past. You stopped running."

I pulled her to me and kissed her hard. I thought that was the best response.

As time went on, I figured that the conversation between Sue and me might have an impact on Amy's view of her relationship with Rachel. I knew it made her think about it, and I expected her to mull it over and marinate on the actions, or inactions, of her life with her ex. Initially, she didn't say a word, but when she did, it was as if the floodgates opened as she recognised the similarities between her experience and mine.

We were curled on her sofa, watching a film, when she suddenly paused the DVD and turned to me.

"The relationship you had with Sue was similar to mine and Rachel's."

At first I was a little confused as to what she meant, as we had already spoken about this. Then I wondered why she had picked that moment to start talking about her past. I quickly realised that the reason was inconsequential. The thing that mattered was that she wanted to talk about it, and however many times she wanted to, I would let her.

"Go on." I shuffled around so I was facing her, my legs pulled up and tucked underneath me.

Amy frowned, not at me, but probably related to something she was thinking about.

"Well, not completely similar. Actually, there were major differences, but the outcome was the same."

I leaned forward and gently took her hand, my fingers threading through hers.

Amy faced me, her lips lifted slightly in a half smile.

"And?" I coaxed her with the one word and an encouraging smile.

"We are who we are, and no one has the right to make us uncomfortable in our own skin, just as we don't have the right to do that to someone else."

My eyes widened. The words had rushed from her, and I was surprised that she had summed up our experiences so clearly in such a small space of time.

"True. No one has the right to make someone feel bad about themselves." I lifted her hand and kissed her fingers.

"I think I should do what you did." I kept my lips on her hand as I lifted my eyes to meet hers. "I should get together with Rachel and have it out with her."

I sat upright and tilted my head to look at her. "Are you sure about this? Are you well enough?"

Amy laughed and I laughed with her, unsure why either of us was laughing in the first place.

"Not right this minute. I'll wait until I can get about on my own before I get in touch with her." She squeezed my fingers. "I need to clear the air with her. I can't ignore what happened between me and her forever. I need closure, just like you did. The only way for me to get that is to understand what actually happened to make our relationship play out the way it did."

I nodded. It was true. There was no point in wondering or surmising what had happened in an effort to understand the outcome. The only way to know for sure was to bring everything to light and find out once and for all why Rachel had acted the way she had.

"Right. Ready for the film?"

Without another word, Amy lifted the remote and pressed play. I just stared at the side of her head for moment, surprised at how Amy had decided to face her past in such a positive and constructive way. A wave of pride washed through me.

Amy turned to me, a smile brightening her face. "Come on. Rest your head on my lap. I'll stroke your hair."

How could a girl resist?

⊱⊰

When she was feeling better, and her broken toes had healed enough for her to get about on her own, Amy arranged to meet Rachel in a restaurant in Cambridge, neutral ground. As she had said, clearing the air with her ex had become a goal that she couldn't ignore any longer. The wait for her return seemed interminable. The hours dragged and dragged, and more than once I had to stop myself from phoning her to see if she was okay. I knew she had to do this on her own, had to take control once and for all and realise she could get past Rachel. The main thing Amy regretted was that she had just up and left. There had been no showdown like Sue and I had, no dramatic punch-ups. Amy just told Rachel she had to go, then cut off all contact for a while whilst she licked her wounds before moving to Norfolk. Burying herself in her work hadn't helped either; it just made her feel more distanced from society. She had left all her friends and family behind, had tried to cocoon herself from the world and its shortcomings, but people are social beings who thrive on interaction. Well, on the whole we do.

I remembered one of the first things she said to me, well, it was when we went to the beach actually. "I'm good at fun." Was that for my benefit or hers? She had also said, "Fun. Something totally distracting. Do things you would never usually do."

It all made sense now. I thought Amy had saved me, but in a way, I think we saved each other that day. When I say saved, you know what I mean—gave each other a purpose, a focus, a chance to start again. The love we shared was not built on a shaky foundation, not the rebound from relationships turned bad—far from it. The love Amy and I shared was born of the wonder of love itself. We were there for each other when we needed it, and then it became so much more.

She came round to see me as soon as she returned to Norwich. Dudley got to her first, like usual—

ball gripped in his mouth and trying to lick her at the same time. Finally he moved his hairy little arse out of the way so I could get my turn.

Kissing her was totally captivating. When she was with me, it seemed as if nothing else mattered; I could take on the world. It grew stronger, the kiss, I mean, and the desire surged inside, almost clouding my reason. But it wasn't the time to follow up on my yearning to make love to her.

Ending the kiss reluctantly, our arms firmly wrapped around each other, I leaned back and looked into her eyes. "How did it go?"

Amy shrugged and sighed. "Pretty much as I expected. Let's get comfy, and I'll tell you."

There was nothing in the world more comfortable than lying on the sofa in her arms, unless it was in bed, or standing, or anywhere, as long as I was in her arms. I stroked her arm gently, my fingertips playing with the fine hairs. My head was snug on her chest, and I felt contented just to hear the sound of her breathing.

"Rachel was pretty much the same as she's always been. I told her how she had made me feel when we were together, and she asked me why I had even bothered to turn up today."

Bitch.

"I told her I just wanted to clear the air, let her know that she had hurt me, and that I needed to forgive her and move on with my life."

I tilted my head and looked up into her face. Amy met my eyes, a smile spreading over those gorgeous lips. But now wasn't the time for thinking about kissing her. Now was the time to let her tell her story uninterrupted.

"She started all sweetness and light, but her attitude changed when she realised I wasn't there to get back together with her. I tried to explain how she had made me feel worthless, and she laughed in my face, told me to grow up. Her exact words were, 'Life is not all sweetness and Mills and Boon novels. Get over yourself.'"

I was glad I hadn't been there. Rachel would have ended up with a nose that was slightly askew, like Sue's.

"But you know what, honey?" Amy asked.

"What?"

"Her taunting didn't affect me. I didn't rise, or sink, to her bait. When she realised that, she became aggressive, brought your name into it."

"What did she say?"

"It doesn't matter. She doesn't matter. I understood completely, for the first time in a long time, that it didn't matter what she thought. That part of my life is dead and buried, gone for good. So I actually did take her advice."

I couldn't believe that she would listen to a selfish, arrogant twat like Rachel. "You did what?"

"Yep. I got over myself." The smile she gave me warmed my heart. "I told her she wasn't worth my time and to stay away from us, then I left. But before I got to the door, she shouted after me, 'And for the record—you were shit between the sheets. Like I was shagging a rag doll.' I stopped, turned, and made sure everyone was looking at either her or me before I said, 'That's no way to speak to your sister, is it?' The look on her face was priceless. I could hear people gagging as I left. Stiffed her with the bill, too."

I sat up sharply, an incredulous grin spreading on my face. "You never said that?"

"Sure did. I knew I had to say something that would stop her in her tracks, and the one thing I knew she hated was to be made to look a fool. There was no comeback for what I said. If she denied it, it would've drawn even more attention to her. She knew I wasn't going to take her shit anymore."

"How?"

"Might have been when I told the waiter to make sure he hid all the knives, or perhaps it was the glass of wine I poured over her head."

"When did you do that?"

"Just before I left the table. Come to think of it, maybe that's why she shouted out what she did."

I threw my head back and laughed, and it wasn't long before Amy joined me. It felt good, so bloody good to laugh at something that could have so easily ruined our lives.

When we eventually recovered so that we were only hiccoughing laughs, Amy caught my hands and held me fast, her expression turning serious. "Beth, I love you so much, so very much." She squeezed my fingers but I didn't mind the pain, especially when she added, "You are the love of my life."

It's amazing how one minute you can be laughing and the next sobbing into the t-shirt of the woman you love more than breathing. Shushing noises whispered through my hair as strong hands stroked my back, and I knew I was home.

છબ

Later that night Amy showed me just how much she loved me, over and over again, and I showed her with every touch and caress, every taste. Skin slipped along skin, breasts pressed against breasts, encompassing all we felt in a climax of unity. There was no her or me, only us. For the first time since we had become a couple, I felt there were no barriers, no guilt, no shame, nothing but the love we shared. We were free to be who we were, free to be ourselves, expecting nothing but receiving everything.

Words like "love" and "forever' slipped readily from our lips between kisses. However long we loved each other, it would never ever be long enough.

Amy was above me, between my legs and looking down at me, but I felt so in control. Weird, I know, but I did. There was no uncertainty—every touch was perfect, every word came from somewhere deep inside. As her fingers slipped inside me, I had the sensation I was filling her. I can't explain it, can't properly describe the feeling. It felt as if we had swapped bodies, but our minds were our own.

And that's the whole point, isn't it?

Resolution Stage:
Generally Known as The Lead Up To The End

I know I said previously that it was four months later, but the four months later is now. Today, in fact.

Amy and my relationship has grown from strength to strength. Every day I wake up and find I love her more than I did yesterday, but definitely not as much as I'll love her tomorrow. Mushy, I know, but true.

All the experiences we shared—some of them when we weren't even together, if you know what I mean—made us realise what we had together. We valued our love, respected each other, trusted implicitly, and readily told each other how we were feeling. Not just the lovey-dovey stuff, but all of it—even the bits that we weren't so proud of.

If Amy did something to piss me off or hurt me, she knew about it, and she did the same back—told me when I stepped out of line. It wasn't a relationship built on pipe dreams or straight from the pages of a trashy romance story. This was real life, and in real life, people get on your nerves, or as my mum would say, "Get on your tits." But even that sounded like a good idea in my book, as long as it was Amy getting on them.

Being in love is the easy part; making it work takes effort, but not in a bad way. We can all become complacent, believing everything is going wonderfully, but ask yourself this. Have you told the person in your life you love them today? Have you showed them? Ruffled their hair...stroked their arm...their back? Made them a cuppa without being asked? What about compliments? "That top suits you" or "You have washed up beautifully." You knew that was coming, didn't you?

Another thing to remember is to never take them for granted, in any respect. I'm not preaching, just sharing what I have learned. To thank someone for making a wonderful meal, for posting your mail, for taking the time to be together although you know they are snowed under at work—all of them relevant for letting your "other" know you appreciate them. And that's part of the love package, alongside respect and trust.

Amy and I still have so much to experience, so much to discover together—along with Dudley, of course. The car crash saw to it that we would always treasure each and every single moment we share, as none of us know when it will be our last. The poor woman in the Ford Mondeo never had chance to say goodbye to her husband and two children. The third glass of wine she had at a business colleague's house turned out to be the reason why. Life is for living, learning, and loving, and when you find that special person, you will want to do all three with them.

Got to go now, as we are going to Fi and Sarah's for dinner. Dudley has got sausages. He loves sausages nearly as much as he loves all of the attention he gets when we are all together. He now sleeps spread eagled on the sofa when Amy comes to stay, but I never close the door. Bless. Must be like all kids—can't deal with his parents making out.

Anyway, a few thoughts before I go. I can hear you groaning. I won't be long, I promise. I'm running too low on tired old clichés to go on for much longer.

Life can throw you a curve ball, sometimes one after the other. It hurts like hell, I know, but never give up trying. Never give up on life. Live it, don't exist. Don't settle for second best and put up with things for the sake of it. Don't stop believing you deserve it.

Don't sit around waiting for the once-in-a-lifetime love; you could wait forever. Go out and look. Remember Harold and Sylvie? They had each found the love of their life, which turned out to be different people, although his was her. A teapot has many different lids: They may not fit perfectly, but they all serve a purpose. They can stop you being scalded or making a mess of things, even though on the outside they don't look quite right. What I'm trying to say, badly, is that if you have loved someone and it didn't work the way you wanted, don't give up. Never think "Once bitten, twice shy." Don't be scared about trying again, whatever mistakes you've made in the past. Learn from them, but don't avoid love. To do that would only hurt one person—you. And *you* have so much to give.

We each have the ability to mould our life, shape it into something we want. If we pass up any opportunity, we become more tentative about our abilities and focus on what we can't do rather than on our strengths.

You only live once, so make the loving *once* matter.
And *once* and for all, be you. You're worth it. We all are.

The End. Finally. Or Is It the Beginning?

About L.T. Smith

L.T. is a late bloomer when it comes to writing and didn't begin until 2005 with her first novel Hearts and Flowers Border (first published in 2006).

She soon caught the bug and has written numerous tales, usually with a comical slant to reflect, as she calls it, "My warped view of the dramatic."

Although she loves to write, L.T. loves to read, too—being an English teacher seems to demand it. Most of her free time is spent with her furry little men—two fluffy balls of trouble who keep her active and her apologies flowing.

E-mail her at fingersmith@hotmail.co.uk
Blog: http://ltsmithfiction.wordpress.com

Other Books from
Ylva Publishing

www.ylva-publishing.com

The Set Piece

Catherine Lane

ISBN: 978-3-95533-376-8
Length: 284 pages (64,000 words)

Amy gets an irresistible offer: Become engaged to soccer star Diego Torres to hide that he's gay and in return get a life of luxury. The simple decision soon becomes complicated.

Diego is being blackmailed, and Amy needs to find the culprit. It doesn't help that Casey, his pretty assistant, is a major distraction. Will Amy watch her from the sidelines or find the courage to get back into the game?

Beginnings
(2nd and revised edition)

L.T. Smith

ISBN: 978-3-95533-337-9
Length: 334 pages (92,500 words)

Lou Turner loves Ashley Richards. Always has and always will. This is Lou's story, a story spanning thirty years...from the innocence of youth to the bitterness of adulthood. But can Lou use her beginnings to shape her future? Only one woman can answer that question. Childhood and friendship, love and belief, and the hope that yesterdays can be what futures are made from.

Damage Control

Jae

ISBN: 978-3-95533-372-0
Length: 347 pages (140,000 words)

When actress Grace Durand is photographed in a compromising situation with a woman, she fears for her career.

She hires PR agent Lauren Pearce to do damage control, not knowing that she's a lesbian.

As they run the gauntlet of the paparazzi together, Lauren realizes how different Grace is from her TV persona.

Getting involved would ruin their careers, but the attraction between them is growing.

Heart's Surrender

Emma Weimann

ISBN: 978-3-95533-183-2
Length: 305 pages (63,000 words)

Neither Samantha Freedman nor Gillian Jennings are looking for a relationship when they begin a no-strings-attached affair. But soon simple attraction turns into something more.

What happens when the worlds of a handywoman and a pampered housewife collide? Can nights of hot, erotic fun lead to love, or will these two very different women go their separate ways?

Coming from Ylva Publishing in 2015

www.ylva-publishing.com

All the Little Moments

G Benson

Anna is focused on her career as an anaesthetist. When a tragic accident leaves her responsible for her young niece and nephew, her life changes abruptly. Completely overwhelmed, Anna barely has time to brush her teeth in the morning let alone date a woman. But then she collides with a long-legged stranger...

A Story of Now

Emily O'Beirne

Nineteen-year-old Claire knows she needs a life. And new friends.

Too sassy for her own good, she doesn't make friends easily anymore. And she has no clue where to start on the whole life front. At first, Robbie and Mia seem the least likely people to help her find it. But in a turbulent time, Claire finds new friends, a new self, and, with the warm, brilliant Mia, a whole new set of feelings.

Popcorn Love

KL Hughes

A prominent figure amongst New York City's fashion elite, Elena Vega is a successful businesswoman and single mother to an adorable three-year-old son, Lucas. Her love life, however, is lacking, as those closest to her keep pointing out.

At the persistent urging of her closest friend, Elena reluctantly agrees to a string of blind dates if she can find a suitable babysitter for Lucas.

Enter Allison Sawyer, a free-spirited senior at New York University.

Elena is intrigued by Allison's ability to push her out of her element, and the young woman's instant and easy connection with a normally shy Lucas quickly earns Allison the job.

After each blind date, Elena returns home to complain to Allison about her lacking suitors. As they bond, Elena begins to realize that the person possessing all the qualities she most desires might just be the woman who has been in front of her the entire time.

The vast difference between the two women's social statuses, however, may be an obstacle not easily overcome.

Once
© by L.T. Smith

ISBN: 978-3-95533-399-7

Also available as e-book.

Published by Ylva Publishing, legal entity of Ylva Verlag, e.Kfr.

Ylva Verlag, e.Kfr.
Owner: Astrid Ohletz
Am Kirschgarten 2
65830 Kriftel
Germany

www.ylva-publishing.com

Revised Edition: June 2015

Credits
Edited by Day Petersen
Cover Design by Amanda Chron

CPSIA information can be obtained at www.ICGtesting.com
Printed in the USA
LVOW11s1713070815

449270LV00001B/74/P